Working It Out

Nicola May

First published in Great Britain by
Nowell Publishing 2011

Copyright © Nicola May 2011

Nicola May has asserted her right under the Copyright,
Designs and Patent Acts 1988 to be identified as the author
of this work.

No part of this publication may be reproduced, stored in a
retrieval system, or transmitted, in any form or by any means,
without the prior permission in writing of the publisher, nor
be otherwise circulated in any form of binding or cover other
than that in which it is published and without a similar condition
including this condition being imposed on the subsequent
purchaser.

This book is a work of fiction. Names, characters, places and
incidents are either a product of the author's imagination or are
used fictitiously.

For Rita May, my beautiful mum,
whose young and vibrant spirit lives on in my heart
and breathes through my writing.

If you cannot work with love but with distaste, it is better that you should leave your work.

Khalil Gibran

Prologue

December 22nd

'I'm so sorry, Ruby. We've done everything we can to keep the department together, but you know how it is. Marketing is a resource, and we are always the first to get hit.'

Ruby bit her lip and nodded as Katy, the Marketing Director of Ritsy Rose Interiors, continued. 'It's very tough out there at the moment.'

'I take it I will get some redundancy?' Ruby managed to offer between gulps. Katy ran a hand through her short blonde hair and looked pained.

'Just the statutory, I'm afraid. Ali from HR is on her way down to see you now. Of course I will give you any glowing references you need – and if things change you know I'll be the first to call you.'

New Year's Day

'Happy New Year, darlin'!'

The tramp tilted his bottle of cider in her direction, hiccupped, then promptly slumped against the front door of the London flat, knocking the holly wreath onto his head as he did so.

Despite her hangover, Ruby smiled and raised the carton of milk she was carrying. 'Happy New Year, Bert,' she replied, stepping over him, 'Maybe you are the Messiah after all.'

Once she was safely ensconced on her newly-purchased Kelly Hoppen sofa with a coffee and an out-of-date mince pie, Ruby Matthews started to cry. In fact, she wept – only stopping when she realised she was in danger of staining the buttery cream suede of the wildly expensive sofa.

'Patrick, why oh why did I have to lose my job the week before Christmas?' Sensing her distress, the black and white furry friend brushed against her legs and purred. 'I knew you'd make me feel better,' Ruby cooed, feeling a surge of love towards the old tom who, over the last ten years, had been with her through thick and thin.

She lay back on her comfy sofa and sighed. She wished she had some wine in the fridge. Self-medication seemed like the only answer at this moment.

It was depressing enough that due to lack of funds she had been forced to spend New Year's Eve at her mother's house. She loved her mother dearly, but cheap plonk and *Jools' Annual Hootenanny* on TV *à deux* didn't set a particularly inspiring tone for the new year, without the added bonus that tomorrow was the first day of the working year and she had to start looking for a job in a recession-ravaged world.

As if catching a whiff of her worries, Patrick lifted a wail in sympathy, leaning his head back and showing off his wonky molar collection in all its glory.

'Hungry, eh? Some comfort you are. Sometimes I think our entire relationship is based on cupboard love. You men are all the bloody same,' Ruby bleated. 'And don't you be expecting mackerel fillets for a while either.'

While Patrick tucked into his value fish flakes, Ruby opened her depleting cupboards to see what she could rustle up for lunch.

'Happy Bloody New Year,' she muttered to herself as she reached for a tin of budget baked beans. Budget. Now there was something she hadn't had to worry about for a while. But with no money coming in she was going to have to be cautious. Ruby swallowed. Having no routine and no incoming finances was already a terrifying prospect.

Chapter One

Ruby woke to the rain lashing against her bedroom window. Despite it being only eight a.m. she forced herself out of bed. She had tossed and turned with worry all night. It had taken her so long to get the deposit together for her stylish maisonette in Putney there was no way she was going to default on the mortgage and lose it now.

Ruby looked in the bathroom mirror. Pushing her hands through her auburn bob, she noticed it could do with a cut. If she intended to start going to interviews she'd better get that sorted.

She pulled back the skin around her eyes in mock face lift style. Her pale skin had few lines and she looked a lot younger than her thirty years. She suddenly felt a panicked surge. What if she was deemed too old or expensive to be considered for another snappy marketing role? While scraping the bottom of her Crème de la Mer moisturizer tub, tears pricked her eyes.

'Don't cry. Be strong.' She said her father's favourite mantra aloud, blinking back the tears that had begun to slowly roll down her cheeks. She shut her eyes momentarily and when she opened them she was sure she could see her father's kind face reflected in the mirror. Thinking to the 'can-do' attitude he had installed in her, she snapped out of her misery and went into 'positive mode'.

'Right,' she said firmly, and headed downstairs. A plan was required. Today she would work out exactly how much money she had left after this month's outgoings. At the moment it would be hard to match her old salary, so she needed to see just how little she could get away with earning in the short term to get by.

Knowing she would have to make cuts, she decided to write a list of what she could live without. As a starter, she was sure she could find a cheaper hairdresser. The Soho one she went to was good, but had been far too expensive anyway. And – if she took the time to study the cosmetic reviews in magazines – she knew she could find a decent moisturiser from Superdrug for half the price of her current one.

She walked through to the kitchen and turned on the television just in time to hear the unemployment figures ringing out from the breakfast news. She clicked the television off and, with a mug of tea in hand, turned to her laptop instead. Just as she was settling down to her job search, her mobile rang.

'Just wishing you a Happy New Year, Ruby.'

'Thanks, Katy. Less than happy at the moment, but hey ho.'

'I've just emailed you a long list of job sites,' her ex-boss continued.

'OK, great. Thanks very much for thinking of me.'

'No worries. Damn, landline going already,' Katy hurried. 'I'd better get back to it. Keep in touch.' Click.

'Yes, she'd better get back to it,' Ruby said aloud to Patrick, who was washing his nether regions at her feet. Back to the world of Ritsy Rose Interiors: ten-hour days, boring board meetings, tedious events, pointless marketing campaigns, and management that didn't know their arse from their elbow.

She typed in her password, suddenly realising that actually it wasn't the job, and all the stress and hassles that came with it, that she would miss, but her work colleagues. They had been a big part of her life for the last three years. She would also, of course, miss the decent salary that a good marketing job in the capital brought in. But thinking back to the many times she'd got home at eight p.m., tired, grumpy, and feeling undervalued, she began to feel better.

She jumped up from the kitchen table, strutted through to her light and airy lounge, and began to pace around. Then it was as if a light bulb pinged on inside her head.

How many times did she tell everyone 'Life is too short,' or 'you're only here for a long weekend so you might as well enjoy it'? She of all people, who had seen her own dad drop dead at fifty-eight of a heart attack, should really practise what she preached.

She had got herself in a rut. A comfortable rut, but a rut no less. Living in a trendy part of London, in a desirable home, affording holidays abroad whenever she fancied one, and not having to think before she bought herself a new outfit.

All of that was great. But had she ever really thought about her future? What it was that she really wanted, what would make her truly happy? Because if she was honest with herself, it certainly wasn't being a single gal festering in the global marketing department of an interior design company.

She went back to her laptop and absent-mindedly typed the words "WORK" and "LOVE" into the search engine. Clicking on the first link it threw up, she smiled broadly as she read aloud the quotation.

'If you cannot work with love but with distaste, it is better that you should leave your work.' Khalil Gibran.

Leaning down to stroke a now purring Patrick, Ruby Ann Matthews, full of inspiration from the poet's words, calmly made a New Year's resolution there and then.

This year, she would be successful in her own personal mission for happiness. Her life would take on a new stance. It certainly wouldn't be easy, but she was more than up for the challenge.

Twelve months, twelve jobs – and by the end of it, she would surely know where her true vocation lay.

Chapter Two

'Happy New Year, Margaret!' Ruby shouted across the road to her neighbour, who was dutifully polishing her brass door knocker.

'Same to you, Ruby.' The white-haired old lady stuffed a duster into her apron pocket, and, as if to balance her stooping shoulders and ample bosom, placed her hands on her hips. 'You're looking very smart, duck.'

'I brush up all right sometimes, you know,' Ruby grinned. 'Anyway, must rush. Looking for gainful employment.'

'Oh, love, I know it won't take you long to find something else,' the old girl said kindly. 'Come in for a cuppa when you have a minute.'

'Will do, Margaret. See you soon.'

'Jesus is alive and living in Camden Town,' Bert shouted after Ruby as she set off at power-walk pace towards Putney station.

'How wonderful, maybe I'll meet Him for lunch,' she retorted gaily.

Thankfully, the local tramp had chosen not to sleep outside her flat last night, as from experience it was quite difficult stepping over him in a skirt.

Reaching the end of her road, she sighed with relief at not having met anyone else on her journey. She was still reeling from her recent embarrassing moment with George, her neighbour from number 28.

The cringeworthy incident had occurred after her emotionally-charged leaving lunch, when she drunkenly gatecrashed a Christmas Eve soiree hosted by Pinch-faced

Pru at number 32.

Ruby had suggested that as George, the gorgeous one, was a landscape gardener and a very handsome one at that, maybe he would like to trim her bush. She had thankfully managed to avoid him since, especially as Pru (the cow) had shown great delight in piping up that Ruby only had a very small roof terrace, with not even a flash of greenery in sight.

George was indeed handsome, but at twenty-four he was far too young for Ruby, and having always gone for professional men in the past, she was sure that apart from having hot sex in a flower bed, she wouldn't have much in common with a gardener.

However, the thought of carnality in the carnations with Gorgeous George made her cheeks flush. She hadn't had a date for over a year, let alone a night of passion.

Her relationship of six years had ended amicably eighteen months ago. That was the problem. No relationship where true love had been involved could surely end amicably?

Retail Manager Dean was without doubt a lovely man, and he adored her. He asked her to marry him countless times. But there was something stopping her committing to him. The rot eventually set in. However, it wasn't until they had been apart for two months that she realised how much she missed him and rushed to take him back. By then, it was too late. Dean had already found someone who gave him all the love Ruby didn't.

Admittedly, she wasn't as heartbroken as when her first love, Richard Spoon, decided to come out to her as gay as they were slow dancing to George Michael's "Careless Whisper" at her eighteenth birthday party.

Post-Dean was a pretty sparce affair. Work became her long-standing lover, and a drunken snog at last year's Christmas party with big-nosed Niall from Accounts was the nearest she had got to any sort of sexual activity since.

Ruby pushed open the door to her future in trepidation.

Petite Recruitment in Richmond seemed to fit the bill for her twelve months, twelve jobs mission, since its strap line was "No job too small, no person too big". What was *that* all about? They had to be quirky to think up something that made no obvious sense. However, to get a good range of opportunities, Ruby figured quirk was required.

'Good morning, dear.' The smartly suited, portly, silver-haired man behind the reception desk held out his hand to her. 'Can I help you?'

She moved forward to shake his hand and noticed he was standing on a stool.

Suddenly the strap line made sense. No person too big!

'I'm terribly sorry, I think I must be in the wrong place,' she spluttered, not wanting to appear rude.

'We do cater for the taller individual too, madam.' The smart man smiled cheekily and Ruby was drawn to him instantly.

Three cups of coffee and several custard creams later, she found out that the smart man's name was Johnny Jessop. Not only did he share her love of the biscuit, he also shared Ruby's wicked sense of humour. He had run Petite Recruitment for the past twenty years with great success. Primarily, he looked after his 'little brothers and sisters', as he called them; he had a vast customer base, mainly in Central London, and his reputation for being fun, fair, and efficient had ensured that he was never short of temporary vacancies of different kinds.

Ruby soon felt comfortable enough to come clean about her twelve months, twelve jobs mission while Johnny perused her CV.

'I won't lie to you, young lady,' he said, without looking up. 'You are over-qualified for most of the jobs I am likely to get you. But if you're willing to be flexible, as you say you are, then I'm sure I can help you.'

'Flexible is my middle name, Mr Jessop,' Ruby smirked.

'But it says "Ann" on here,' Johnny replied dryly, pointing to her CV. 'What's this about one of your hobbies being tropical fish?'

'Oops. I meant to take the hobby bit off. That's actually a lie. I used to have a goldfish called Ken, until Patrick decided to eat him.'

Johnny smirked. 'Patrick?'

'Oh, he's my cat.'

Johnny was now laughing out loud. 'Ruby Matthews, I think I'm going to enjoy helping you with your mission.'

They chinked their cups in celebration. Ruby felt that she had found the perfect mentor for her mission.

'Now, we can't waste any time,' Johnny continued in business-like fashion. 'Month one is already two days old, and as it happens I had a role come in this morning that I need to fill as soon as possible. It will involve getting your hands dirty, but can you start on Monday?'

Chapter Three

'David Ketwell, what a bargain, what a bargain!' Ruby joined in with the 24,000-strong throng at the Madejski Stadium, as the centre-forward scored another excellent goal. She had been in lust with the handsome fellow ginger ever since he scored his first Premier League goal against Middlesborough for her beloved Reading FC. She pulled her blue and white scarf closer to her face as the cold air began to nip at her nose. Her brother Sam gripped her hand tightly. He chose not to go in the disabled area of the stand as he wanted to experience the same vibe as everyone else did.

'Talk me through it again, sis, talk me through it.' Ruby could sense his delight at the bristling atmosphere of the crowd. Her own eyes filled with tears, she relived the goal through her brother's sightless eyes, loving that he preferred her personal commentary to the one on his headset. It was during moments like this that his blindness really got to her. Sam had contracted Leber Congenital Amaurosis shortly after his birth, so he had experienced more black moods than he had ever seen blue skies or green fields. He was, however, the most inspirational person Ruby knew. He was on a work placement at the local university, being trained by the IT department. He too was a handsome ginger and his affable personality ensured he had a plethora of good friends. Without fail, he was always dressed smartly, never faltering on his addiction to trainers and designer dark glasses. Ruby's love for him was infinite.

Eleven years Ruby's junior, nineteen-year-old Sam

lived in Reading with their mother Laura, as Ruby had done until she was eighteen and decided that the draw of the big city was more appealing. She tried to visit as often as she could to catch up with Sam and to give her mum a well-earned break. This weekend she was particularly glad of the diversion, not wanting to think about her pending new career path until Monday came around.

She always took the chance to get in as many Reading home matches as her life would allow. After a celebratory one-nil victory, Ruby guided Sam through the crowds to catch the bus back into town.

'I'm getting a guide dog,' Sam announced once they found a seat. 'Scary, but also exciting, don't you think?'

'That's great news, Sam. Is Mum OK with having a dog in the house then?'

'Yeah, she's really excited. Since Dad died, she's been going on about wanting a dog but was always worried it would get in my way. This way we get the best of both worlds. She's quite taken with my Dog Mobility Instructor too, I think. She got a bit giggly when he came over the other day.'

Ruby felt the familiar burn in her throat whenever her dad was mentioned. His death had been the most terrible shock to them all. One minute he was carving the Christmas Day turkey, the next he was lying dead on the floor. He was very greatly missed and as much as Christmas had always been Ruby's favourite time of year, it would never be the same again.

Laura Matthews was still young at heart, and at fifty remained a very striking woman, with her light brown wavy hair (thanks, Dad, for the ginger genes) and enviable figure. She had, however, always relied on her husband with regards to finances and the like, and had become quite shy and retiring since his death, finding it hard to go out into the world again.

Sometimes, Ruby got really down about her

relationship with her mum. Without a doubt Laura deeply loved her daughter, but even though Ruby was now thirty, she felt she lacked the parental guidance her father had always offered. In fact, because Laura had been so wrapped up in her own grief, Ruby felt like she was the parent to both her mother and brother. She craved sometimes to be told off for something, or to be able to confide her worries in her mum.

But on the other hand, Ruby wanted to protect her mum from worry, so she decided not to mention the twelve job mission to her at this stage.

She wondered what her dad would have thought of her madcap idea. Then again, if he was still here, would this be the direction her life would have taken?

Maybe her lack of commitment to Dean and total commitment to work was a telling symptom of Bereavementitus. Perhaps this change of direction was her first dose, four years on from her loss, of much-needed medicine.

'So, come on, tell me all about it. When do I get to meet the new furry member of the Matthews family?' Ruby asked Sam brightly.

'The instructor is going to be at the house when we get back. He wants a final chat before we start training together next week. His name's Ben, by the way.'

Ruby used her key to open the front door to their homely terraced house in Princes Street.

'Hi, Mum! It's us,' Ruby called out, so as not to startle her.

'Hello, loves – cup of tea? You both must be freezing.' Their mother's soft voice drifted through the house.

The siblings walked through to the kitchen and Ruby stopped in her tracks, causing Sam to bump into her, cussing as he did so. The reason for her halting was leaning against the cooker. He must have been about five foot ten, ideal for her five foot six frame. He had short blond hair with a Tintin-like quiff in the front, and big brown eyes that she could feel herself drowning in. His lips were full and his face was open and kind. He was wearing baggy indigo jeans with a grey Gap sweatshirt. Ruby Matthews was in lust for the second time in one day, with possibly the most handsome man she had ever come across.

She took a deep breath and smiled openly. 'Oh, hi, you must be Ben.'

The handsome man laughed out loud. A laugh so full and hearty, she wanted to grab him and kiss him passionately right there and then, even in front of her own mother.

Sam was laughing out loud too. Ruby was confused.

'You div,' Sam uttered. 'Ben is a Golden Labrador. This is Graham.'

'Don't call your sister a div, dear, that's not very nice,' Mrs Matthews piped up. Ruby noticed that she was wearing a new pink jumper, with lipstick to match.

The god of a guide dog instructor held out his hand. 'Pleased to meet you, Ruby. I've heard a lot about you from Sam.'

Ruby, red to her roots, held his hand slightly longer than she probably should have, and felt her heart beating fast beneath her thick coat.

'So, where is Ben then?' she enquired.

'He's not here yet,' Graham told her. 'I just wanted a last chat with your mum and brother to make sure they know exactly what's involved in having a guide dog. I'll bring him round on Monday to introduce him to Sam and if all goes well, we can start the training then.'

'Graham has got it all under control, don't worry.' Laura smiled openly at Graham, flicking back her hair as she did so. Then, turning to Sam, she asked, 'So how was the match?'

'Bloody brilliant,' he replied animatedly, and much to

everyone's amusement proceeded to run around the kitchen, arms outstretched as if he was flying, shouting, 'Come on, you R's! Come on, you R's!'

'So, you support Reading then, Graham?' Ruby asked, praying that he did so she would have one thing in common with him.

'No, I'm a Manchester United man.'

'Pah,' Sam scoffed light-heartedly. 'All these Southerners who support a Northern team.'

Graham poked him in the ribs. 'Ben's a Reading fan, though. He says he likes to stick with the underdogs!'

Everybody laughed.

The warmth of the hot tea soon had brother and sister removing their coats and thawing out. They chatted in the familiar front room, while their mother checked on the chicken and roast potatoes in the oven and Graham laid the table in the dining room. Ruby felt content.

How easy it would be to rent her place out and come to live back here for a while. But no. Part of being thirty was about independence and creating a happy and fulfilled life for herself. Tomorrow's start to her twelve month, twelve job mission would hopefully be the first step towards that goal.

Chapter Four

January, Job One: Auxiliary Nurse

'You all right today, Ginger?' Bert called from his horizontal position on next door's step. 'You've got a smile on that freckly face for once. Usually it looks like a smacked arse.'

Ruby turned back to shout something equally abusive at him, and without looking where she was going, bumped straight into Gorgeous George, who was single-handedly carrying a lawnmower to his van. 'Whoa. Easy, tiger.' George steadied her with his spare hand and smiled at her. 'A nice smacked arse though, I'm sure,' he said cheekily in his Cockney lilt.

'Language!' Margaret shouted from across the road. She was washing her front step, a wide, toothless grin on her face.

'Sorry, Margaret,' they said in unison. The interruption thankfully allowed Ruby's face to turn from a deep shade of red to a more subtle pink.

George was five foot six. His jet black hair was cropped short and he had the brightest blue eyes. He was the proud and somewhat cocky owner of one very fit body. Despite him being the same height as her (she didn't usually go for short men) Ruby often fantasised about him being her own personal Tom Cruise look-a-like or pint- sized Diet Coke man.

Ruby tried to respond to the gorgeous one's previous comment with something witty, but remembering her misdemeanour on Christmas Eve, words failed her.

'Did that mad cat of yours get your tongue?' George joked, which made Ruby laugh.

Brushing a few stray grass clippings off her bottle-green trench-coat, she told him, 'Me and my smacked boat race are off to start a new job today.'

'Oh well done, bird,' George said kindly. 'And Bert's right – you do look happier than usual. Where are you working anyway?'

'Let's just say, Georgie boy, that if you ever need a bed bath then I'm your girl.' And, without waiting for an answer, she strutted off to the end of the road.

'Show us your uniform and I might trim that imaginary bush of yours!' George shouted after her. This time she didn't turn around but kept walking, wearing a very large smirk.

Ruby followed Johnny's concise directions from Twickenham train station. It took her exactly nine minutes, as he had predicted. It was part of Petite Recruitment's general procedure to provide every temporary worker with a page of notes informing them of directions, contact details, and duties within each particular employ.

She reached the designated address and looked up. The blue sign told her she was in the right place. She began to walk up the long drive, feeling anticipation as she did so, and when the door to the large greystone manor house was thrown open before she had a chance to knock on the huge brass knocker, she felt as if she was on the film set of a Jane Austen adaptation.

A yapping Jack Russell ran towards her and jumped at her legs.

'Down now, Montgomery, be a good boy.' A tall distinguished-looking gentleman followed. He was wearing a grey three-piece suit with a top hat and sported a brass cane. He tipped his hat at Ruby and twirled it down towards her feet as if he were a ringmaster. It was certainly a different start to her day than the low grunt of the security man at Ritsy Rose Interiors.

'Good afternoon, madam. My name is Lucas Steadburton. I am a resident of this Parish.'

Ruby smiled. 'A pleasure to meet you, Mr Steadburton, I'm sure,' she replied, speaking as if she was an extra on the film set, and almost bobbing a curtsey.

'Mrs Hornsby didn't say you were a redhead,' he said rather sternly, and walked into the magnificent grounds, whistling for Montgomery as he went.

Although she was taken aback by his comment about her hair – cheeky old devil – Ruby managed a smile and walked through to the grand main hall. Her desire for the quirky was already far exceeding her expectations here at Dinsworth House – retirement home to the stars. Tentatively, she made her way to the cluttered reception desk and rang the antiquated brass hand bell that stood upon it, thinking as she did so, that this place felt more like a country hotel than an old people's home. Apart from the awful memory of her father's death, Ruby loved anything Christmassy, and the huge Christmas tree, ablaze with twinkling lights, that towered towards the twelve foot high ceiling made her warm inside.

Ellie was the receptionist of the day, according to the plaque next to the bell. When a lady appeared from a door behind reception, Ruby thought quickly to herself, maybe not quite *Sense and Sensibility* but *Fawlty Towers* instead. The lady in question was tall, willowy, and extremely glamorous. Ruby thought she must have been at least seventy-five. She had soft white hair, gathered back in a perfect French pleat. Caked in make-up, her bright pink lipstick – with matching nail varnish and even brighter pink blusher – clashed considerably with her red feather boa. She was wearing a long purple dress with billowing sleeves, and Ruby imagined her bursting into song at any minute.

'Oh, it's Ginger Rogers! I didn't realise you were coming today. Is Fred Astaire with you?' the lady asked in a forced posh voice.

Ruby blinked but carried on regardless. 'Oh, hello there,' she replied politely, not sure exactly how she should react. She decided to play along. 'I'm actually going to be working here for a few weeks. I've been asked to meet with Mrs Hornsby in the first instance. Mr Astaire couldn't make it, I'm afraid.'

'Ah, yes, poor old Fred – it's probably his gammy hip playing up. One moment, please. I will summon Mrs Hornsby for you.'

The old lady floated back through the door behind reception and slammed it shut. As she did so, Ruby noticed a sign on the door.

Your life lies before you
Like freshly fallen snow
Be careful how you walk
For every footprint will show

How very true, and how very wonderful, Ruby thought. She already knew she was going to like it here. However, after fifteen minutes, when there was still no sign of Mrs Hornsby, she began to get a little concerned. She was now five minutes late for her nine thirty start. She rang the bell again, and this when time the door opened she was greeted by a ruddy-cheeked plump lady with brown hair, wearing navy trousers and tunic and a white plastic apron tied loosely around her waist. She wiped her right hand on her trousers, offered it to Ruby, and shook hers with gusto.

'Hello, dear, you must be Ruby. So sorry to keep you waiting. I'm Mrs Hornsby, the Matron here, but please call me Trish.'

'Oh, thanks. I'm sorry I'm late,' Ruby uttered. 'I did ask the lady with the red feather boa to ask for you.'

Mrs Hornsby smiled. 'Oh, that's our Dolly. Alzheimer's, bless her. She occasionally sneaks down here to meet and greet. She'd have forgotten all about you by now.'

Ruby smiled warmly as Mrs Hornsby continued in short, breathless bursts, 'Ellie, who's usually on the front desk, has got the sickness bug – in fact, the same bug that half of the residents have, I'm afraid. Follow me, follow me.'

And they were off! Ruby followed the Matron at high speed down a long passageway, each side of which was adorned with black and white photos of the late and greats from theatre and film.

'We are all having to muck in – "muck" being the *mot du jour*,' Trish Hornsby said over her shoulder as they reached the day room, which, Ruby noticed, was aptly named the Doris Day Room.

Ruby grimaced; she knew now why Johnny had said she might get her hands dirty.

The day room had long, wide windows that looked out over the mansion grounds. Two swans were swimming regally on the far side of the ornamental lake. Ten or so residents sat dotted around on comfy-looking high armed chairs; one of them appeared to be singing to herself and two others were sleeping soundly. Ruby noticed that the majority of the women wore full make-up, and the men sported bow ties. All around were elaborate antiques and a huge plasma television was taking up nearly an entire wall of the room. The other housed a small stage, where a short man wearing a bowler hat and carrying a cane was performing a tap-dance routine in slow motion. The television sound was up so high that Ruby couldn't imagine how anyone could sleep, let alone hear themselves think.

'Now, off to the staff room – it's on the corner of the corridor down that way.' Mrs Hornsby pointed. 'Grab yourself a uniform and an apron from the pegs.'

Ruby dutifully did as she was told. 'Oh, and make sure you have some plastic gloves at the ready,' Mrs Hornsby shouted after her.

Ruby's vision of being Florence Nightingale – mopping fevered brows and administering drugs sedately from a trolley – were already fading fast. As she scurried back to the Doris Day Room, Ruby thought that she looked less like Barbara Windsor in *Carry on Doctor* and more like Victoria Wood in *Dinner Ladies,* in her pale blue tunic and baggy trousers, with a fetching white plastic apron. She would have to pray that she didn't bump into Gorgeous George again until she could afford to get a 'proper' uniform from Ann Summers! As she was holding that thought, she was startled by a deep voice and a grey cardboard bowl being thrust into her hand.

'Quick, get over to Dolly – red feather boa.'

Propelled by the urgency in the voice, Ruby ran as fast as she could to the old girl, who proceeded to bring up her porridge and prune breakfast into the cardboard bowl. It brought tears to Ruby's eyes that the glamorous lady had to suffer this indignity in public. 'It's all right, Dolly. Let's get you cleaned up, shall we?' Ruby said gently, not minding half as much about the unsavouriness of it all as she thought she would.

'Good shot, Ginger!' Lucas hollered as he arrived back into the room, rosy-faced from his walk and Montgomery yapping at his feet.

The deep voice was now beside her. 'Yes, well done. I'm Justice. I won't shake your hand for obvious reasons.' He smiled broadly, showing the most perfect set of white teeth Ruby had ever seen. 'You are indeed a fine redhead and it suits you, so don't listen to Lucas.'

His long black dreadlocks were tied back in a ponytail and his ebony skin was blemish-free. Ruby smiled back, taking in his strong cheekbones. At near six foot two, he towered above her and his shoulders seemed nearly as wide. He put a big hand on her shoulder.

'Can't tell you how glad I am to see you. It's madness here with this bug going around.'

'Well, you just tell me where you want me and I'll assume the position,' Ruby chimed innocently.

'Oo-er, missus,' Justice winked.

Who did he think he was? Ruby thought. Kenneth bloody Williams? Flushing pink on realising what she had said, she also suddenly felt a warm surge of activity in her nether regions at the closeness of her new compadre. What was wrong with her lately? Maybe the liberation of leaving a full-time job had sexually liberated her.

While the pair of them cleaned up Dolly, Ruby was able to establish that Justice was actually a jobbing actor. However, after only managing to seal a voiceover for hair restorer and an advert for oven chips in the past two years, Dinsworth House remained his main source of income.

Just as they were finishing up, Mrs Hornsby appeared in the doorway. 'Ruby, could you come and give me a hand please?'

'Sure.' Ruby washed and dried her hands in the bedroom sink and followed the Matron dutifully.

Leading her into another bedroom, Mrs Hornsby addressed the old lady sitting in a chair next to the bed. 'Connie,' she spoke loudly. 'This is Ruby. Ruby is going to be helping us here for a while.'

Age had shortened the old lady. Propped up against a large pink cushion, she looked like a little girl. Big brown eyes sat in a heart-shaped face, and despite her ill fitting, curly blonde wig, Ruby could tell that in her youth, she would have been extremely beautiful.

She looked slowly at Ruby. 'Lucy. That's a pretty name, dear.'

Mrs Hornsby smiled at Ruby. 'Deaf as a post,' she said in her normal speaking voice. Then, shouting again, 'I said

Ruby, not Lucy, Connie.'

'Oh, sorry, Looby, dear. I've got it now – like Looby Loo off *Andy Pandy*?' Connie shouted back.

'You've got it!' Ruby smiled, thinking if they carried on they'd be here all day.

'Well done,' the Matron interrupted, completely on Ruby's wavelength. 'While I'm taking Connie for a bath, please can you strip and remake her bed? There's clean linen in the laundry cupboard, next to the kitchen.'

As Trish Hornsby helped the old lady out of her seat, she turned to Ruby. 'Now, young Looby, if there's one thing I wish I'd done when I was younger …' She paused. 'It was my pelvic floor exercises.'

This wasn't quite the pearl of wisdom Ruby had been expecting, and she had to stop herself from laughing. 'I'll remember that, Connie, thanks.'

Once alone, Ruby pulled back the duvet to reveal a large wet patch on the bottom sheet. Poor thing, she thought, as she continued with the task in hand, replacing the plastic undersheet and making the bed up again in able fashion.

Over a well earned coffee break, Ruby and Justice chatted in the cosy staff room. Audrey Hepburn, Elvis, and Burt Reynolds watched over them from the cluttered walls. Alongside the old greats was a list and photo gallery of all twenty patients. Their appropriate health charts were stored neatly in a tray underneath.

'I really love it here now,' Justice stated. 'You do become quite attached to the old codgers, and the fact that they have all been in the entertainment industry allows them to tell some amazing stories.'

Ruby nodded. 'I admire how you cope, to be honest. I feel emotional already, but it does make such a pleasant change to help people.' She took a slurp of coffee, and added, 'Bit of a shock with the bodily fluids though, I have to say. The closest I got to that in marketing was when somebody spilt their drink over me.'

Justice laughed heartily as Ruby continued, 'By the way, I bumped into Lucas when I arrived. What a lovely old boy – he seems hilarious.'

'He is a very funny man and underneath his pomp and circumstance, there is a lovely warm person. He's got terminal cancer, though. I shall miss him when he goes.'

Justice could sense Ruby's discomfort..

'Its part and parcel of working with old folks, I'm afraid,' he told her gently. 'Mind you, we've only lost two since I've been here. Must be all the Caribbean food I get the chef to cook.' There was a sparkle in his big brown eyes.

Ruby laughed. 'So where are you from then?'

'Ilford. Do you know it?' Justice's wide grin was contagious.

Ruby poked his ribs flirtatiously. 'You know what I mean.'

'Saint Lucia, the finest island in the Caribbean,' he drawled in a deep, ethnic accent for effect.

'Gorgeous!' Ruby exclaimed. 'Such a beautiful place. I went on holiday there a few years ago. You must miss it so much.'

'I try and get back at least once a year. Ma and Da are still there. I came over for work. Employment is not great over there.'

'Surely, though, with all those hotels, there's some sort of entertainment role for you?' Ruby enquired with interest.

'I did work at one of the new golf resorts once, but the hours were so long and the money so poor that I gave it up. I also want the big time, baby, and sadly I couldn't see me making my break on my beautiful isle.' Justice smiled that smile again and Ruby felt that feeling in her nether regions again.

'Justice, Ruby, come quickly!' Mrs Hornsby shouted with urgency from the Doris Day Room. 'It's Lucas – he's collapsed.'

Chapter Five

Lucas lay dazed on the floor of the Doris Day Room while Montgomery barked beside him. Some of the other residents were shuffling towards him to see what the commotion was. He looked up at Ruby quizzically.

'What the deuces am I doing down here, Ginger?'

'I think you must have tripped on the edge of the rug.' Ruby winked at him.

'Ah, yes, that damn rug. Justice, old fellow, get it sorted, won't you?'

'See it as done, Lucas. Now let's get you up, shall we? Does anything hurt?'

'Only the pride, dear boy, just the pride.'

They walked Lucas slowly to his room and got him comfortable. Mrs Hornsby did the necessary nursing checks and gave him his some painkillers. She then scuttled off to check that everyone else was happy, and Justice went back to reception as the bell was ringing.

As Ruby quietly pulled the curtains closed in Lucas's room, she noticed various photos on the windowsill, including one of him collecting a BAFTA. He looked extremely smart, handsome, and proud. It made Ruby sad, thinking about getting old. All the memories you collect and share – and then it's all over. She shook herself to get rid of her morbid thoughts.

'You OK, Ginger?' Lucas whispered weakly.

'Look at you worrying about me. I'm fine, Lucas. You get some rest, that was a nasty fall.'

'Bloody rug.'

'Yes, bloody rug,' Ruby agreed. 'I'll bring you a cup of

tea later on.' She touched Lucas's hand gently and turned to leave the room.

'Ginger?'

'Yes, Lucas?'

'Could you stay with me a little longer?'

'Of course I can.' She noticed his crammed bookshelf at the back of the room. 'I can read to you, if you like.'

'How simply marvellous – a poem would be divine. How about "Daffodils"? Yes, Wordsworth and his "Daffodils", please.'

Ruby surveyed the shelf and pulled out the poetry collection. It was slightly daunting to be reading to a classically trained actor, but she would do her best. She sat on the chair beside Lucas, cleared her throat, and announced, "I Wandered Lonely as a Cloud" also known as "Daffodils" by William Wordsworth.'

Her nerves disappeared as she began to read. The beauty of the words took her out of the room and out of herself.

I wandered lonely as a cloud
That floats on high o'er vales and hills,
When all at once I saw a crowd,
A host, of golden daffodils;
Beside the lake, beneath the trees,
Fluttering and dancing in the breeze.
Continuous as the stars that shine
And twinkle on the milky way,
They stretched in never-ending line
Along the margin of a bay:
Ten thousand saw I at a glance,
Tossing their heads in sprightly dance.
The waves beside them danced; but they
Out-did the sparkling leaves in glee;
A poet could not be but gay,
In such a jocund company:

I gazed – and-gazed – but little thought
What wealth the show to me had brought:
For oft, when on my couch I lie
In vacant or in pensive mood,
They flash upon that inward eye
Which is the bliss of solitude;
And then my heart with pleasure fills,
And dances with the daffodils

Lucas's eyes began to close. 'The best show I ever saw, Ginger, the best show,' he murmured. Ruby smiled as he continued. 'Ever been to the Lake District?'

She shook her head. 'No. It's somewhere I've always wanted to go to, but haven't made it yet.'

'Make sure you get there one day, you promise me that.'

'I promise, Lucas. I promise.' She pulled the covers around him and he began to snore quietly. She looked at him for a few minutes and began to cry, not only for the loneliness of this old man, but for her father's lost years. Oh, how she wished she could have him back for even one day. Just to feel his strong reassuring arms around her, telling her that whatever happened it would be all right. To see the expression of joy on her mum's face when he told her daily that he loved her. But this would never happen. She shut her eyes and took deep breaths to try and extinguish the fire within that loss brought.

Eventually, she got herself together, checked on Lucas one last time, and made sure that Montgomery was settled in his basket in the corner of the bedroom

She bumped into Mrs Hornsby as she was quietly closing his door.

'You all right, love?' the kindly nurse asked.

'Yes, just tired,' Ruby replied wearily.

'I should think you are, your shift ended an hour ago. Now, home with you. See you at midday tomorrow.'

'Goodnight, Mrs Hornsby.' Ruby could not call her Trish. Collecting her coat from the staff room, she began her short walk to the station.

What a good start to her mission, Ruby thought. An hour over her normal working hours and for once she didn't begrudge it.

Chapter Six

'The usual, Ruby?' the shopkeeper enquired from behind the counter, holding out a magazine and a packet of custard creams.

'Can't afford the luxury of the magazine at the moment, I'm afraid, Raj. Got to be sensible this month. So just my biscuits, please. Oh, and a packet of Polos for Margaret.'

Ruby felt lucky that despite being in a big city, she still felt some rare sense of community spirit in her immediate vicinity. Gill's convenience store was on the corner of her road and the proprietors Raj and Suki Gill had made her feel welcomed from day one. She loved the fact that she only had to walk five minutes and could buy virtually anything she needed, at practically any time.

'No Arun tonight then?' Ruby enquired after the Gills' handsome son, another dishy benefit of this flexible outfit.

'No. He's out playing football tonight,' Raj yawned, rubbing his neck.

'Always busy, our Arun,' Suki piped up from the back of the shop.

Yes, Ruby thought. Far too busy to get involved with someone without a proper job now.

As Ruby started walking to the door with her negative thoughts, Suki called out.

'Hang on a minute, Ruby, I've got something for you.' The pretty forty-something Indian lady reappeared from behind the counter with a carrier bag. 'Here. I'm done with these.'

Ruby glanced in the bag, and saw the last four weeks'

issues of her favourite weekly magazine. She felt slightly overwhelmed.

'Thanks so much, Suki. That's really kind of you.'

'It's nothing. Now you enjoy. Well done on getting some work so quickly, by the way.'

'Thank you. See you soon,' Ruby called back, stepping into the bitter January night homeward bound.

Ruby walked briskly up Amerhand Road. Despite feeling dog tired, she realised she hadn't caught up with her old friend Margaret for ages, and ought to pay her a flying visit.

Since the day Ruby had moved into her flat two years ago, Margaret had become part of her life in Putney. As soon as Ruby had waved goodbye to her removal truck, the old girl brought her tea bags and biscuits. Plus, more importantly, she had managed to cease Patrick's wailing with a piece of cooked liver. And so a beautiful friendship began.

Ruby thought it was like having a wonderful auntie to confide in, without the worry of her mother finding out her deepest, darkest secrets. Not that her mother would ask – nor that Ruby had any too exciting to mention, for that matter!

Seventy-five years on the planet had made Margaret wise. She was non-judgmental and a good listener, and it was obvious that she thought the world of her red-headed neighbour.

Ruby gently tapped on her neighbour's window the usual four times, so as not to startle her. No response.

'Margaret, it's me,' she called out.

On hearing how loud *Eggheads* was blaring out from the television, she knocked harder. The TV was turned down, and Margaret shuffled to the front door and opened it. She was sucking a Polo in and out of her near toothless mouth. Her white hair was pinned back in a tight bun.

'Who sang "Bleeding Love"?' Margaret immediately

demanded, walking back through the hall into the lounge.

'Leona Lewis,' Ruby replied straight away, following her.

'Bleeding cheek, more like. No wonder those Eggheads beat me again – shouldn't be allowed to use all those modern questions. Anyway, nice to see you, duck.'

'You too, Margaret.' Ruby kissed her crinkly face. 'How are you today?'

'Thinking I'd be better off as a fish, what with no teeth or feet to speak off.'

'Oh, bless you and your bunions,' Ruby responded.

'I shouldn't complain, really. The padded slippers you got me do ease them a bit.'

Margaret pointed to her purple, out-of-shape footwear and sucked her Polo in and out furiously. 'And I don't regret a single dance or any of the beautiful shoes I used to wear that caused them,' she reminisced, 'Anyway, enough of my ramblings. Let's have a cuppa. You can stimulate my diminishing brain cells with what's going on with you.'

'Lovely.' Ruby hung her coat up on a hook behind the front door. 'I've brought some custard creams. Oh, and some Polos for you too.' She pulled the biscuits from a carrier bag and placed both them and the mints on the coffee table.

Despite being knackered, Ruby insisted on making the tea. Once she had brought in the brass tray with the customary metal teapot, knitted cosy, and flowery bone china cups, she plonked herself down in her usual armchair, sighing with relief as she took the weight off of her feet.

She loved coming to visit her neighbour, especially in the winter when her open fire was roaring. Margaret and her husband Stanley had lived in the same house all of their married life. When he died of a stroke ten years ago, his wife had never even thought about finding anyone else.

He had been her one and only love, and that, she said – unless a Burt Reynolds look-a-like came along – was how she wanted it to stay. And, despite her only son Greg moving to Australia with his work years ago, the old dear never once said she was lonely.

Her furniture had definitely seen better days. The arms of the chair Ruby was sitting on were threadbare, and she could feel a spring underneath her. On the hearth was a plethora of brass; brass jugs, brass horses, brass cow,s and a magnificent brass poker. Every perceivable wall space was covered in oil paintings housed in thick gold frames. In the corner opposite the television was Ruby's favourite piece; an old fashioned horn gramophone. The only downside being that Margaret had just one record to play on it – Frankie Vaughan's "The Garden of Eden". And, whenever she had a sherry or three, she would play it over and over until it drove Ruby slightly mad. Despite her surroundings being worn, number 25 Amerland Road was very homely, and with Margaret being a fanatical cleaner, everything was spotless.

'Are they sugar-free?' Margaret enquired, taking the packet of Polos from the table. Ruby stifled a giggle.

'Now I know what you're thinking, my girl. Why does the silly old bat want sugar-free when she has no teeth? Well, duck, this is *my* new year's resolution. The reason I have just two teeth is that I have eaten too much sugar all my life and that's what made 'em fall out in the first place. It has to stop. Two teeth are better than none, and I ain't getting no second-rate falsies.'

'OK,' Ruby said, smiling. 'I'll make sure I get you sugar-free in the future.'

'Good, good. Now, come on, spill the beans, girlie. Found yourself a fella yet?'

'What are you like, Margaret?' Ruby tutted. 'It's only two weeks since I last saw you.'

'Well, a lot can happen in that time, duck. I mean, look

at that girl on *Coronation Street* – she got married and pregnant in the space of three episodes.' Margaret reached for her tea and let out a squeaky fart. 'What about that lovely new neighbour of ours, surely he's worth a look?'

'I reckon he thinks I'm a trollop,' Ruby said soulfully.

'Oh, duck, what on earth have you done now?'

'I asked if he wouldn't mind trimming my bush for me, when we were having Christmas drinks at Pinch-Faced Pru's place.'

'Dear me.' Margaret grimaced slightly. 'But he doesn't have to know you don't have a garden.'

'The pinch-faced one had great delight in telling him that I didn't!' Ruby exclaimed.

'Ooh, she's a nasty piece of work, that one,' Margaret replied. 'Well, don't you worry. I'm sure he took it as a bit of fun. Thinking on it, I might ask him to trim mine for me too.'

'Margaret!'

'My *rose bushes*, young lady. My feet are too bad to stand out in the cold for too long.' The old girl chuckled. 'Mind you if I was forty years younger …' She let out another fart and put her hand to her mouth. 'Oops, cabbage, that is. Good job he's not here now.'

Ruby was used to her neighbour's habits, and without batting an eye at the distinctive hum now engulfing the room, she stood up.

'Right, I really must be off. I've got to get some rest.'

'Oh, come on, have one more cuppa,' the lonely old lady insisted. 'I want to know how you really feel about losing your job. You don't have to put a brave face on with me, you know that.'

'I'm fine,' Ruby replied sulkily and plonked herself back down on the chair.

'Fine, my fanny,' Margaret scolded, and on noticing Ruby's sullen face added, 'You're thirty, not thirteen.'

'I was gutted that they didn't fire Katy instead of me, to

be honest. I worked far harder than she did. There, I said it.'

'I don't blame you being pissed off about that, love. But as my old Stan used to say, "You won't ever be remembered for the extra hours you did in the office."' Ruby nodded as Margaret continued, 'She probably had the Chief Exec. looking at her own interiors, that's why *she* stayed.'

'Margaret!'

'Well, why else wouldn't they want to keep you, darlin'?'

Ruby smiled. 'Right, lovely Margaret, I really must go. Patrick will be eating his own tail.'

'OK, duck. How is the new job? At least I've been good preparation for having to talk to old biddies all day?'

By the time she had given Margaret an account of her twelve month, twelve job mission, updated her about Graham, the luscious dog trainer, plus given her a full rundown of the goings-on at Dinsworth House, Ruby's flying visit had turned into two hours and she could barely keep her eyes open. She said her goodbyes and wandered across the road to her flat.

Just as she arrived back home, her mobile rang.

'So?' Johnny enquired tentatively.

'Tiring, but I love it.'

'Better than being a corporate cog?'

'Without question. Thanks so much, Johnny.'

'Look, I'll leave you be as you must be shattered. I'm here if you need me. Mrs Hornsby thinks you're great, by the way, so well done.'

Ruby flopped down on her chair and stroked a purring Patrick. 'They like me, Patrick, and I like them. No distaste, just love. Good old Khalil.' She promptly fell asleep, mouth gaping open.

Chapter Seven

'Morning, Looby Loo.' Justice greeted Ruby with his electric smile at the entrance to the Doris Day Room and handed her some disposable gloves. 'Cyril's just had an accident of the brown variety, I'm afraid. I'll have to leave you to clear him up. I'm in the middle of sorting a sickly Dolly.'

Ruby screwed her face up then smiled. 'Do I get to fill out some sort of job satisfaction form at the end of the day?'

Justice laughed. 'Go on. Just hold your breath and think of England.'

Despite it being her second week, Ruby still had not been able to control her gag reflex when faced with a 'poo job'.

'Hello, Cyril,' she said breezily, going into his bathroom where he was sitting on a chair at the sink, wearing just a white vest and his bowler hat. His soiled pants were on the floor next to him. This was the first time she'd had to clean him up and she pulled her gloves on in readiness.

Cyril had a round face, and what was left of his dyed black hair was sleeked back with Brylcreme. He had what Ruby would describe as a "cheeky" face, the lines adorning it telling a merry tale of life on the boards, she guessed. He quite often could be seen tap dancing slowly on the stage in the Doris Day Room. Frustratingly, his arthritis would not allow him to go at full pelt any more. Cyril was one of the more colourful characters in the house, and would flirt with any female, given half the chance. His bedroom, like many of the others, was adorned with old black and white photos, mainly of beautiful women. Amongst them, amusingly, he had one big colour poster of a topless Linda Lusardi.

'I messed, Nurse, I'm sorry,' he said matter-of-factly, keeping his back to her. 'Bloody age – catches up on you, you know, dear. One minute you're running round the stage, limbs everywhere, blink and the next minute your legs hardly move and there's number twos running down them. Blooming annoying, if you ask me.'

Again, Ruby had a tear in her eye, not certain if it was brought on by the emotion of it all or from the particularly pungent stench rising from the discarded underpants on the tiled floor by her feet. 'Right, let's get you sorted, shall we?' She retched as quietly as she could, pulled a plastic bag out of the pocket of her tunic, and reached tentatively for the dirty Y-fronts.

'Would you like me to bathe you?' she asked softly, retaining her composure in order to retain Cyril's dignity.

'I can't think of anything I'd like more, but I'm so stiff from my dancing yesterday I can barely move,' he replied. 'Would you be a love and just wash me in here?'

Ruby nodded and began to fill his sink with warm water. She suddenly felt a bit awkward being faced with a naked man, despite him being eighty-five and needing her more than anything to help him. She'd only cleaned up a couple of the ladies before. She took a deep breath, looked out to the frosty grounds through the bedroom window beyond, and began the task in hand.

She knew that Cyril was sitting on the area that needed the most attention, but, due to the stench, decided to delay the main task. She started with his face, gently wiping him clean, rinsing the sponge out as she went, all the while trying to stop herself from gagging at the ripe odour that still enveloped the room. Cyril kept his eyes shut with a half smile on his face. When she tentatively reached his groin area put the sponge under his balls, the old man suddenly began to breathe heavily. Ruby pulled the sponge away in alarm, thinking he was about to have some sort of fit. 'Are you all right?' she asked urgently.

'Of course, nurse, I'm more than fine.' Cyril then let out a huge sigh.

Relieved, Ruby turned to the sink to rinse out the sponge under fresh running water.

Returning to her patient, she suddenly gasped, for there, standing large and proud, was Cyril's shriveled penis.

'Up periscope!' he said loudly, and laughed.

At that moment, Justice walked in. Ruby looked at her charge open-mouthed, pointed to his erection, and handed her colleague the sponge. Cyril's eyes were still closed and Justice silently shook with laughter. He waved Ruby out of the room and she blew him a kiss flirtatiously as she left.

'Cyril, are you misbehaving as usual?' Justice talked to the randy old devil with a smile in his voice.

'Oh, Justice, trust you to come and spoil my fun.' Cyril then opened his faded, knowing eyes, grinned, and let out an enormous fart.

Ruby walked to the staff room and put the kettle on. She checked herself in the mirror and laughed out loud. This job was surprisingly giving her more satisfaction than she thought possible. However, she was sure that flirting with a handsome man didn't quite have the same effect with a blob of dried poo on your cheek!

Quickly downing a cup of coffee and two custard creams from the stash she'd brought in earlier, she went to check on Lucas.

'Ginger! Just the girl.' He greeted her with a huge smile, and not to be left out, Montgomery jumped up from his basket, tail wagging, and came over for a pat.

Since his fall, every day without fail Ruby would make time to sit with Lucas. He was such good company it was quite often the highlight of her day. Today, she noticed how big his hazel eyes looked in his now hollowing face. Cancer was so ravaging, so cruel. Lucas was pale and shrinking by the minute; however, he always managed to look smart in his paisley smoking jacket, and still insisted on a daily shave.

Just being with the lovely Lucas made her question her own mortality. If she reached eighty – at a push – that actually wasn't that many years on the planet.

Three years at Ritsy Rose Interiors, six years with Dean, that was almost a tenth of her life taken up on things that did'nt make her happy! She certainly didn't want to waste any more time, and was now surer than ever that she had made the right decision to change her life's direction.

Ruby placed a cup of tea and a few custard creams on Lucas's bedside table.

'Dear girl, you really are quite wonderful,' he said camply, immediately dunking one of the biscuits and biting into it with relish. 'Now, myself and Monty need to ask a favour of you.'

'Fire away,' Ruby said chirpily.

'Well, it's damn frustrating but I don't seem to have the energy to walk the pup on the grounds any more, and we were wondering …' He looked down at his beloved pet who began to yap and wag his tail furiously, as if knowing they were talking about him. 'Well, we were wondering if you'd mind awfully helping us out.'

'Oh, Lucas, of course! It will be a pleasure. I'll be glad of the fresh air.'

Lucas grinned. 'Hmm. Yes, this place – *odeur de cabbage et piss*. Really quite vile!' Reaching for the old-fashioned perfume atomiser on his bedside table, he proceeded to spray a wonderful scent around the room.

Ruby put her hand on top of his. Feeling his thin, smooth skin, she became conscious of how fond she had grown of both Lucas and his best friend Monty in such a short time.

'Would you like me to read to you first?' she asked softly.

'That would be simply divine, dear girl. Simply divine.'

Chapter Eight

'Jesus is alive and kicking and living in Greenwich,' Bert shouted from the door of number 32, swathed in a blanket and swigging from a bottle of cider.

'Great,' Ruby replied. 'Maybe He'll beat Usain Bolt in the Olympics.'

At that moment, Pinch-faced Pru appeared on her doorstep, shooed Bert off, then sped away in her BMW convertible, without even acknowledging Ruby.

'Moody bitch,' Ruby said out loud.

'Oi oi. Bit early for that sort of talk, innit?' George bounded down his front steps on the other side, carrying a strimmer. 'How you doing anyway, bird? Haven't seen you for a while.'

'I'm fine, thanks – just completely knackered. It's not easy being a tart with a heart, you know.' George laughed as Ruby continued, 'Last day today though – and then all change next week.'

Margaret appeared at her front gate, waving her duster at them both. Ruby noticed that she was wearing a thick layer of bright coral lipstick. She had arched it into a bow on her top lip, and with her sugar-free Polo appearing in and out at regular intervals, it made her look like an exaggerated cartoon character,

'All right, Margaret?' they hollered in unison.

'George, would you be a dear and come and look at my bushes sometime? They really could do with a bit of a trim,' the old lady shouted across the road.

The cheeky gardener whispered to Ruby. 'Got it, you see, bird. Whatever age, they still want me.'

Ruby shook her head at him in mock disbelief, as he called out, 'Yeah, sure, Margaret. I'll try and pop in after work today.'

Margaret, ever the perceptive, piped up, 'Thanks, duck. By the way, Ruby, enjoy your last day with the big black man.' She winked and shuffled back indoors, leaving Ruby, cheeks a-burning and George looking at her quizzically.

'Well, have a good 'un, Rubes. You *and* the big black man.' He leapt into his van, cranked up his stereo, rolled down his window, and grinned. 'See ya, sexy!'

'Yeah, see ya, sexy,' Bert mimicked as he staggered down the street.

Ruby grimaced and set off walking to the station. What on earth would George think of her now? Requesting him to trim her unmentionables, and thenMargaret's implications about Justice. Hussy – that's exactly what he would think.

But why was she worried anyway? Sexy and handsome he might be, but at twenty-four, he really was far too young for her thirty years, and he wasn't even her type.

She couldn't believe it was her last day at Dinsworth House. Although she would have quite happily stayed on there, her mind was made up: she would follow through with her original plan of trying twelve career paths. Of course, there was a sense of turmoil within her. She felt sad at the prospect of leaving not only the residents, but also Justice.

Her friendship with him had developed nicely into an attraction, but other than being a mild flirtation, she didn't think he felt the same way that she did about him. But she had been glad of the savoury distraction amidst the occasional unsavoury aspects of the work.

Yes, Ruby decided, despite her reluctance to leave, she still felt strongly compelled to complete her mission. Twelve months, twelve jobs. One down – eleven to go!

'Got a minute to chat, Ginger?' Lucas enquired from his bed as Ruby stroked Montgomery, then sent the Jack Russell to his basket in the corner of the bedroom.

'Sure. It's my last day today.' Ruby had spent most of her shift having a last chat with all the residents, saving her favourite for the end.

'Last day, eh? I'm going to miss you, Ginger,' Lucas said meaningfully in his posh voice.

'And me you, Lucas. I promise to come and visit lots, and of course still take Montgomery out for walks.'

'Good, good, dear girl. That's what we like to hear.'

'I've always meant to ask you one thing, actually.'

'Fire away, Ginger, fire away.'

'Why "Montgomery"? Is he named after some sort of Lord?'

'Of sorts.' Lucas laughed heartily. He shifted himself to a sitting position. 'Montgomery Clift, have you heard of him?'

Ruby shook her head.

'He was a fine Hollywood actor, partial to both the ladies and the gentlemen, rumour has it.' Ruby smiled as Lucas continued in his animated fashion. 'He was such a fine specimen of a man that I likened Montgomery's kissable little face to his.'

'That's sweet,' Ruby cooed.

'Shame he met such a tragic end though,' Lucas said thoughtfully. 'The drink and drugs got him. It was said that even Marilyn Monroe didn't feel as if she had problems compared to his.'

'Oh dear,' Ruby said seriously. 'Well, we shall certainly make sure that the canine Montgomery Clift will not have any such difficulties. He shall be kept squeaky clean on a diet of dog biscuits, his only vice being the occasional cup of lukewarm tea.'

'Good show, Ginger, that's the spirit. Only the best for our little man.'

Ruby gently moved Lucas forward and plumped up the pillows behind him. 'You can tell me to stop being a nosey old bag if you like, Lucas, but do you have any family?' Ruby had been saddened that since starting at Dinsworth House four weeks ago, her favourite resident had not had even one visitor.

'That's the trouble with being a homo, my dear Ginger,' he explained without bitterness. 'Sometimes it can be a lonely old life. I'm an only child, and of course had no children of my own. Lots of friends, mind, but as you get older, and especially with the lives we used to lead, they all popped off early.'

Ruby looked at him forlornly, and he grinned at her, exclaiming, 'Oh, Ginger, do cheer up! I've had the most amazing life. I also had the most amazing love. Gerald was his name. He was the most terrible tart. Fat old queen too, but his personality was his draw. He was a stand-up comedian, incredibly funny, and despite his promiscuity I knew that his heart always lay with me. He left me his beautiful cottage in the Lakes too, in a pretty village called Millbeck. The pair of us had some bloody marvelous times there. Two old *daffodils* together.' He paused as if remembering the good times. 'Damn shame it's so bloody remote or I'd be there now, rather than in the suburbs of the big smoke any day.' It all became clear to Ruby why Lucas had such a love of the Lake District. 'He died of AIDS, you know. Terrible business.' A tear ran slowly down his left cheek. 'I still miss the old bugger.'

Ruby went to the sink and got a warm flannel. She gently wiped his face.

'Would you like me to read to you?' she asked quietly.

Lucas slipped back down into the bed, ignoring her question, and began to quietly sing "My Way", about the final curtain. He turned on his side.

'Ginger, tuck me in, dear girl, would you – and pull the curtains.'

She did as she was asked, then reached for the Wordsworth poetry book. Sitting next to Lucas, she held his hand and read his favourite poem. As she reached the lines 'And then my heart with pleasure fills, and dances with the Daffodils', a wonderful smile spread across his face ... and then he was gone.

Ruby took a deep breath as a flood of tears filled her green eyes. She leant down to kiss her beautiful friend's now peaceful and relaxed face, and then opened the window wide to let his big spirit free.

Chapter Nine

Justice held Ruby close in the staff room as she wept loudly.

She could feel his warm, big body against hers and suddenly felt very safe.

'It's OK, angel,' he soothed. 'He didn't suffer for long. We had no idea he was so close to the end. The doctor saw him just a couple of days ago and said he might have another six to eight weeks.'

Pulling her closer to him, Justice began to stroke her hair comfortingly. After so many months of abstinence Ruby suddenly became aware of her built-up sexual tension. She stopped crying and lifted her head to face him. He looked down at her lovingly and put his big soft lips on hers. She closed her eyes in ecstasy and pushed herself against him. All of a sudden, the door to the staff room burst open. Then *WHACK*! – There was a slap to the side of her head and then *WHACK*! – A slap to the side of Justice's head.

'What the hell do you think you're doing, Justice, you cheating, lying, no-good bastard?'

'Whoa now, Ellie, it's not what it seems,' he said, holding his hands up in an appeasing way. 'I was just comforting Ruby. She was with Lucas when he died.'

'Oh, so you stick your tongue down everyone's throat to comfort them, do ya!'

'Ellie-Ruby-Ruby-Ellie,' Justice floundered.

Ruby could see the angry whites of Ellie's eyes. She was a large black lady with a shock of cropped blonde hair.

'So while I'm stuck with my reception duties, you've made it your business to get jiggy with some limey red-headed slapper of an auxiliary.' She lifted both hands in the air and waved them around madly. 'Failed your nursing exams, did you, sister?'

With that she careered down the corridor, sending both Marilyn Monroe and Greta Garbo flying as she did so.

'Thank goodness you *didn't* get jiggy with this limey red-headed slapper, eh?' Ruby chewed on her nails, still in shock. 'Or we'd probably both be meeting Lucas again, sooner rather than later!'

Johnny phoned as Ruby reached Putney station and she explained what had happened. She had had no idea that Justice was already spoken for. Luckily, Mrs Hornsby hadn't caught wind of the incident, so her reference from Dinsworth House would remain excellent.

'Anyway, *c'est la vie, chérie,*' Johnny chuckled, taking her tale of woe in his stride. 'It's February first tomorrow – new job, new knob and all that.'

'You've got me another job already? That's great.'

'Um, well, not quite yet. There's not a lot around, as you can imagine, but I'm on the case, on the case.'

Chapter Ten

The *Deal or No Deal* theme tune was blaring out of the television when George arrived at Margaret's. He pulled his West Ham scarf and Puffa jacket tightly around him and shivered. Being a landscape gardener was great in the summer, but definitely had its downsides in the winter. Today, he felt chilled to the bone.

Pushing back his non-existent fringe, he knocked loudly with the gleaming brass knocker. Margaret turned the television down and shuffled to the door in her slippers. Her coral lipstick was now even thicker, and she was wearing a smart brown dress and long string of pearls. In George's honour? He sincerely hoped it wasn't. Maybe he shouldn't have tempted fate and jested with Ruby earlier about the old girl's intentions.

'I mean, why would anyone deal at ten grand when the quarter of a million's still there?' Margaret announced, Polo flying in and out of her mouth, leaving George bemused at what she was on about. He never had been one for quiz shows.

'Just look at you, all wrapped up and handsome.'

She squidged his chin with her right hand. Oh God, maybe it was for him! She carried on her monologue. 'Noel Edmonds and you all in one day, what is a woman to do?'

She laughed and George smiled slightly uncomfortably.

'Sorry I'm so late, Margaret – ended up working in the East End, so I took the chance to pop into me old dear's.'

'Oh, it doesn't matter, darling. Why don't you come in and have a cuppa with *this* old dear now? It's far too dark for you to see out the back, especially as my sensor light has broken.'

George took off his jacket and scarf, and made himself comfortable on the armchair with the threadbare arms.

Relishing the heat of the open fire, he looked around and noticed the archaic gramophone. Loving music so much, he couldn't even imagine life without his iPod. The antique pictures and cluttered hearth reminded him of his Nanny Stevens' house, and he felt momentarily sad that she was not around any more. Margaret shuffled in from the kitchen with a brass tray, housing the customary metal tea pot and flowery bone-china cups and saucers.

'So do you have an old man, as well as an old dear?' she asked, smiling.

'Yeah. Very happy they are too. Me old man is a postman. He was enjoying having a bit of time off today, after the Christmas rush and all that.'

'Brothers and sisters?' Margaret paused. 'I'm sorry, duck. Listen to me, sounding like a nosey old neighbour.'

George realised that Margaret probably was quite lonely. But she seemed so homely and kind that it didn't seem too much of a hardship to spend some time with her.

She had introduced herself to him the day he moved in, bringing to his door a pint of milk and some teabags. 'I know you boys, I bet you're not prepared,' was all she had said and left him to it. Since then, their waving ritual had continued until today, two months later, when she had actually asked him for his help and he was happy to oblige.

'No brothers and sisters, just me,' George offered.

'So, if your roots are in the East End, why did you choose to live in Putney?' she continued.

'Most of my regular clients are over this way, so it just made more sense. I like it over here too. Far enough out of town if you want a bit of peace, but near enough if you want a big night out.'

Margaret nodded. 'Although, since my feet have been bad, I haven't been up West for ten years. Got a dream of having tea at The Ritz one day. Keeps me going, that one does,' she carried on thoughtfully.

'Do you have any children, Margaret?'

The old lady nodded. 'Just the one son. Greg, his name is. He's in his forties now. Lives in Australia with his wife, so I rarely see him. No grandchildren to miss, so that's a blessing, if you know what I mean.' She paused and suddenly looked very sad.

Leaning down and rubbing her protruding bunion through her slippers, she continued, 'Can't any of you youngsters around here get on with it? I could do with some babysitting duties.'

'Don't look at me with children in your eyes,' George laughed. 'I'm only twenty-four, and enjoying being single, thank you very much.'

'I can't believe you don't have a glint in your eye for Miss Red-Head next door though. She's such a bonny girl.'

'Ruby?' He screwed his face up. 'Ruby's just Ruby,' he replied nonchalantly.

The old lady looked at him knowingly, deftly sucking her Polo in and out.

'Don't look at me like that. She's a good laugh and all that, but she's definitely not my type, and she's at least five years older than me.'

'Nincompoop!' Margaret exclaimed loudly. 'You young 'uns. With age comes sage, I say. Mind you, liver spots too,' she laughed.

'My dear Margaret, if you do want me to trim your bushes I suggest you leave it there.'

George grinned as he said it, but the old girl was no fool and knew when to shut up.

He stood up from the armchair. 'Right, I'm getting off. Ta for the tea.'

'OK, duck. Could you put my record on for me before you go, please? These damn feet of mine.'

'Course I can.' George walked over to the gramophone. 'I'll pop round in the morning to look at your garden, and check what's up with your sensor light too. Probably just a bulb.'

'You're a darling. Thank you.'

When George had eventually worked out how to use the archaic music machine, Margaret shut the door and began to sing aloud the lyrics to 'The Garden of Eden'.

George shivered as he walked to his flat, the dulcet tones of Frankie Vaughan ringing in his ears, and filthy thoughts of Ruby Matthews beginning to run through his mind

Chapter Eleven

'Your new usual, Ruby?' Raj enquired from behind the shop counter, holding up a packet of custard creams.

'Actually, Raj, today is a monumental day, as from now onwards, I would like my old usual please – some biscuits *and* my *Oh Yeah* mag.'

Raj laughed.

It was a novelty to feel the excitement of pulling a shiny new magazine off the shelf. In the past, Ruby had become complacent with how lucky she was, and would never have believed that getting home and immersing herself in the world of ultra-skinny celebrities and glitzy marriages that were destined to fail would become classed as a treat. At least it would help her forget about the awful day she'd had.

She was still by no means cash rich, but this month, having started her twelve-job mission, she was at least able to keep her head above water. She just hoped that Johnny would be able to find her something as soon as possible so that the mission could continue as planned.

'I'd better take some sugar-free Polos for Margaret too?'

'You are joking, aren't you?' Suki enquired from the back of the shop. 'She's got no teeth to worry about.'

'Don't ask,' Ruby laughed. 'That reminds me. I said I'd do a shopping run for her tomorrow. I'll drop a list in.'

'OK, no problem. See you tomorrow.'

'Good night,' Ruby shouted as she made her way outside into the freezing night air.

With the upset of losing Lucas and the Justice drama that had ensued, Ruby was utterly exhausted when she pushed open her front door. She fed a wailing Patrick, who bolted his food and shot out of the cat flap, made herself a cup of tea, and lay on the sofa ready to read her magazine. She was cold. Thankful that she could still afford her heating bills, she wandered to the kitchen and turned her heating up high.

An hour later, she awoke with a start to hear somebody banging loudly on her front door. 'Ruby? Ruby – you in there?' the male voice demanded urgently. Still half asleep, she pushed the magazine off her face, pulled herself out of her chair, wiped the dribble from the side of her mouth, ran downstairs quickly, and opened the door. Her eyes were almost closed and her now greasy hair stuck up on end. Too dozy to be mortified, she was faced with a frantic Gorgeous George.

'What on earth's the matter?' she managed to mumble.

'Ruby, you have to come quick. It's Patrick. I was turning in off of the main road and he ran out. I really had no chance to miss him. I am so sorry.' He had tears in his eyes.

'Is he …?'

Ruby didn't really want to know.

'Is he still alive?' George said for her. 'Yes, he is. Quick, I wrapped him in my scarf and left him on the road. I was worried about moving him.'

Slamming the front door behind her, she grabbed George's hand and ran as fast as she could to the end of the road.

'No, oh no.' She went down on her knees to cradle her beloved furry friend. There was blood coming from his mouth, and one of his front legs was bent behind him awkwardly. 'It's OK, darling boy,' she soothed. Patrick looked up at her with his big amber eyes. 'Can you take us to the vet's, George?'

'Of course I can. You stay right here. I'll get my van.'

Two hours and one hundred and ten pounds later (which George had agreed to cough up), Patrick had eight lives left. He had a bump on his head and his leg was in a splint, but the vet said he had been very lucky.

George pulled up outside his place and they both got out. 'I am so sorry again, Rubes.'

'If you'd have killed him then you would be,' Ruby said in all seriousness. 'Right, I'd better get the old boy in.' She cradled Patrick gently in her arms. 'Oh shit!'

'What is it?' George asked, concerned.

'In the hurry to get to Patrick, I've locked myself out. The only spare key I have is at my mum's in Reading.'

'Shall I take you there?' George's guilt was making him far too generous.

'No, it's far too far away, and far too late, and I'm still too skint for a locksmith's call-out charge. Oh bloody hell!'

George locked the van and put his arm around her shoulders. Patrick was shivering. Margaret, pulling her bedroom curtains, looked out and saw them together and held herself in glee.

'Come into the warm,' George said kindly. 'We can make up a bed for Patrick and you can have my flatmate's room – he's away for a while.' He paused. 'And as it's you, I promise to keep my hands to myself. Don't worry about your key either. I've got a mate who'd be able to break in without causing too much damage.'

Tired, hungry, and freezing, Ruby could do nothing but nod in agreement. She couldn't even be bothered to get into a conversation about George's flatmate. She was sure she'd never seen anyone else going in and out of his place.

George pushed open his front door and stepped aside to allow Ruby and her precious cargo through. Trying not to jolt Patrick, she stepped carefully over the pile of lads' mags in the hallway and walked straight up the stairs and into the lounge. George threw her a towel and she made her furry patient a makeshift sleeping area on the comfy blue sofa. For once, the old Tom didn't make a peep. He just looked up at her with his big yellow eyes as if to say thanks. Ruby thought what could have been, and realised there and then just how much she loved him.

She up to the bathroom, and wasn't sure if she was more shocked by the scum ring around the bath, or by what a fright she looked. She was still wearing her sick- stained tunic and her hair was sticking up like a cock's comb. She put some toothpaste on her finger and roughly ran it around her gums, wetted her hands and pushed her hair down as far as it would allow her.

Her nosiness got the better of her, and instead of going straight downstairs, she peeped into the bedrooms. The smaller of the two was very tidy. The double bed was covered with a plain white duvet and a black roller blind was pulled down over the window. Aftershaves sat in a neat row on a chest of drawers, and a law textbook rested open and face down on the bedside table. The other bedroom wasn't quite so neat. The king-size sleigh bed was unmade and there were clothes all over the floor. A West Ham calendar hung from the wardrobe door, and a *Nuts* magazine and half full glass of stale water were on the bedside table. A portable Bose sound system sat on a chest of drawers.

On coming downstairs, she walked past the kitchen, and noticed the pile of dirty dishes stacked in the sink. She hadn't been inside a bachelor pad for ages. It must be an age thing, she thought, but she had an amazing urge to pull on a pair of rubber gloves and start cleaning.

Maybe if it wasn't a rented flat they'd take more care of it, she thought. She had been quite disappointed when Margaret had told her that George didn't actually own it. Whatever age, a man with assets was always far more attractive to her than one without.

She could hear George in the front room talking to Patrick.

'She's not bad, your mum, is she, mate? And she loves ya, that's for sure.'

Ruby managed a secret smile.

'Nice uniform,' George smirked when she appeared in the lounge doorway. 'But I think I might pass on a bed bath this time.' She threw a cushion at him.

'Oi, mind your pussy,' he warned her. 'Don't want to get him too excited, do we?' He held his hand up to protect Patrick and laughed. 'Do you want me to wash your uniform for tomorrow?' he enquired.

Ruby nearly fainted. Men didn't normally think out of the box like that, did they?

'No, its fine,' she replied. 'Last day at Dinsworth House today, remember. That's a point, I should have given the uniform back, but with all the drama …' she hesitated.

'Drama?' George enquired. Ruby burst into tears.

'What is it, Rubes?' George went to her side.

'Lucas, one of the residents, died today. I'd become really fond of him.' She continued to sob.

George took her in his arms and comforted her. Burrowing into his chest, he rubbed the top of her hair affectionately. She turned her head to face him and sprang on him the most passionate kiss she had ever given anyone in her life.

But this wasn't enough for Ruby Matthews. Feeling a huge surge of life, that only witnessing someone die can bring, Ruby pushed George back firmly on to his sofa and kissed him again.

All the while Patrick snored peacefully beside them.

When George's hand began creeping up her tunic, reality hit home and Ruby jumped up like a jack-in-a-box, words tumbling out of her mouth at one hundred miles an hour. 'Oh my God, I'm so so sorry, I really don't know what came over me. That was just so out of character for me.'

George, still gaining his breath back, smirked. 'Well, if that character wants to come back again, then she's really welcome.'

'I h-have to leave,' she stuttered.

'You've got nowhere to go,' he told her.

Flustered completely from her advances, and the fact that she had become a serial snogger in her hour of need, she laughed nervously. Her immaturity even shocked herself at times. Changing the subject completely, she managed to regain her composure.

'So, this mate of yours who can break into my house – is he a locksmith then?'

'Something like that.' George tapped the side of this nose. 'Ask me no questions, I will tell you no lies. Now get your clothes off and get into that spare bed. Unless you want to get in mine, of course?' He fetched her a clean pair of boxers and a big T-shirt. 'Mind you, your big black man might not like you staying at a strange bloke's house. Whoever he is.'

'Ask me no questions, I will tell you no lies,' Ruby said smugly, forcing George to laugh out loud.

'Smartarse!' He playfully punched her on the arm.

'Jealous are you?' she pushed.

'Jealous? Me? Don't flatter yourself, love,' he grinned. 'Now do as you're told and get your clothes off.'

'Goodnight,' Ruby shouted breezily through the now closed door of the spare room. 'Thanks for helping me out,' she called, leaving a somewhat bewildered George to study his *Nuts* magazine.

Chapter Twelve

Attending Lucas's cremation a week later had brought with it a day of mixed emotions. As he had no family, Mr Bentley, the owner of Dinsworth House, had made the arrangements. Ruby had sneaked in the back as Justice had told her his girlfriend would be attending, and she didn't want to bump into Ellie and cause any sort of commotion. She did, however, sing at the top of her voice to "All Things Bright and Beautiful", as she knew it was one of Lucas's favourites. Justice held on to Montgomery, who wore a fetching pink bow on his collar and appropriately yapped the whole way through the hymn. Ruby thought it would have been a terrible shame for such a great man to leave this world to too small an audience, and was heartened to see as many residents present were able to attend. Mrs Hornsby and a few of the other nurses were also there.

As she watched the curtains shut on Lucas for the final time, Ruby prayed that he would soon be meeting Gerald, and that they would have a fine old time laughing and quaffing champagne together on a cloud of daffodils.

Margaret was sweeping her front step as Ruby slowly walked up Amerland Road. The old lady could sense her sadness.

'Cuppa, duck?' Ruby nodded and followed her inside, to the comforting sight and sound of a roaring fire. As soon as the door was shut behind her, Ruby started to cry. Margaret awkwardly drew Ruby into her ample bosom. The scent of mothballs and Brasso felt strangely comforting.

'Rum old thing, death.'

'It just makes me think of my dad every time I'm faced with it again,' Ruby blubbered.

'I know, duck, and I can't say it gets any easier the older you get. There's not a day goes by that I don't miss my Stanley.' Margaret held her tightly and added, 'Well, let's hope Lucas is in a better place now.'

'Yes,' Ruby sniffed, wishing that somebody, some day, would actually prove there was a heaven. 'I won't stay for tea if you don't mind, Margaret,' she went on. 'I've got loads of chores to get on with.'

'You do that, duck. Maybe George will come round and comfort you later.'

'What makes you say that?' Ruby asked.

'I saw you coming out of his doorway the other morning.' Her faded blue eyes twinkled. 'Do I need to start saving for a hat?'

'Margaret! What are you like? We're just friends,' Ruby blushed.

'Oh, right, and I've got a set of filmstar veneers,' the old girl laughed, and gave her a wet kiss on the cheek. 'Take care, love. Always here if you need an ear.'

Patrick was purring in the front window, looking out at the birds like the King of Sheba when Ruby arrived home. George had insisted on buying the red velvet cushion for him as he took sole responsibility for the animal's broken leg. There had been no mention of the kissing incident. Ruby had put it down to spur-of-the-moment madness in her grief, and because George hadn't said anything, she guessed he wasn't that bothered either.

After she had fed her pampered pussy cat, she lay back on her sofa. She had chores to do, but now she was home and sat down, she couldn't be bothered. She sat back and thought over the last few hours.

Tonight, she really fancied going out. Ruby had hoped

that there would be some sort of wake for Lucas, but Justice had told her that for some reason Mr Bentley hadn't arranged one.

Although Johnny had paid her, current outgoings still only allowed a couple of nights out a month and she didn't want to waste one on not having anywhere in particular to go. Johnny had texted earlier to say he was still on the search for job Number Two, and she prayed that he would find her something and fast.

Her landline rang. It was her brother. 'Big sis! How the devil are you?' Sam asked. She felt too sad to relay the story of today's events, so put the onus back on her brother, a common occurrence when discussing death in the Matthews family, she noticed. They barely discussed their father's death, as the pain was still so intense even after four years. They all realised this probably wasn't healthy, but nobody ever took the initiative to start talking about it, for fear of bringing the hurt to the surface and doing more harm than good.

'Sam the man!' she exclaimed. 'More importantly, how are you and Ben getting on?'

'Just fine. He is the most amazing dog and I can't tell you the freedom it's given me. I get the bus to college without a second thought now. It's freed up lots of Mum's time too as she doesn't feel she has to chaperone me everywhere.'

Ruby felt forever humbled by her brave, forthright brother. Here she was feeling sorry for herself, and really she led a very blessed life. She often felt guilty about her completeness and wished she could change places with him, even just for one day.

'I'm really chuffed for you, Sam,' Ruby said, and she meant it. 'I actually have some news for you too,' she went on. 'Don't faint but I've been working as a nurse in an old people's home for the past month.'

'Bloody hell, sis. Not like you to get your hands dirty.'

'Oi, Samuel Matthews!'

'Bet you smelt of piss and cabbage when you got home at night,' Sam continued to annoy her.

'Sam! Well, yes – and sick and poo too. But do you know what? The sense of satisfaction I got from helping people was worth more than working on a bloody million boring marketing campaigns.'

'Well, I'm really pleased for you, sis.'

'Anyway, is Mum there?' Ruby enquired. 'I'd better fill her in on what's going on with me.'

'She's out, actually.'

'Where's she gone?' Ruby said with surprise. Her mother never usually went out after dark unless it was with one of her children.

'Not sure. Graham picked her up around seven. Think they were going for a meal.'

'What – Graham from the guide dog place?' Ruby remembered his gorgeous face and how she had felt when she saw him. 'He's a bit young for Mum, isn't he?'

'He's thirty-five. What's fifteen years between friends, eh? But I'm sure it's not like that. You know what Mum's like, she's probably just discussing my well-being.'

'Yeah, I expect so.'

'There was actually another reason for my call.'

'Go on,' Ruby urged.

'Well, Graham thinks it would be a good idea for Ben and me to come up to London with him to face some different obstacles – in particular the Underground. I was wondering if maybe we could crash at yours and make a weekend of it?'

'Yes, yes of course that's fine.'

'Cool, thanks. That's great, Rubes.'

'I'll give you a buzz tomorrow and let you know which weekend is good.'

'OK, but don't let it clash with the Mighty Royals' next home game.'

'As if!' Ruby exclaimed. 'See you soon. Really looking forward to it.'

Once she had finished yet another cup of tea, she ran a bath. Lying back, she closed her eyes and luxuriated in her Royal Jelly bubble bath, a much appreciated Christmas gift from her mother. As the warm water soothed her tired body, she thought about poor old Lucas and suddenly felt very depressed. Then, realising that he wouldn't have wanted her to be sad, she began to have romantic thoughts instead.

She imagined frolicking on the white sands of Saint Lucia with Justice. Dave Kitwell blew her secret kisses from the pitch as Graham tenderly held her hand while Reading beat Manchester United. She even fantasised about Gorgeous George trimming her bush with his strimmer.

'Shit!' Ruby sat bolt upright. Here she was, thinking about all these men in her life when she really should be thinking about her best friend Fi. She had forgotten to return her New Year's Eve text – and with everything else going on, she hadn't made any effort to call her for the whole month.

Patrick happened to limp into the bathroom as his mistress leapt out of the bath, covering him from ears to tail in bubbles. Meowing in dismay, the Tom made a mental note that he really must call the RSPCA himself in the morning.

Chapter Thirteen

'Darling girl, the Sauvignon Blanc cabaret has arrived!' Fiona O'Donahue pushed past Ruby and opened the fridge, depositing four bottles of her favourite tipple on the top shelf. 'I can't believe the lovely little man in the corner shop knew what wine you liked best. I just went in there, mentioned in conversation I was visiting, and he filled my box, so to speak. He also put in this week's *Oh Yeah* and some custard creams, and said you could pay him in the week. However, being the marvellous friend that I am, they are obviously a gift from moi!'

Ruby smiled at her outlandish friend. 'Who'd have thought the day would come when a bottle of wine would be a luxury item in this household? Good old Raj. And thanks, mate.'

Fi's uncontrollable afro hair (her parents had no idea where it came from) was scraped back, wild strands making their escape. Her kohl eyeliner was smudged and she constantly reapplied lipgloss to her rosebud lips. Her one green and one brown eye made her look strangely exotic.

Ruby loved having her around. Fi hadn't changed from the moment they had randomly met in the Hairy Lemon, a roaring pub in Dublin, two years previously. Ruby had gone on a last-ditch weekend with her ex-boyfriend Dean, thinking they could rekindle their dwindling relationship.

Meeting the hilarious Fi had made her realise that she would have much more fun being single. So, a dull old relationship ended and a beautiful new friendship began.

Furthermore, much to Ruby's delight, after spending

countless weekends in London with her friend, Fi decided she loved it enough to move over from Dublin. She had found a job straight away working for an event company who arranged high-profile celebrity launches and parties. It was the ideal job to suit her exuberant personality.

'Get some glasses out, darling,' she said. 'We must have a drink to celebrate my arrival.'

Ruby laughed and hugged her. 'Sorry for being such a shit friend.'

'Well, yes, you are, but I do accept the apology. I would also like to announce that I think it's bloody amazing that you stayed in a job for a whole month wiping old people's arses.' Without allowing Ruby to get a word in, she continued, her Irish lilt rising the more excited she got, 'I am also *so* jealous of you snogging a gorgeous black man. You must fill me in. Did he have a big one?'

'Fiona O'Donahue. You really are quite vulgar.' Ruby thought back to that magical moment. 'But yes, as it happens, he did,' she admitted. 'Sadly, I only felt it pushed against my ribcage through two sets of clothes, as his girlfriend – who, I might add, I was completely unaware of – disturbed us and ruined the moment.'

'Oh, how bloody annoying. Do you think there's any chance of a reprisal?'

'No way!' Ruby exclaimed. 'The size of his willy was nothing in comparison to the size of his girlfriend.'

They both fell about laughing.

'It's good to see you, mate,' Ruby managed once they'd stopped laughing.

'You too,' Fi replied. 'Now remind me of tonight's plan?'

Before she could answer and go on to tell Fi about 'the kiss' with George, there was an almighty commotion at the front door as Sam let himself in. Patrick hissed and wailed his disapproval at another animal daring to enter his territory. Ben, as calm as a guide dog could be when faced with the maddest cat in London, held his head high but looked quite perturbed by the whole situation.

'Hi, sis.' Sam kissed her on the cheek and stood very still. 'You haven't moved anything around since I was last here, have you?'

'Darling brother, of course not. I think we'll all be fine with furniture negotiation even after a skinful.'

Her brother unleashed Ben, who surreptitiously began to suss out the geography of the flat.

'I can smell Fi – where is she?' Sam asked innocently.

'What do you mean you can smell me, you eejit?' Fi shrieked.

'Coco Mademoiselle today, isn't it?' Sam announced, quite chuffed with himself. Fi was always smothered in beautiful perfume and for this reason, plus her *joie de vivre*, he'd had a crush on her since he was a fifteen-year- old schoolboy. In fact, way back, he had made a point of learning all the new fragrances just so he could impress her.

'Where's Graham?' Ruby asked Sam.

'He's got to work till seven. Said he'd call when he gets into Paddington later.'

'Who's Graham?' Fi's ears pricked up at the mention of a new man.

'He's Sam's guide dog instructor. Completely gorgeous, but rumour has it he's dating our mother.' Ruby laughed.

'No! How old is he then?' Fi asked.

'Thirty-five,' Sam replied.

'Same age as me, eh?' Fi raised her eyebrows. 'Well, good on her, I say. Top girl your ma is, and she deserves all the happiness.'

'Knock, knock,' Gorgeous George said loudly through the already open door.

'Come in, George.' Ruby waved her arms towards Fi. 'George, Fi – Fi, George.'

'Ruby, I already know who Fiona is,' George reminded her. 'I met her at Pinch-faced Pru's Christmas drinks.'

'Nice bod,' Fi mouthed to Ruby, who could feel herself blushing.

'Shit, yeah, of course you did. I seem to have had total memory loss from that night. Well, nearly.' She reeled inside again at her most recent unruly behaviour and quickly turned to Sam.

'Sam, this is Gorge –' she managed to stop herself in time. 'I mean, this is George.' She paused. 'My neighbour and friend.'

'All right mate?' George shook Sam's hand. 'Glad to say that the Mighty Hammers are whipping those not so Mighty Royals' arses in the Premier League.'

'Oi!' both Sam and Ruby said in unison.

'Drink before we go?' Ruby asked. 'I've got white wine or white wine.'

Chapter Fourteen

Ruby awoke to the sound of very loud snoring in her left ear. Her head was pounding from the copious amount of wine she had consumed the night before. She turned over, expecting to see the tangled offerings of Fi's afro strewn on the pillow next to her, but instead was faced with a cropped black head of hair.

The black head of hair turned over and Ruby screamed. 'Oh my God, did we do it?'

'Keep the noise down, bird,' George slurred. 'My head's banging.'

'Well, did we?' she repeated, swearing to herself that that was the last time she was ever going to drink to oblivion again.

'Rubes, I'm quite hurt that you find the thought so repulsive, but no, *we didn't do it.*' He dropped his Cockney accent and adopted her English rose tone. 'Well, I don't think we did anyway,' he teased. 'You were well up for it *again* though.' Ruby closed her eyes in disbelief as her handsome neighbour continued, 'And we did have a good old fumble. You've got quite decent tits!'

Ruby hid her head under the covers.

'And you definitely *could* do with a bit of a trim.' She stayed there as George continued. 'I was actually quite surprised not to see a flash of grey.'

And then, as she continued to groan in agony at the sheer embarrassment of it all, George looked down at her. 'But being the gentleman that I am, I didn't think it right in your semi-conscious state to go any further.'

Ruby, albeit mortified by her antics, let out a sigh of

relief. It wasn't that she didn't think George was very sexy. In fact, lying there next to her with his buff chest on display, she quite easily could have ravished him stone cold sober.

However, with the good friendship developing between them, she didn't want to ruin that. Well ... that was what her head was telling her anyway.

She sat up in bed and then promptly slid back down again, realising that she was only in her underwear. 'Please go and get me some tea, George. I feel like I've licked the bottom of a parrot's cage.'

'Maybe that's not all you licked.' The cheeky gardener laughed loudly as Ruby whacked him with a pillow.

While George boiled the kettle, she swiftly pulled on her shirt. On his return, they sat back in his sleigh bed like an old couple, propped up drinking tea.

'Oh shit, some of it's coming back to me now.' Ruby began to remember the night before and held her head in her hands.

'Well, brace yourself, Rubes, you're not going to like what you're about to hear.'

'Oh no.' Ruby moaned. 'Tell me everything that happened.'

'Well, in short, we all ended up in The Collection on the Kings Road – poncy bar if you ask me, but Fi insisted. Anyway, your mum called to confess that yes she *was* in a relationship with Graham and was very happy. You happened to get something in your eye and Graham was leaning over you. In my drunken state I thought he was trying it on with you so I stupidly told Sam, who became angry at Graham for betraying your mum and for taking advantage of you when you were hanging. He went to punch him, missed, fell against a table, and knocked a beer over some city twat.'

'Bless him, poor Sam,' Ruby uttered.

'Well, it actually got worse, because the City twat

starting taking the mick out of Sam for wearing dark glasses inside. That's where I intervened and told him that actually *he* must be blind, as the bronzed bimbo he was with was more of a dog than Ben. I proceeded to lump him right on the jaw. Needless to say, we all got chucked out.'

'I can't believe I don't remember that,' Ruby whined.

'By this time, you were so drunk your head was resting on the table.'

'Classy!' Ruby uttered. 'So where did everyone sleep?'

'Ruby. OK, please keep calm. To be honest ... I'm not actually sure where everyone is.'

'Oh no. Please tell me Sam is safe,' Ruby screeched. George remained silent.

'Well, is he?' Ruby was near tears.

'That's the thing,' George said guiltily. 'Amongst the entire fracas, Sam managed to find his way out of the bar with Ben chasing behind him. Graham and I searched for them for around an hour but with no joy. I gave Graham the spare key to yours as you were insistent that you wanted to play the Diet Coke Man game with Gorgeous George.'

Ruby managed a slight smile, then realising the urgency of the situation, jumped out of bed. 'We have to get up right now and find Sam,' she croaked. 'He may have gone home but I daren't call Mum for fear of worrying her in case he didn't.'

'Does he have your address here?' George enquired, slightly concerned now.

'Yes, of course he bloody does. Let's go to mine now, in fact. He may be there and we're worrying for nothing.'

While George went to the bathroom, Ruby wandered into the kitchen in her knickers and shirt in search of her jeans. She had a raging thirst. Not able to find one clean mug amongst the pile of washing up, she bent right over the sink. With one foot on the floor and her thonged arse in air, she gulped the cold water straight from the tap.

'Think these may be what you were looking for, pet.' A male Geordie accent rose from the kitchen table and Ruby nearly fainted with shock. She whipped around, and sitting there was a man shielding his face with a tea towel in one hand andher jeans in the other.

Bless him, Ruby thought gratefully. Most men would have just sat there and had a right old gawp. Mind you, she didn't know how much he'd seen before the aforementioned towel had been surreptitiously positioned. Grabbing the jeans, she held them in front of her to cover her embarrassment.

'Why-aye, lass, I'm James – George's flatmate.'

'Oh, um, hi, James.' Ruby was blushing to the roots of her hair.

James looked like an older version of Harry Potter, and appeared very studious with his small round-framed Gucci glasses. He had what her mother would call 'a friendly face', and short brown hair tinged with flecks of grey. He was tall and gangly, with day old stubble on his chin. Even in his faded blue dressing gown, Ruby found him quite attractive in a geeky sort of way.

'This isn't how it looks, you know.'

He laughed and Ruby noticed the sweet little crinkles at the corner of his eyes. 'I'm not your brother, pet. It's none of my business what you get up to.' At the mention of the word 'brother' Ruby started to cry. James immediately went into 'I'm a man and I'm not sure what to do with a woman's emotions' mode. 'Oh shit, I've made you cry and I don't even know your name.' He awkwardly stood up and went to comfort her. In his shyness, and trying not to touch her bare legs or bum, he accidentally put his hand directly on her right breast. 'Oh shit, pet, oh sorry!' he exclaimed, then 'Oh, let me leave you to sort yourself out now.' He turned and rushed to his bedroom.

Just then, George appeared in the doorway. Noticing her tearstained face, he said, 'Bloody hell, Rubes, what's the matter?'

'I'm fine, fine. It was just something James said. I'm so worried about Sam. We have to find him.'

'James? I didn't realise he was back this weekend.'

'Oh, it doesn't matter, let's go round to mine pronto,' Ruby stressed.

'See you later, mate,' George shouted up the stairs.

He could hear the shower running, so without waiting for an answer, he grabbed his keys off of the side and hurried to the front door.

On arrival at her maisonette, Graham staggered down to the door looking grey and tired. He opened it and went upstairs to slump back on the sofa. A disgruntled Patrick ran in, his leg seemingly completely healed. Wasn't it cats that were supposed to have nights out on the tiles? the animal thought, and proceeded to wail and brush his tail around Ruby's legs for both attention and food.

'Any news?' Graham asked the pair, concern evident in his voice.

'Nope,' they replied in unison.

'I've phoned Laura – I mean your mum,' Graham told Ruby shyly. 'I acted really normal and upbeat and said we'd all had a great time. Sam is definitely not there, she would have said something.'

'Do you think we should call the police?' Ruby asked, now frantic with worry.

'Call the police about what?' Sam appeared in the lounge doorway, holding Ben firmly by his harness and with a pint of milk in the other hand. Without giving anyone a chance to speak, he launched into his little speech. 'Boy, what a night! Firstly, I want to say sorry, Graham, for even thinking you would hurt our mum. I was drunk and an idiot.' He lifted his dark glasses and rubbed his eyes. 'God, I need to sit down.'

He held out the milk, which Ruby took from him as Graham got out of his seat. 'Can you make me a cup of tea, please, sis? I'm parched.'

George helped Sam to the chair. 'So, where did you go, mate?'

'Well, I remembered Ruby telling me once that there were some good bars in Soho. Ben had luckily caught up with me by this time, and nudged me to show I was safe. I asked someone to hail us a cab and asked the driver to take us there.'

'Puts a new spin on being blind drunk, I guess,' Ruby joked. 'Anyway, go on,' she urged.

'Well, we wandered around for a bit, listening to the vibe of the West End, and then a really nice lady, who from the sound of her voice echo, must have been in a doorway, asked if we would like to stay with her for £75. She said she'd feed and water Ben, so who was I to say no?' he smirked.

'Oh, Sam, please tell me you didn't,' Ruby cringed.

Sam paused for effect. 'I wish I could see all your bloody faces! Of course I didn't!'

Everybody laughed.

'Although how cool would it be to tell the boys at college that I'd lost my cherry to a Soho pro!' Sam added comically.

'So where *did* you stay?' Graham piped up.

'On the bloody floor! My wayward sister was obviously too drunk to sort out a blow-up bed for me as promised, and I didn't think you'd be too chuffed if I got in with you.'

'I'm really sorry, darling.' Ruby leant down and put her arm around her brother, feeling even worse that her bed had been empty all night.

'Patrick was driving me mad this morning with his incessant spitting and wailing for food, so I decided to go out for a walk to get away from him. I really do think a bump on the head has made that moggy even more mental.'

'Where's Fi, by the way?' Graham asked innocently.

'Oh my God, where *is* Fi? With all this worry over you, I completely forgot about her!' Ruby screeched.

'She'll be fine,' George reassured her. 'I can't imagine her not finding somewhere to lay her hat.' Sam laughed and then stopped, suddenly aware that she might be with another man.

'I must check my phone,' Ruby said, then added, 'Shit, it's at your house, George – I left it by the bed. Be a love and go and get it, please.'

George dutifully did as he was told. Shutting the door behind him, the gardener's attention was drawn to the other side of the road.

Despite it being a cold February morning, there, beaming from the doorway of number 30, was Bert.

'Jesus is alive and living in Putney!' Bert bawled, raising his can of cider as if in triumph. Fiona O'Donahue, mad hair everywhere, snuggled a little closer to him, pulled the tramp's dirty mac up to her neck, and let out a big snore.

Chapter Fifteen

'Al lright mate?' George bounded up the stairs and greeted his flatmate.

James, feet up on one of their sofas, was drinking from a bottle of beer and watching the Sunday afternoon match on Sky Sports.

Wye aye, lad, there's beer in the fridge if you want one,' he said, without looking up.

'Cheers.' George went to the fridge, and put his feet up on the other sofa. 'I'm fucking knackered.'

'I bet you are. Leave you alone for five minutes and you're shagging old ginger next door.'

George laughed out loud. 'Actually, I didn't nail her. She's a good girl, Rubes is, and she does make me laugh.'

'Well, be careful. Once they hit the big 3-0, their body clock starts going overtime. She'll be wanting to marry you next.'

'Oh, shut up. She's not my type. Bit of fun, that's all, and she said herself she wants to be just friends. Nice tits though.'

Adverts blasted out from the plasma screen on the wall.

'What's the score anyway?'

'Chelsea, one nil up. Terry scored a cracker forty minutes in. Before that it was quite a dull match.' James took a swig of beer.

George yawned, 'I ought to go tackle the washing up.'

'Yeah. I did wonder if we'd been burgled when I got home yesterday,' James said, eyes still glued to the screen.

George jumped up off the sofa. 'Right, let's get another

beer down us and watch Chelsea beat the Gunners. The pleasure of that may even give me the incentive to do the dishes.'

Chapter Sixteen

Ruby's mobile rang just as she was leaving the flat.

'Hey, Johnny. How you doing?' she asked breezily, adorned in her navy Gabbana suit and white shirt. Despite the icy pavements from a fluttering of snow the night before, she had braved kitten heels today.

George wolf-whistled from his van and she stuck her middle finger up at him jovially. Margaret broke from polishing her knocker and waved a duster at her.

'Just checking you're all set for this mission, madam? Month two, job two already,' Johnny said in her ear.

'I love it when a plan falls into place,' Ruby told him. 'But yes, I'm all set, albeit a little nervous at this one.'

'Well, variety is the spice of life, my dear,' Johnny guffawed in his usual cheerful manner. 'Just make sure you take care if you fraternise with any of your charges on *this* particular assignment …'

February, Job Two: Sexual Health Clinic Receptionist

Harley Street was to be the location for Month Two. The Fairdale Clinic was, in fact, a beautiful Queen Anne-style building, situated in well-kept grounds with an ornate pond. Ruby went in through the imposing front door, which stood open, and, rounding a corner, found herself in a small waiting area. She was amazed at how plush it was, beautifully decorated in a soothing pale blue with deep purple velvet curtains. Exotic plants were dotted around the room, and each seat appeared to have its own separate cubicle with a coffee table adorned with magazines, the type that even when Ruby was working, she thought of as a luxury – namely *Wallpaper*, *Vogue,* and *Sunsoaker Monthly*.

There was a woman sitting in one of the waiting booths. All Ruby could see was a pair of long, slender legs that ended with elegant black patent stilettos. The rest of her was disguised by a fully opened *Financial Times*. In another booth, a man was sat as far away from the woman as he possibly could. *Sunsoaker Monthly* was concealing *his* face, and he was wearing a very smart, dark grey pin- striped suit.

Ruby approached the unmanned, glassed-in reception desk and rang the bell. Even without having eyes in the back of her head, she could feel the man and woman discreetly looking her way. She stood and waited for a minute or so until she heard footsteps bounding up behind her. Turning around, she came face-to-face with a short Asian man. Ruby reckoned he must have been in his early forties. He was wearing black skinny jeans, crocodile loafers, a bottle-green velvet jacket, and a yellow bow tie. His wispy black hair could easily allow him to pass as a Tibetan monk with regrowth. He virtually jumped on Ruby.

'Ruby, Ruby, Ruby, Ruby!' he sang loudly to the tune of the Kaiser Chiefs' hit, and then carried on in the same loud vein. 'So sorry to have kep you waiting. I am …' A pause for effect – or maybe to remember who he was. 'Tony Choi. You will be sitting beside me for the next three weeks, while Julia, my usual partner in grime, is shagging her way round the world with a new husband.'

Ruby stifled a laugh.

Johnny Jessop, I think I love you, she thought. This was going to be hilarious.

Tony ushered her round to the side of the reception desk, and through a private door. Despite the obvious money and discretion involved at the hospital, there was still a door and glass screen which separated 'The Sexers' – Tony's words for the patients – from 'The Receptors' – Tony's words for himself and his employees. He explained that before the screen had been put in, there had been a terrible incident in which he had been almost throttled by a man insisting that he see his wife's records. The husband had found her appointment card, which had led him to the Fairdale Clinic. His own guilty conscience had convinced him that she too was having an affair, and had passed on an STD to him. It turned out that *he* was the one with the sexually transmitted disease, and that she was actually secretly having an unsightly wart removed in the unit next door. The man got his penicillin, swiftly followed by his marching orders. Rumour had it the now smooth- skinned wife settled for half of Berkshire.

Tony scurried about in the back office. He shuffled papers around on a desk and dropped several onto the floor. Leaving them where they fell, he reached to the top of a filing cabinet and grabbed a black appointment diary.

'OK. Rules of the establishment,' he shouted at Ruby, and pointed to the two swivel chairs behind the screen. 'That is your seat, this is mine. And this is the list of Sexers for the day.' He opened the diary and pointed to today's date. 'And let's take it from there, shall we?'

'OK, no probs,' Ruby replied, wishing that Tony would stop shouting quite so loudly.

As if reading her mind, he turned his head around so that she was looking directly into his right ear. 'Hearing aid, you see. Little bit, how you call it? Old sheep on this side.'

Old sheep? Ruby thought hard and then laughed to herself. Mutt and Jeff (mutton) – Cockney rhyming slang for deaf, of course! How bloody funny. If George had been here he'd have known straight away.

George's cheeky face and honed body came to the forefront of her mind. She was still reeling slightly from the fact that they'd actually gone to bed together and 'fumbled', as he called it. She believed that they hadn't gone the whole way, as despite his cocky exterior Ruby knew that he wouldn't take advantage of her. Oh shit, what if they *had* gone the whole way? She already realised, looking at the many warning posters on the office walls, that rubber should definitely be the male genitalia material, of choice. However, she and George most certainly wouldn't have thought to use contraception – well, in her drunken state, she wouldn't have anyway.

Ruby suddenly felt an itch in her nethers. Psychosomatic, it must be, she thought. She convinced herself again that she should trust her gorgeous neighbour. Plus, if she did have something, would she itch anyway?

Despite this sudden irrational fear, she still wished she'd been sober enough to remember what the 'fumblings' had felt like. If it was anything like his kiss she would probably have internally combusted. But then again, if she'd been sober, she reckoned her head would have stopped her. Just as she was imagining what George looked like completely naked, a shout came from Tony.

'If I make too much noise you tell me, Ruby, yes? Julia usually throws this fish at me.' He pointed to a battered stress-relieving object in the shape and colour of a goldfish.

'Of course I will.' Ruby suppressed a snort. 'Oh, and have you got any leaflets so I can start getting my head around symptoms et cetera, please?'

'Sure thing,' he suddenly said very quietly. And then, raising his tone a few decibels, he continued, 'Right, we better get on, Ruby.' He lifted both arms in the air and waved them around madly, as if performing some sort of ritual. 'As I say every day: Ready, Steady, Gonorrhea!' He flung the hatch back and hollered, 'Mrs Smith to wrception, please.'

Chapter Seventeen

'Ready, Steady, Gonorrhea!' Tony shouted, patting Ruby so hard on the back she nearly choked on her tea. She had hoped day two might be a bit quieter, but there was no chance. Her lively workmate threw open the hatch. 'You have a boil on your *what*?' Tony blasted, and then felt the sharp thud of the goldfish landing on his head as Ruby tried in vain to hush him.

These poor people, Ruby thought. One night of passion without using a condom, and now they had to face not only the fear of disease, but also the embarrassment of Tony Choi telling the nation. Luckily she had managed to stay out of the 'front line'. She ably assisted with the necessary paperwork and showed patients to the relevant nurses and doctors. Her other role was to ferry blood and urine to the labs for testing. The sort of money these people paid warranted a speedy service.

The whole experience made her seriously think about how easy it was to disrupt your life overnight thanks to one silly error, and she felt lucky that none of her nights of oblivion had ever brought her to a place such as this.

There had been one incident this week that had really shocked her. A very respectable-looking lady came in frantic with worry that she had contracted chlamydia on a recent holiday. She asked to be tested for everything and it came to light that actually she was HIV positive, and had been for two years. Ruby comforted the patient, trying hard to hold back her own tears, while waiting for a counsellor to arrive.

When she had gone, Ruby made it her business to look

up everything about the disease. She was heartened by how many treatments were available to keep the condition from developing into full-blown AIDS, but was equally shocked at how the incidence of heterosexuals contracting the disease had risen.

Tony, without fail, took his hour for lunch. Come rain or shine he would sit on the balcony overlooking the grounds and eat the same things every day: cheese and pickle sandwiches, salt and vinegar crisps, a yoghurt-based drink, and an apple.

It was while she was looking through the patient list for that afternoon that she saw the familiar dark-haired figure walking bold as brass towards the front line.

'Oh my God. Oh my God,' she panicked under her breath. In her hurry to get away from the situation, she fell right off of the reception stool and flat onto her face, amazingly, managing to slam the hatch shut as she did so. At this moment, Tony, lunchtime over, bounded through the back office and saw her lying under the reception desk face down. 'Ruby! Ruby! What have you done? Who have hurt you?'

'Shh, shh, ignore me, ignore me!' Ruby hissed, gesturing wildly to the hatch. Tony thankfully realised that for her to be face down amongst the samples must warrant a definite emergency situation. With his Cheshire Cat-type smile in place (usually only reserved for patients who annoyed him), he opened the hatch calmly.

'All OK, Tone, mate?' George smirked through the opening.

'Helo, George. You all right? You been having some apples and pears for your lunch?'

George laughed out loud.

Oh no, Ruby thought. They're on first name terms. Her handsome neighbour must be a regular! She felt herself start to itch down below again. What if he had given her something? She crawled into the office on her hands and knees, just as Tony moved out of the way to reach for the appointments diary.

'I'd recognise that pert little arse anywhere. Is that you, Ruby?' George asked in amazement.

'Why are you down there?' Tony asked, having no understanding of what was going on.

'What *are* you doing?' George continued, looking at Ruby as if she had gone completely mad.

'I'm … er … working here. I … er …' She continued with the first lie that came into her head. 'I dropped one of my contacts.'

'I didn't know you wore contacts,' George quizzed.

Tony squished his face up and tried to help her. 'Oh, yeah, she's always losing her contacts. I say, "Ruby, write your contacts down or you'll lose them."'

'Anyway,' Ruby said boldly, 'more importantly, what are *you* doing here?'

'I'm, er, working here,' George mimicked.

'Working?' Ruby queried.

'Yeah, he working here.' Tony nodded frantically, still not knowing what on earth was going on.

'I tend to the grounds here once a month. Give the bushes a bit of a trim, you know.' George winked at Ruby, who flushed red and burst out laughing.

'And there she was thinking you had the crabs in your pants!' Tony chuckled, as the goldfish whistled past his good ear.

Chapter Eighteen

Ruby shivered and pulled up the collar of her bottle-green coat. It was cold and dark, and she longed for the clocks to spring forward to bring lighter evenings. She felt a sense of relief when she reached the end of her road. Tony was a lovely man and the job was great; a complete eye-opener for her, but tonight, she was tired and her ears were still ringing from her colleague's constant shouting. Walking towards her flat, she noticed that George wasn't home. Pinch-faced Pru revved her engine as she sped past and flew into a tiny parking spot outside her house in the tightly packed no through road. At times like this, Ruby was glad she didn't have a car, as with her limited reverse parking skills it would take her all night to find a space wide enough. Plus, she probably wouldn't even be able to afford petrol at the moment.

As she approached her flat, she heard the familiar sound of a dog yapping. Then, all of a sudden, running towards her, tongue lolling as if in a big smile, was Montgomery, and close behind was Justice, his hulking frame comically being dragged at top speed into the gloaming.

'Hello, you two,' she said in surprise, smiling wildly.

'Hello, gorgeous red-headed one,' Justice flirted.

'What brings you here then?' Ruby asked.

'I have something to give you,' Justice replied.

'Oo-er, missus,' Ruby mimicked from their first meeting. 'You'd better come on in.'

Margaret, who was shutting her curtains, saw Ruby and her guests under the street lamp, waved a duster at her, and winked.

At the sound of the door opening Patrick flew from his velvet cushion to greet them, and on sight of Montgomery, his back lifted and bristled and he began to spit wildly. The small dog, hardly intimidated by this black and white ball of angry fluff, started barking frantically, placing his two front legs down on the floor as if he was going to pounce.

'Patrick, stop it!' Ruby shouted. Then, suddenly feeling sorry for him, she swept his scrabbling body up and carried him into the bedroom. She put some Crunchies with him and pushed the door to, soothing him as she did so. Justice took in his surroundings.

'Nice place you've got here, Ruby.'

'Yeah, well I used to be on a "nice" salary,' she smiled, then continued. 'Cup of tea?'

'Coffee if you've got it, please.'

Justice let Montgomery off the lead and the soppy mutt jumped right into Ruby's arms. After a big fuss from her, he hopped down and began to run around her flat, sniffing anything and everything he came across. Patrick's wails could still be heard from the bedroom.

With hot coffee and custard creams on a tray, Montgomery settled on Ruby's lap on the sofa while Justice perched on a leather cube. The tale began to unravel.

'Did the girlfriend forgive you then?' Damn, Ruby hadn't wanted to mention her at all but the question seemed to fly out of her mouth.

'Thankfully, yes. And that's not a slur on you at all, Rubes. I think you're gorgeous, but I've been with Ellie forever and I do love her. Thanks for keeping out of her way at the funeral, though; it made my life a lot easier.'

If she was honest with herself, Ruby did feel slightly hurt at his admission. However, she even shocked herself with the adult response that came out of her mouth.

'It's OK, Justice. I think we both got a bit carried away in the moment, what with Lucas dying and everything. Just to have your arms around me was lovely, and it was me who instigated the kiss.'

'Mates?' Justice turned his big brown eyes on her soulfully.

'Mates,' Ruby confirmed honestly, and continued, 'So, how you knew where I lived? Why are you here?'

'So many questions.' Justice laughed. 'Right. Well, firstly, Mrs Hornsby knew where to find you through Petite Recruitment, and secondly, apart from confirming that there is no bad feeling between us, this is the reason I'm here.'

He held out a smart white Basildon Bond envelope, handwritten with her name and address. 'Mr Bentley asked if I minded delivering it by hand to ensure it got here. Montgomery needed a walk and I'm getting paid for being here, so why not?'

'Don't put yourself out, eh,' Ruby said sarcastically with a smile. 'I know you mentioned Mr Bentley before as being the owner of Dinsworth House and he arranged Lucas's funeral, but tell me more. I like to be kept up on all the goss.'

'The place has been in his family for generations; he rents a very small part of it out for residents. He usually keeps himself to himself.'

'Oh, I had no idea. I just assumed it was some National Trust-type set-up and that he ran the lease or something.'

'Did you talk to him at the funeral?' Justice asked.

Ruby shook her head. 'I was so upset I didn't even notice him.'

Justice continued, 'If you somehow ever get to meet him you'll realise – apart from getting a substantial income from the old people – why he prefers to rent out the house than open it up to the public.' He stood and held one arm up dramatically. Oh, how one *detests* the thought of the

Great Unwashed scuffling through the Bentley corridors of history.'

Ruby laughed at Justice's emulation of the eccentric English gentleman. 'If he's so bloody rich then why didn't he fork out on some sort of wake for Lucas?'

'I guess it costs a lot to run the place,' Justice answered.

'Sounds like a mean bastard if you ask me,' Ruby stated.

Justice leant forward expectantly. He pointed to the envelope. 'Well – go on. Aren't you going to open it? I'm as intrigued as you are, to find out what it's all about.'

At that moment, Patrick escaped from the bedroom, shot down the stairs, and through the cat flap, wailing as he went. Montgomery, now being held tightly on his lead, let out a whimper and ran to Ruby's outstretched hand as she offered him a custard cream.

'Ruby, will you just open the letter,' Justice urged.

Ruby pulled open the envelope, not at all sure what she might find, and began to read aloud.

Dear Ms Matthews,

I firstly would like to thank you for all your hard work at Dinsworth House. The staff and residents spoke highly of your time here, albeit short. You were a special favourite of Mr Lucas Steadburton, hence the reason for this letter.

Mr Steadburton used to visit me every day whilst walking his beloved Montgomery. He knew his time was short and wanted his pet to go to a good home when he passed. I would have gladly taken him on if I wasn't so damn allergic to fur of any kind. So – to this end Lucas said he couldn't think of anyone else he would rather share Montgomery's life with than you.

You should already have a lead. I trust you can purchase your own dog bowls.

Happy walking!
Domenic Bentley Esq.

'Bless Lucas,' Ruby uttered with tears in her eyes.

'No wonder Bentley was so adamant I took the dog for a walk,' Justice replied.

She patted Montgomery. 'Looks like it's me and you, kid.'

Just then, Patrick crept back in through the cat flap, saw Montgomery, arched his back, and started to spit. He could only be pacified by a fresh portion of fish flakes.

'Lucifer here ain't gonna like it,' Justice said, scrunching his face up.

'It's certainly going to be interesting,' Ruby grimaced.

'Anyway, Rubes.' Justice stood up. 'As much as I'd like to stay in your charming company all evening, I'd better get back to my shift or Mrs Hornsby will be sending out a search party.'

Ruby got up off the sofa and he leant down to kiss her cheek.

Ruby followed him down to the front door.

'Bring Montgomery to visit us sometimes, won't you?' Justice said gently. 'The residents would love it too.'

'I'll do that.' Ruby shut the door behind him and as she did so, noticed an interesting looking pink envelope on the floor.

On realising the date, she suddenly felt very excited. What with being so busy with her work, she hadn't even remembered that it was Valentine's Day.

Patrick finished his snack and looked up. He started to hiss and spit when he realised that Montgomery was still there. Barking his head off, the dog leapt up from the beanbag he'd taken residence on and chased Patrick through the cat flap. Ruby opened the door and followed him as she really didn't want to upset the old Tom.

The aggrieved pussy stopped in his tracks, looked back

at his owner, and meowed pitifully. And Ruby knew exactly what he was saying. 'Either he goes or I do.'

She went back inside and shut the door. Rubbing her hands over her face with tiredness, she walked to the kitchen and poured herself a large glass of wine. She was just about to open the card when her mobile rang.

'Ruby darling, it is I, the cute Celtic one,' Fi trilled.

Ruby laughed. 'Hello, stranger. Haven't heard from you for a while. Thought you might have eloped with Bert.'

'How fecking funny was that? I ached for a week after. How the devil I didn't get frostbite I don't know,' her mad friend continued. 'Anyway, I'm calling you 'cos I've had my air miles statement today.'

'And?' Ruby interrupted.

'I've got enough for two flights to Dublin. So when do ya fancy going?'

Ruby started to justify the expense out loud. 'Oh shit, I don't know if I should. I'm just getting myself back on track, and now I've got Patrick *and* Montgomery to think about.'

'If bullshit was music, you'd be a brass bleedin' band. I was only talking about a weekend – of course you can come!' Ruby raised her eyebrows at her friend's indignation. Fi went on, 'My brother Darragh is away working in New York at the end of the month and he says we can have his apartment in the city centre. So all you need is some spends. Come on, Ruby, it'll be a gas!'

Ruby gave in. 'OK then. We'd better get those flights booked.'

'I'll do it right now. And by the way, Rubes – who the bejaysus is Montgomery?'

Chapter Nineteen

'I'm glad I caught you,' Ruby puffed as she power-walked home from the park. Montgomery yapped at her heels and leapt up at George with delight when he saw him. Maybe he was a gay old dog, just like his namesake, Ruby thought.

Despite not having another job lined up, she was actually quite relieved that her stint at the Fairdale Clinic had come to an end. It was only Wednesday too, so she had two glorious days off to get herself ready for Dublin. Seeing George, she blushed as she thought of the Valentine card she had received a fortnight ago. On the front there was a picture of two iced cakes with cherries on top, and inside in print, were the words NICE BUNS, a big kiss, and a scribbled "Guess Who?"

It had to have been from him. After all, he was the only one who had got within an inch of her body in months – well, apart from Justice's interrupted kiss, of course.

Realising that romance was still missing from her life, she embraced the fact that she was happy with her currently successful job mission. Yes, it would be nice to have a man, but it had to be the right man, and at the moment he hadn't come along.

Two assignments had been completed without incident – well, almost without incident – and a weekend away was approaching where she could afford to buy her own drinks again.

'Go on, what is it, bird?' George asked.

'Got a massive favour to ask you.' Ruby put her hands on her hips and got her breath back.

'Sounds dubious,' he said, eyeing her suspiciously.

'Could you look after Montgomery for me?' She gave him a doe-eyed look and explained, 'I'm going to Dublin with Fi for a couple of days and there's no way I can leave him in the house with Patrick – they'll kill each other. It's bloody hard keeping them both happy as it is.'

George leant down and ruffled the little dog's head. 'Of course I will, Rubes. He is just the best. I s'pose you want me to feed that pesky cat as well, do you?'

Well, if he'll let you in the door, knowing you're the one who ran him over, that would be really helpful. Thanks.'

'Just leave me a key and instructions and I'll sort it all for you.' George gave her his cheeky smile. 'Be good eh, Rubes – and if you can't be good …'

'Yeah, yeah … be good at it!' They both laughed. 'You are the best neighbour a girl could ever have, do you know that, George Stevens?'

Leaning over, Ruby kissed him full on the cheek. She knew just how to play her tough little East End neighbour when she needed to. God, he smelt divine – where was that flower bed when she needed it?

Just as she was walking down the steps to her flat, Margaret shouted across to her, 'Got a minute, love?'

'Sure.' Ruby turned around and headed across the road. Margaret stood at her closed gate.

'Sorry to be a pain, but would you mind popping to Gill's for me? The cold's playing havoc with my feet and I could do with a few bits.'

'Course I can, Margaret. I'm glad you caught me now, I'm off to Dublin with Fi for a couple of days.'

Margaret put her hands on her hips. 'Ooh, how wonderful. All those lovely Irish boys for you.'

'Margaret. Tut tut. It's not all about men, you know.'

'Well, I see you had your big black man round the other day.' She sucked her Polo in and out of her mouth furiously.

Ruby laughed. 'Yes, he quite madly brought me a Jack Russell. Bloody chaos in my flat now. I'll explain all when I'm back.' Ruby knew that if she started talking to Margaret, she wouldn't get away for hours. 'Right, give me your list and then get out of this cold.'

'Did you get any more Valentines?' Margaret enquired, trying to stall her for as long as possible.

Ruby's eyes widened. 'Actually, yes, and I think it could only have been from our very own sexy landscape gardener.'

'No!' Margaret exclaimed. Despite the mutual denials of affection, she could feel the spark between her lovely young neighbours, and wanted more than anything to ignite it.

'Yes!' Ruby laughed out loud at Margaret's excitement. 'Now, much as I'd love to gossip with you all day, I've got to get ready for my weekend.'

'Maybe you should act on it, Ruby?'

'What – the card?'

'You'll lose him if you don't,' the old lady said knowingly.

'Margaret! There's nothing to lose. And he's a big enough boy to act on it himself if he really wants to.'

Margaret shrugged her wise old shoulders. 'You're not getting any younger, duck.'

Ruby playfully poked her arm.

'Now what did you want from the shop, you old matchmaker?'

Chapter Twenty

'Jaysus, I'm freezing my tits off up here!' Fi shrieked, her hair trailing wildly behind her in the bitter Dublin wind. She then pointed to the statue by the Ha'penny Bridge; two women sitting on a bench engaged in conversation, their shopping bags at their feet.

'Look, Rubes, that's us that is,' she laughed. 'They are known as The Hags with the Bags.' Ruby smiled as Fi recommenced her rant. 'Why on earth I let you talk me into this, I will never know.'

Ruby, despite her love of open top bus tours in whichever city she visited, had to admit that her red nose and blue fingers indicated it was time to give in.

'Let's get off at the next stop,' she shouted. 'We can warm our cockles over a drink or three.'

The girls ran down the bus steps, laughing, the driver shaking his head in disbelief that they had even considered the top deck.

They spotted a bar straight away, and quickly made their way through the throng of shivering smokers outside. Relishing the feeling of relief as the cold air was taken over by the warmth of their new surroundings, Fi and Ruby walked towards the bar. The relaxed minimalism of the décor – dark, oak and cream and the comfiest-looking sofas – immediately appealed to both. Fi signalled Ruby to grab a sofa which had just come free by the door. She did so, placing her bag territorially on the low table in front of her.

'A fine pint of Guinness for the lady,' Fi announced, handing a glass to her friend. 'Now this'll put hairs on those buns of yours,' she added, reminding Ruby of her Valentine's card as she sank down into the comfy sofa.

'Pints? How very student!' Ruby uttered.

'When in Ireland and all that,' Fi answered.

'Do you reckon it was George who sent the card, Fi?'

'Yeah, to be sure. Did he get your hole the other night anyways?' Fi wiped the Guinness moustache from her top lip.

Used to Fi's vulgar colloquialisms, Ruby told her. 'No, we didn't do it. Well, he insists we didn't anyway. I was so bloody pissed I can't remember.' She took a big swig of her drink.

'So would you want to do it?' Fi enquired seriously.

'I think he's really fit and he does make me laugh, but something's stopping me.' Ruby looked into space, trying to work out why. 'I guess it's just he's become a really good friend and I would hate for us to have a fling and fall out.'

'Not that you like him too much, and if you went out with him you'd be scared he'd leave you?'

'No,' Ruby said abruptly, then undid her coat and continued animatedly, 'I forgot to tell you about his flatmate, James. He's quite sexy in a geeky sort of way.'

'Oh yeah?' Fi responded with interest. 'You must introduce me when we get home.'

'When I get over the embarrassment having my naked arse in his face, that is.' Ruby relayed the story of the morning after the night before and both girls went into hysterics. Ruby managed to contain herself enough to take another slurp of her drink.

'And anyway, on a serious note, Fi, after working in that clinic, we really mustn't just have sex for the sake of it, and if we do, we must be safe. It's too easy to pick up something nasty these days.'

'The way our track record's going it would be a bloody miracle to pick up *anything,* nasty or not, at the moment,'

Fi snorted. Ruby, lifting her glass to her mouth, laughed so hard that a mouthful of Guinness went all over her face.

'Now that's what I call a classy lady.'

Ruby looked up, straight into the eyes of something very naughty indeed. She hurriedly pulled a tissue from her bag and wiped the offending froth away. The naughtiness moved nearer to her and held his hand out.

'Ciaran O'Shea!' Ruby suddenly recognised him. 'I remember you. Ritsy Rose Interiors – You did the *Irish Luxury Homes* magazine shoot for us.'

'Rosy, I'm sorry I didn't recognise you with your clothes on.'

'Jaysus, you've got the blarney in you.' Fi grimaced as Ruby told him. 'It's Ruby, not Rosy, and no, Fi, he was photographing beds not bods.'

Ciaran was a very handsome man. He was over six foot and sported a mop of curly dark hair. His twinkling blue eyes were surrounded by deep-set laughter lines. His skin was very fair and he had matching freckles. He was wearing stylish dark baggy jeans and a grey cashmere v-neck jumper. Ruby had been seeing Dean at the time of the shoot, but thinking back, she did remember a lot of the other girls swooning over the dark Irish one.

'Can I join you?' he asked, suddenly a lot less full of it.

'The more the bleedin' merrier,' Fi piped up. 'Mine's a Guinness, tanks.'

Several drinks later and the three of them could barely string a sentence together. Fi had hit the whisky and Ruby knew it was just a matter of time before she became a nasty drunk and find venom in her tongue. Usually, Ruby would drag her back home before this stage, but her own selfish drunken need to be near this handsome man stopped her.

Ruby was now leaning heavily on Ciaran's shoulder for support.

'Well, if you're gonna carry on with him, then I'm back to Darragh's,' Fi suddenly spat irrationally. Here we go, Ruby thought and before she had a chance to say anything, her feisty friend had turned on her heels and hot-footed it back to her brother's flat. Ruby knew that Fi would go home and crash out and all would be forgiven and forgotten in the morning, so didn't bother to go after her.

'Oh dear. Your friend must be havin' the PMTs,' Ciaran said snidely, and smiled sweetly at Ruby. 'Another pint of Guinness for the fair lady, please,' he said, leering at the pretty young barmaid's chest as he ordered.

Ciaran sat back down and rested his hand between Ruby's thighs. She was now dizzy with excitement. All her previous resolutions about not drinking to oblivion and memories of stark lessons from the Fairdale Clinic evaded her with one single stare into the blue pools of sexiness in front of her. Ruby finished her Guinness, and let out a huge hiccup.

'Hey there, sexy. I'll take you home,' Ciaran said, helping Ruby to her feet. She leaned her weight against him as they edged their way out of the busy warm pub and into the freezing air.

Once outside, she stumbled against a wall and put her hand to her head. 'Look, Ciaran, I think we'd better call it a night,' she slurred. 'Can you get me a taxi, please? I need to lie down.' She shut her eyes and opened them again quickly to try and lessen her dizziness.

As soon as they were in the taxi, she put her head back on the seat. The traffic was still quite bad, even at this time of night, and she suddenly noticed them going past the road where Darragh's flat was.

'Ciaran,' she said faintly, pointing to the street in question. 'That's where I'm staying.'

'Don't you worry your pretty little ginger head, you hear me? I'll be looking after you.'

'Okie-dokie, David Bailey,' Ruby slurred. 'The night is

young and we can have more fun,' she said really slowly, raising her right hand floppily in the air. Her head lolled on to his shoulder.

'That's my girl,' Ciaran grinned, resting his hand on her left breast until they pulled up outside his apartment building.

Chapter Twenty-one

Ruby woke up with a start, feeling very groggy indeed. She lifted her head slowly, with the sudden awful realisation that she had no idea where she was. The bed was king-size and the sheets were black silk. The ceiling was mirrored. She was naked and felt an alien soreness between her legs.

'Hey, beautiful,' Ciaran said softly, walking into the room. 'I made you a coffee.'

'Th-thanks,' Ruby stuttered. She raised herself on her elbows and winced in pain, a large bruise evident on her upper arm. She had no recollection of what had happened after drinking that last pint of Guinness. Her brain ached trying to bring some sort of memory to the forefront of her mind. But nada, nien, nothing.

'I'm gonna take a shower, sweet cheeks,' Ciaran said carelessly.

'Sure.' Ruby nodded, on autopilot, wanting to be a million miles away from here.

Ciaran appeared again in the doorway and schmoozed. 'I've got a shoot in London next month. I'll look you up. Be rude not to do it again.' He winked and sauntered back into his plush en-suite bathroom. 'Come and join me if you want!' he shouted through to the bedroom.

Ruby shot out of bed and grabbed her clothes, then went from the bedroom into a large lounge to try and find her handbag. On the wall at one end of this room was the largest plasma screen Ruby had ever seen. A big pile of DVDs, mostly porn, were scattered on the floor underneath. She was horrified. What on earth had they got up to?

She dressed quickly, and too mortified to even say goodbye, she quietly closed the flat door behind her, making her way downstairs and out of the communal entrance of the plush apartment block.

Once in the city centre, Ruby felt immediate relief, and when the taxi turned into Darragh's road, she saw the modern block of flats where he lived.

Although minimalist in design, Darragh had made his one-bedroom flat very cosy. Knick-knacks from various work trips abroad were strewn around the lounge, and one of the kitchen walls was covered in photos of friends and family.

Fi was already waiting by the front door and they hugged each other tightly.

'So?' Fi asked when she had made them both a cup of coffee.

Ruby sat on the sofa and put her hand to her head. She felt terrible. Fi sat by her side and put her arm around her.

'I'm so fecking sorry, Rubes. You know what I'm like when I'm drunk, a complete eejit. I can't believe how selfish I was, walking out and leaving you.' She sighed and took a swig of her coffee. Was it good though?' Fi smirked. 'He is bloody handsome, I'll give you that.'

'I don't know!' Ruby wailed. 'I was all over him in the pub. I woke up in his place and I don't remember a bloody thing. I'm covered in bruises and without a doubt we must have done the deed. What I do remember is being so drunk I could barely stand when I came out of the pub, and I'm sure I asked him to drop me back here.'

'Oh, Rubes.. He is a bastard if he has taken advantage of you.'

'I can't believe I fell for his blarney, that's all. Oh God.' Ruby put her head in her hands. 'And I bet we didn't use a condom.'

Once she had taken a long, hot bath and had another

cup of coffee in her hands, she sank back into the big cream sofa at Darragh's, let out a huge sigh, and said to Fi, 'This has to be a lesson to us both, you know. I for one am going to try my best not to get so hammered any more. It's too bloody dangerous.'

They clinked mugs and said, 'Deal,' in unison.

Ruby was close to tears when she saw kind, caring George waiting dutifully for them in Arrivals at Heathrow. He beamed as soon as he spotted her. In the car park he brushed grass clippings off the seat of his van and George, Ruby, Fi, and a very excitable Montgomery all squeezed in together after securing the luggage safely in the back.

'Have my babies been good?' Ruby enquired, fussing over the excitable mutt and suddenly thinking about Patrick.

'More interestingly, have *you*?' George retorted, looking straight at Ruby. When both girls remained silent; he looked out of the driver's window momentarily, and then turned up the chart show on Radio 1.

'We're just knackered. Sorry, George,' Ruby managed guiltily.

Montgomery started to lick Ruby's face and she squealed in disgust. George laughed out loud. 'You can't be cross with him; he's such a character, Rubes. Patrick hates him though. He scratched his nose quite badly last night. Look.'

Ruby checked out the dog's injury. 'What a nightmare. I feel really bad but was actually thinking on the plane that maybe I should find him another home. It's just not fair on him.'

'Bout time that mad cat was taught a lesson,' Fi suddenly piped up.

'God, Fi, I didn't mean Patrick,' Ruby said, shocked. 'As much as I adore him, Monty will be the one who has to go.'

'Look, I can't have him long-term Rubes,' George told her, 'but to help you out, let me take him until we find a good home for him.' He put his hand on Ruby's leg and added, 'We'll make sure it's someone Lucas would have approved of.'

'You're a star, George Stevens, and I promise I'll pay for his food and take him for walks.' Relief suddenly washed over her.

Ruby was shattered when she eventually said goodbye to the others and trotted down the steps to her front door. She stepped over Bert gently so as not to wake him. 'Poor old sod,' she muttered. She sometimes thought that she should invite him in for a bath, but felt sick at the thought of having to clean it afterwards. Maybe she should suggest it to George, seeing as his bath was filthy already.

It was a particularly cold March night so she went inside, found an old duvet, and laid it over the still sleeping tramp. He let out a small grunt of pleasure and continued to snore loudly.

She wondered what had led him to end up here. She had been lucky to find work, she realised that – but guessed if some people couldn't find work and didn't have savings or family support, it actually wouldn't take that much to put you on the street. The thought made her shiver.

She made her way inside and fed a pleasantly purring Patrick, who was delighted to see her, and even more delighted *not* to be seeing Montgomery, who was spending the night at George's.

She still felt decidedly groggy and drank down a pint of water to ease her dehydration headache.

She crawled into bed and sank into her comfy feather pillows. This was it now. She had learnt her lesson. She had to be more sexually responsible. She couldn't believe the way she had acted, especially after her stint at the Fairdale Clinic.

Rain began to lash against the bedroom window and she suddenly felt very alone and frightened. What if no work came in – how would she manage? She thought back to Dean. He had loved her so much he would have supported her whatever happened. Job, or no job.

And then her mind wandered to Gorgeous George. On paper, he didn't fill any of her criteria, apart from being good-looking, that was. He didn't own his own house. He was short. He was a gardener. He probably didn't earn loads of money. He was a bit rough round the edges and his flat was dirty. And he was only twenty-four.

However, in her heart he ticked all the boxes. He was kind, thoughtful, funny, loving, sexy, exciting, generous. But he was far too young, and had so much living to do before he would even think of settling down, and why would he want to settle down with someone as over the hill as her anyway? On the other hand, what if he did fancy her and they did make a go of it? Fi was right – the very worst thing that could happen to her *was* that he could leave her. To Ruby that *was* the very worst thing.

That awful sense of abandonment when somebody you loved was no longer around was just too much to bear a second time around and right now she didn't think she was strong enough to take that chance.

Patrick jumped up on the bed and curled in around her legs, purring loudly.

'I know, I know, at least I still have you. Goodnight, Patrick.' And within seconds they were both snoring softly.

Chapter Twenty-two

March, Job Three: Waitress

Piaf's was exactly how Ruby imagined an old-fashioned teashop to be. As she walked off the bustling Covent Garden side street, the door made a bell behind the counter chime. The main focus of the establishment was the large glass counter that curved its way right around the small shop, and the walls were adorned with glamorous pictures of the shop's namesake, Edith Piaf.

Under the counter, shielded by glass, was the most delicious array of cakes and pastries that Ruby had ever seen. She could feel herself salivating as she eyed her favourite lemon Danish pastries, as well as old-fashioned cream horns, chocolate éclairs, and iced finger buns. At the far end of the shop were amazing homemade cakes set on pretty bone china plates: coffee cake, carrot cake, lemon drizzle cake, chocolate cake, and plain old Victoria Sandwich.

She found it highly amusing that the lady who owned the tea shop was another friend of Johnny's, and that was how she had got this particular job. He owed her some money for party catering, so he had sent Ruby 'in kind' to pay off his debt and Johnny was to pay Ruby at the end of the month.

Waiting on people had never been on Ruby's agenda, but needs must and all that. She would go in with a positive fashion and prayed that nobody clicked their fingers to get her attention, as that was her pet hate.

The enticing aroma of fresh coffee made her feel

almost high, and the selection of every sort of tea imaginable in pretty, nineteenth-century tea caddies excited her senses. She hoped that an 'eat-in' or 'takeaway' perk was a given in this job. It would certainly beat the Dinsworth House fayre.

A lady, who Ruby assumed to be in her early seventies, was looking into an ornate antique mirror and tidying her hair, humming as she did so. She stood at just four foot eleven and still had the beauty and grace of a much younger woman. Her hair was dyed jet black, hanging around her shoulders in coiffured waves. She had false eyelashes, and bright red lipstick. She was wearing a long sleeved, black, lacy knee-length dress, with lace-up black pointed boots and a crisp old-fashioned white linen pinny. Ruby likened her to a beautiful 1940s screen goddess. The lady stopped humming.'Hello, dear girl. Ruby, is it? Johnny was right. He said you were presentable enough.'

Ruby stifled a giggle. She could just imagine Johnny befriending this woman, who was brusque and full of energy.

'Welcome to Piaf's, home of fine tea, cakes, and gateaux. Oh, and home to me, of course.' The little lady's laugh rose and fell as if a bubbling spring. She had a childlike innocence, full of gaiety. She carried on, 'I am Daphne du Mont. Owner of this wonderland.' She threw her head back and laughed again. Ruby thought she was a joy to behold. Johnny was right; she loved her already.

'Now, Ruby – what a pretty name, by the way – just so that you are clear, these are the rules of my domain.' Daphne delivered her next monologue at top speed, without taking a single breath. 'I need you from seven thirty till four thirty, Monday to Friday. You have a half- hour break at one thirty. The customer is always right, the coffee is always hot, the cakes are always fresh, and the tips are always shared. OK, dear?'

'Er, yes, that's totally fine.' Ruby was quite taken back

by the energy of this little woman. But tips, how fantastic. Her contents insurance was due this month. Hopefully, if she worked hard enough, she could cover that.

Daphne went on to tell her, 'I'm without fail up with the tits. I always get the urn on, the fresh cakes on display, and the tables laid before you arrive. At the end of the day, you just need to make sure that any tablecloths that are dirty are put in the back kitchen for washing, and that the cakes are all covered.'

Ruby noticed the pretty white lace cloths and the red and white checked napkins. It made her feel as if she had stepped back in time to a Parisian Left Bank café.

'Come, come, Ruby,' the old lady said. 'Let me show you the back kitchen.'

She lifted a hatch on the counter and Ruby dutifully followed her. 'This is where you throw the dirty tablecloths.' She gestured at the washing machine. 'And here you do any washing up.' She then pointed to the dishwasher. 'Pamela will be here to help you from eight. She leaves at five. She can be a lazy little vixen sometimes, so do tell me if she plays up.' Daphne du Mont took a breath. '*This* is the tip box.' She shook a money box in the shape of a pig with gusto. 'Get madam to empty it when she arrives and then from Friday, you must share the bounty between the both of you.' She wasn't finished yet, but carried on relentlessly, 'Oh yes, and just one more thing. If there is any lifting of boxes required, just ring this bell and Norbert will be right down to assist you.'

She gave a small bell on a shelf at the bottom of the stairs a quick shake. As soon as she had put the bell down, Ruby heard someone tearing down the stairs from the living quarters above.

'You rang?' the husky German accent comically addressed Daphne. Ruby was quite taken aback. With a name like Norbert, she had imagined a short, balding man with glasses. Instead, in front of her was a lanky, six foot four beauty in his mid-thirties, with tousled, dark, shoulder-length hair and pointed features. He was wearing baggy tracksuit bottoms, trendy horn-rimmed spectacles, and nothing else. Good cheekbones, Ruby thought, trying hard not to stare at his hairy chest.

'False alarm, darling, sorry.' Daphne put her arm on his. 'This is Ruby, by the way. She's helping out while Katerina is away.'

'*Guten Morgen*, Ruby. Ve are learning my lines at the moment. New West End musical. Just ring loudly and I'll be as quick as I can.' The tall German turned to go back upstairs and Daphne smacked his bottom with a resounding thud, making him shriek in delight as she chased up after him.

The dark old horse! Ruby laughed to herself. Surrounded by every cake under the sun, and a charming toy boy to boot – she could think of worse ways to spend her days.

And then Pamela arrived.

'Oh, hi, y'all – you must be Ruby,' the tall willowy girl greeted her. She threw her coat off and launched it over the lift-up hatch in the counter so it hit the floor. She had shoulder-length, over-highlighted hair which looked like it had been ironed, and she was frantically chewing gum. Her black T-shirt was so tight over her 36DD breasts that you could have used her nipples as coat hooks. She was wearing black knee-high boots over her clinging leggings. 'I really must have some war-tar before I do anything,' she uttered in her New England drawl, grabbing a bottle of water from the fridge behind the counter, tipping her head back, and downing the cold liquid.

Taking an instant dislike to the woman, Ruby breathed deeply. 'Mrs du Mont is wonderful and I'm not going to let Johnny down now,' she repeated three times to herself, and then smiled broadly at Pamela. 'Oh, are we allowed to help ourselves to drinks?' she enquired innocently. 'I forgot to ask before Mrs du Mont disappeared.'

'We're allowed tap water and as much tea and coffee as we can drink, but the silly old bag won't know if you take the odd bottle out of the fridge. She's too busy shagging the kinky Kraut to realise *anything* at the moment.'

Dislike had in one minute turned to hatred, as the drawl continued without expression. 'Oh Gahd, my skin feels just so tight. I think Dr Robb overdid me on the Botox last night. Hey, Ruby, does my butt look big in these pants?'

Ruby wasn't sure if a stick insect actually had a 'butt'; however, she managed to retain politeness in the shape of a non-enthusing, 'You're fine, Pamela,' all the while wondering how on earth she was going to last four weeks working alongside the American without beating her to death with a rock cake.

Chapter Twenty-three

'What're you doing here?' Ruby exclaimed on encountering Margaret in Gill's.

'I was going stir crazy in that house so I bound up the bunions and headed forthwith.'

She wobbled slightly, and Suki ran around from behind the counter with a chair. 'Here, Margaret, rest a while. I'll get Raj to bring the car round to the front and he can drop you home.'

'Good, he can take me too,' Ruby said cheekily.

Margaret put her hand on Ruby's. 'You all right, love? You looked the worse for wear this morning.'

'I … er …' Ruby stuttered. At that moment the shop bell rang and George came bounding up to the counter.

'All right, Raj, I'm parked on the double yellows round the corner, so gotta be quick.'

'What can I get you today, mate?' Raj enquired.

'A case of your finest Stella, please, gov.' George suddenly noticed Ruby and Margaret. 'Hello, ladies. Didn't know there was a Neighbourhood Watch meeting going on today.'

Ruby was sure that Suki blushed.

George threw a twenty pound note at Raj. 'Would love to chat to you lovely people, but can't risk another ticket. I've already 'ad two this month.' He grabbed his lagers and ran back towards the door.

'I bet that young lad has broken a few hearts in his time,' Suki gushed, not realising that George was still in ear-shot.

'Broken hearts? Me? Nah.' George looked back,

grinning. 'They all skip away knowing they've had the pleasure of my company for a while.' He laughed out loud, shutting the door behind him.

Suki blushed again. Ruby smiled. Margaret said quietly to herself, 'She'll lose him.'

Raj, oblivious to the whole scene, walked around from the counter, car keys in hand.

*

Ruby saw Margaret into her house, and stoked up her fire.

'You've had some logs delivered, I see.'

'Yeah, bless young George. He was cutting down trees at the weekend, so dropped some round. He's a good boy, that one.'

'Yes, he is,' was all Ruby could manage. 'Anyway, I must get back, Margaret. Patrick will be climbing the walls to be fed.' She held up the tin of cat food she had just purchased from Gill's.

If she was honest with herself, she really didn't want to get into a conversation about Dublin. It wasn't anything to do with Margaret judging her – Ruby knew she wouldn't.

'You don't want to talk about it, do you, Rubes?' an ever-knowing Margaret asked.

Ruby shook her head. 'I've just been a silly girl, Margaret, that's all.'

'I've been around the block enough times for nothing to shock me; you should know that by now.' Margaret kissed her on the cheek then threw her arms around her, engulfing her in a comforting hug. Ruby felt safe and secure against her ample breasts.

'Unsafe sex with a near stranger,' Ruby offered, her face still hidden.

'Back to the Fairdale Clinic and make a note when your period is due,' Margaret replied matter of factly.

Ruby, touched by the frankness of her wonderful neighbour and suddenly overwhelmed by the worry of not having a 'proper' job, let out a huge sob and held the old lady tighter.

Margaret stroked her red hair gently, until her heaving body subsided and she pulled away.

'Now, home with you and learn from you experience.' Margaret wagged her finger at her. 'There's ten good 'uns out there for every bad one. You've just got to let the right ones in.'

Pinch-faced Pru's car jolted to a halt outside her flat in Amerhand Road. She almost fell out of the car onto the road. When she hung onto her wall to balance herself, Ruby realised she was drunk. 'You OK?' she asked.

Pru immediately burst into tears. Ruby being Ruby thought she couldn't just leave her neighbour in this state. 'Come on,' she said kindly. 'Let's get you inside before anyone reports you to the police for drink driving.'

Without an argument, Ruby fished Pru's keys out of her bag and put them in her door. 'Will you come in for a minute?' Pru asked and hiccupped loudly.

'Sure,' Ruby replied.

Pinch-faced Pru's flat was how Ruby had imagined it to be. Black and white and minimalist with lots of clean lines. There wasn't a cushion out of place or one stray magazine lying around.

Pru, despite being quite drunk, managed to make them both a cup of coffee.

While she was in the kitchen, Ruby looked around the front room and noticed a photograph above the modern fireplace. It was of the pinch-faced one sitting next to a pretty, blonde girl with similar features. It looked like they were perched at the top of a mountain and were wearing large smiles and bobble hats. When Pru reappeared with the drinks, Ruby said, 'Nice picture. Is that your sister?'

The pursed lips wobbled and Ruby wished she hadn't opened her mouth. 'That's the reason for this.' Pru pointed at her tear-strewn face and began to wail again. 'She's finally bloody left me. Been seeing someone she campaigns with at Stonewall.'

Ruby remembered Fi mentioning an event she'd done for Stonewall a couple of years before, and knew they were an organisation focusing on gay and bisexual equality. Ruby had put Pru down as a few things, but never a lesbian.

'Oh, Pru, I'm so sorry. How long were you together?'

'Three years, but she confessed tonight she'd been leading a double life for two of them. I can't believe it. We were talking about having children soon and everything.'

She began to cry again. Ruby went to comfort her. She put her arms around her crumbling neighbour and held her until the sobbing subsided. Ruby smelt her expensive perfume and felt how soft her cashmere jumper was.

'Oh, Ruby,' Pru suddenly said, lost in the moment, her head pressed firmly against her red-headed neighbour's 34B breasts. 'This feels so good.' She moved her head slowly around and placed her pursed lips on top of Ruby's, who in turn immediately leapt up from the sofa in panic.

'I'm sorry, Pru, I …' Ruby stuttered. 'They may be a pain, but I like men far too much to even consider this.'

Pru suddenly sobered up. 'Oh God, Ruby. I'm so sorry. I don't know what came over me.' She began talking in a manic fashion and Ruby checked there was a quick route to the front door. 'It's just I see you every day. You walk past always looking gorgeous and so in control.' She sniffed loudly. 'And then I see you with that scruffy little gardener and I don't want you to waste your life with him. I think you're beautiful, Ruby.'

It all made sense now – the dirty looks and speeding off. It was a misguided love which would never be reciprocated.

Regardless, whatever Pru was going through now, Ruby would not take her being rude about her Gorgeous

George.

'That "scruffy little gardener" happens to be one of my best friends, and is a sensitive and kind man,' Ruby said fiercely. 'One shouldn't always judge a book by its cover – and you for one should know that, Pru.'

'Oh, Ruby, forgive me. I'm just drunk and not thinking what I'm saying.'

Ruby stood up. Her intuition about Pru had been right. There was something about her that she didn't like very much.

'I have to go now, Pru. I hope it all works out for you.'

Pru got up slowly and saw Ruby to the door. With her drunkenness dulling all form of common sense, she smacked Ruby lightly on the bottom. 'Nice buns!' she called after her, laughing manically.

Ruby shut her front door behind her as quickly as she could and put her back against it. She couldn't wait to see George's face when she told him that the Valentine card she had thought was from him had actually been from her pinch-faced lesbian of a neighbour all along.

Chapter Twenty-four

Daphne du Mont sang her favourite Piaf song with passion as she dusted the pictures of her heroine covering the walls of her beloved teashop.

'Only regret the things you don't do,' Daphne relayed to Ruby, who smiled at the sheer energy of this lovely lady.

The vibrant teashop owner put down her duster and began one of her morning soliloquies. 'Edith Piaf, the Little Sparrow. You really must read up on her, Ruby. Such a wonderful voice, but such a tragic life. One of her lovers died in a plane crash on his way to see her, you know.'

'Oh, that's sad.' Ruby bit her bottom lip. Daphne was now on a roll.

'She's buried in Paris. Amazing churchyard! Norbert and I met there, actually. Anyway, Ruby, you really must go one day. Jim Morrison is also buried there. His fans have created a complete shrine for him. Rumour has it that Edith Piaf died in the French Riviera and her second husband drove her body back to Paris secretly so that fans would think she had died in her hometown. What romance, what tragedy.' She carried on dusting.

'Hi y'all.' Pamela arrived, late again, 'Gahd, these London subway drivers, always on a go slow.' She threw her coat over the hatch; it fell to the floor as usual. Daphne raised her eyebrows at Ruby and disappeared upstairs.

'Jeeze, I need a caw-fee before I do anything, I'm bushed.' Pamela poured herself an espresso and whipped a chocolate éclair from under the counter. Ruby couldn't imagine why Daphne didn't get rid of this lazy prima donna but the customers loved her – well, the fickle male advertising types seemed to, anyway – letching over her plumped-up lips and huge fake breasts. Daphne certainly wasn't stupid.

Ten o'clock on the dot, the door dinged and in walked Mrs Connolly, a regular customer. Ruby loved this time; the shop was buzzing and it was a great place to people- watch when she wasn't rushed off her feet. She waved to Glen, another regular – a car salesman in his forties who had recently lost his job but was too scared to tell his wife as she had just had twins and he didn't want to worry her.

'Ouch!' Ruby flinched as the hot steam from the tea urn made one of her burns from yesterday smart, and realised why there was always a ready supply of aloe vera ointment in the back kitchen. At least her life at Ritsy Rose Interiors hadn't caused her any injury. Here, she was getting covered in burns and scalds. At Dinsworth, she had been covered in poo! All part of life's rich tapestry, she supposed.

'Here comes the old flea bag,' Pamela drawled, supping on another bottle of water.

Mrs Connolly was anything but an 'old flea bag'. In fact, Ruby had become quite fond of her. Every day at this time, the old lady would come in and sit at the same seat right near the door. Daphne made sure that a reserved sign was always on it. Her back was slightly hunched and she had pure white curly hair. She always wore a shade of purple – pale lilac today, Ruby noticed. She would order a pot of Earl Grey and a cream horn, and would make it last for exactly one hour, always sneaking the end of the horn under the table to her sweet little Yorkshire terrier, Chester. Daphne had overruled any sort of health and safety ruling on having a dog on the premises as 'dear Mabel' (Daphne's words) had been coming to Piaf's for the past twenty years since her husband had died, and she and Chester were now as much part of the furniture as Daphne was.

Every day, Mrs Connolly would quietly ask for *The Times* from the rack at the back of the shop. She was a lady of few words, but Ruby could see the kindness in her eyes, and could tell without a doubt that Chester was her life. Bless her, losing her husband when she must have been still young, Ruby thought. Life was sometimes so unfair.

Pamela was clearing tables when Mrs Connolly handed her back the pay plate with a crisp ten pound note on it. Ruby was refilling the urn and happened to notice Pamela putting the incorrect change back on the plate. Ruby was just about to open her mouth when Pamela grabbed her wrist. 'Don't you dare say a word. I told her that the cream horns had gone up months ago; the extra goes straight into our tip box. And if you think of telling Daffers upstairs then don't bother, 'cos it'll be your word against mine.'

Ruby was dumbfounded. What a cow! Just as she was about to aim a suitably hard rock cake at her head, the shop door flew open.

'Ooh, look at you with your fancy outfit on. New shoes and everything.' Fi smiled, her wild hair up in a bun with loads of rogue strands flying around her face, disturbed by the cold March wind. 'Cup of your finest builders brew, please. And make it strong, none of your weak English tea. I've managed to sneak out on break and thought I'd come and say hello.'

'I forgot how close your office was.' Ruby took the money for the tea. 'Here you go. Pop yourself up on the stool. I've time for a quick chat.'

'I guess that's Barbie over there?' Fi nodded towards Pamela.

'Yeah, that's her. Amazingly, she's actually doing some work.' Her American colleague was clearing tables.

'Anyway, Rubes, this is not purely a social visit. I need

to run something by you.'

'Go on,' Ruby urged.

'Well, we – as in the Sparkle Events we – are working on a celebrity birthday party and well, the demands are so great for this bash – all stuck up their own fecking arses if you ask me – that I could really do with some help.' Ruby's eyes lit up in anticipation. 'So how do you fancy Month Four, Job Four being an event organiser to the stars?' Fi continued. 'Money no object on this one; I don't think they even know what the words "credit" and "crunch" mean.' Fi raised her eyebrows and continued, 'The biggest perk, of course, is that you will be working with yours truly.'

Ruby did a little jump up and down and then ran from behind the counter to hug her friend. 'Oh my God, how bloody exciting. Thanks, Fi.'

'I take it that's a yes, then?' Fiona smiled at her excitable friend and realised just how much she loved her. 'Right. That's a done deal. Have a good day. Just need to find a driver now.'

At this, Glen's ears pricked up and he rushed over to Fi.

'Sorry to be so forward, love, but I'm out of work and am more than qualified to be a driver, whatever you need. Just let me know where and when.'

Fi looked to Ruby, who nodded wildly.

'Flash me your driving licence right now and you are my official parker.' Fi smiled as Glen did as he was told. How times had changed, Ruby thought. People really were desperate for work.

Ruby walked to the door and held it open for Mrs Connolly and Fi.

'Thanks, dear.' Mrs Connolly put her gloved hand on Ruby's. Chester barked. Fi followed the old lady out and waved goodbye through the glass, pointing and making a lunging action with her hips as she noticed one of the good-looking advertising types drinking a cappuccino in the window of the tea shop.

As Ruby scoured the tables to check that everyone was happy, she suddenly realised why Pamela was so keen to clear the tables during a busy spell. She made sure the lazy one couldn't see her, then began to watch her every move.

Bold as brass, Pamela speedily filled the front pocket of her apron with the majority of the tips, just leaving a few paltry silver coins on the main plate. She strutted over to the counter, smiled at Ruby, and tipped these dregs into the china tip-share pig.

Ruby managed to keep her temper in check as she thought– Revenge is a dish best served cold. Pamela Hampton might think she could get away with fleecing little old ladies and fair employers, but there was no way she was going to get away with short-changing Ruby Ann Matthews.

Chapter Twenty-five

Daphne mouthed Edith Piaf song lyrics as she danced cheek to cheek with Norbert around the empty tea shop. Ruby didn't bat an eyelid as she pushed open the door. She was used to the eccentricities of Daphne and Norbert's relationship and loved them both for it.

'Morning, Rubes,' they said in unison, breaking away from their waltz.

'Your last day, Ruby, yes?' Norbert asked. 'We will be sad to see you go.'

'Yes, we will indeed, young Ruby,' Daphne agreed.

'Although we love our Katerina, having you here has been a breath of fresh air.'

Ruby felt warm inside. It had been a long time since she had felt so wanted in the workplace, and so far Johnny's choices had given her a hat-trick of appreciation.

'Right, we are going back upstairs for a while.' Norbert grabbed Daphne by the hand and dragged her towards the stairs.

Daphne, giggling like a teenager, shouted back down to Ruby, 'Just ring the bell at ten to eleven and we'll be ready.'

Plan PamAm was fully in place for eleven sharp. The stick insect was going to be crushed without one single rock cake being thrown.

Ruby opened up and greeted the customers with her usual jovial manner. She was fond of her regular clientele, and none more so than Mabel Connolly and Chester.

Ten o'clock on the dot and here they were. Ruby carried the Earl Grey and cream horn to their reserved table. 'Morning, Mabel. Here you go. It's on the house today. In fact, Daphne says it will be on the house for the next month – and you know why.'

Mabel nodded, then put her finger in a straight line against one side of her nose as if she was in the Gestapo. 'Oh yes, I know why.' She took a loud slurp of her tea, and then whispered loudly, 'We're all set.'

'Good stuff,' Ruby whispered back, handing the old lady a Christmas cracker, which she quickly hid in her handbag.

The door chimed. Ruby looked up and did a double-take at the gorgeous man who walked in. Pamela, hurrying as fast as her high heels would allow her, tried and failed to get behind the counter to him first.

'Cup of the normal filter stuff, please. Black with two sugar.'

They were the perfect plum tones of an English gentleman. He was in his late forties; tall and perfectly groomed, with dark brown hair that was neither short nor long. His expensive-looking dark grey coat and brass cane, combined with his observant, pale blue eyes and perfect teeth, made him look like he just stepped off the set of a period drama.

Ruby, taken aback by the sheer presence of this man, stuttered, 'And, er, would you, er, like anything else, sir?'

'Spit it out, girl,' the posh man snorted. 'I'll take a slice of that lemon drizzle cake over there too. Looks simply divine.'

Ruby bent over to reach the cake slice. Completely ignoring Pamela's pouting, the handsome man casually leant across the counter and smacked Ruby on the bottom with his cane. 'I just couldn't resist it,' he said, and laughed heartily. Ruby didn't make a sound. She was in complete shock, but quite alarmingly had to admit she'd rather enjoyed it.

'I ... er ... don't know quite what to say,' was all she

could muster, as she rubbed her tingling buttocks.

The man carried on as if nothing had happened. 'Anyway, my dear, I've come in to see the du Mont woman. I spoke to her last week. She's sorting some cakes for a party I'm having at Dinsworth.'

'What – Dinsworth House in Twickenham?'

'You know it?'

'I used to work there, in the retirement home.' She wiped her floury hands on her apron and held out her hand over the counter. 'I'm Ruby Matthews.'

'Ruby? You must be Ginger, of course. Lucas spoke very highly of you. I looked out for you at his funeral but I must have missed you. Now, how is that lively hound of his?' He cleared his throat and before Ruby had time to answer, he said, 'Do forgive me for not introducing myself first. How very rude. I'm Domenic Bentley but please call me Bentley. I'm the owner of said house.'

'I'm very pleased to meet you, Bentley,' Ruby replied politely. 'And Montgomery is very well, thank you.'

She rang the bell. Norbert came running down, shirtless and breathless. 'Is it time?' he asked.

'No, no. There's a Mr Bentley here to see Daphne about some cakes.'

Daphne was listening at the top of the stairs. 'I'll be down in five, dear.'

As Daphne chatted to Bentley at the end of the shop, Pamela was in a complete strop, wondering how much she'd have got from a lawsuit if he'd dared to spank *her*.

Eleven o'clock came. Mrs Connolly got Ruby's attention and pointed to the clock. Ruby rang for Norbert, who came down dressed this time, and signalled to Mrs du Mont, who excused herself from Bentley for a minute and came over to the counter. She mouthed, 'Ready?' to her accomplices. They all nodded.

'Pamela, dear, would you mind just sweeping over by the front door?' Mrs du Mont requested. 'Chester seems to have made an awful mess under the table today.'

Pamela grabbed the broom from the back office, huffing and puffing with distaste at having to do manual work. Ruby gave Mrs Connolly the nod. The cracker was pulled under the table; Chester, shocked by the sudden loud bang, ran out as fast as he could, tripping Pamela right over as he did so. She flipped in the air and all of the change came flying out of the front of her apron, as well as three £10 notes.

While Pamela was flailing in embarrassment and discomfort on the floor, Norbert grabbed the loose change and put it in the tip pig. He took the notes and checked them. They had all been marked with the letters E.P. (for Edith Piaf), as Ruby had been instructed to do every time she put money into the till. Pamela struggled up, puffing and panting, her Botoxed face remaining expressionless.

'Pesky dog!' she seethed.

Daphne waved the marked notes in front of her face. 'Piaf's has no room for deceit. You're a thief and a cheat and you're fired!'

Mrs Connolly clapped her hands together in joy and shouted, 'Bravo!' Chester ran around his owner's feet, barking loudly. The stick insect grabbed her coat and sped to the door. 'You plain ginger bitch. How dare you!' she screamed at Ruby as it slammed shut.

Mrs du Mont started singing a Piaf tune at the top of her voice, while giving out fresh cream slices to anyone who had witnessed the drama.

'Bloody good show.' Domenic Bentley patted Ruby on the back. 'And I'd much rather a plain ginger bitch than a pumped-up, blonde slapper with no arse any day. I say, do you fancy coming out to dinner with me one night?'

'I … er …' Ruby floundered, flushing to her roots.

'It's OK, dear girl,' Bentley intercepted. 'You don't have to give me an answer right now.' He pushed a business card into her apron pocket, tipped his hat to Mrs du Mont, and headed out into the cold March air.

Four thirty quickly came, and it was time for Ruby to say her goodbyes. As she put on her coat, Daphne came downstairs and turned the door sign to Closed. Norbert followed closely, carrying a square, white cake box.

Daphne planted a big wet kiss on Ruby's cheek. 'I don't want to cry, darling Ruby, so all I am going to say is, I'll see you soon.' She pulled a lace hanky from up her sleeve and dabbed her eyes.

Norbert presented the cake, announcing, 'Ruby, we love you and we want you to come back to work or play anytime you like.'

Ruby smiled. 'You won't get rid of me that easily, I promise that. Now, what have we here?'

She opened the box and laughed out loud. There, looking up at her from a sea of bright green icing, was the Reading football team. Their blue and white tops were perfectly formed out of coloured marzipan. David Kitwell, red icing for hair, had his left arm raised.

'See your Kitwell man, he blow you the kiss, Ruby,' Norbert declared.

'Ooh, and just think – I can lick him all over later!' Ruby grinned. 'Thank you, thank you so much.'

'It really has been a pleasure working with you, my dear,' Daphne said with emotion.

'And you too,' Ruby said meaningfully, Realising, as she skipped out into the cool spring evening, that her twelve-month mission to happiness had definitely been the right decision.

Chapter Twenty-six

'The ref needs effing glasses!' George was shouting up at the big screen in O'Neills when Ruby walked in, followed by Fi. 'Bastards.' A penalty kick flew past the West Ham keeper.

'Calm down, love, you'll have a heart attack.' Ruby put two pints of lager down in front of the boys.

'Cheers, bird.' George sat back down.

'Thanks, Ruby.' James smiled at her.

'You a Newcastle supporter then, James?'

'Aye, of course. A magpie man through and through.'

'Never mind,' Ruby jibed and turned to George. 'Anyway, how are the Mighty Royals doing today?'

'One nil down last time I looked,' he replied, eyes glued to the screen.

'Can you all fecking shut up about football now please?' Fi scraped her hair up into a bun, holding hairgrips in her mouth as she did so. 'It bores the shite out of me.'

'What you drinking anyway?' George asked, suddenly aware that Ruby didn't have her usual glass of Sauvignon Blanc.

'White wine and soda,' she answered quickly.

'I didn't put you down as a girl who did mixers.' He winked at her. Ruby didn't want to dwell on this conversation, as since Dublin, she was trying her best not to drink as much as she used to. She felt that having soda would make her drink last longer.

'Now, young James, we don't know much about you now, do we?' Fi shifted a little closer to him and he looked slightly uncomfortable.

'Well, what do you want to know, pet? Just ask away.'

Fi held a pretend microphone up to his mouth. 'So tell me, Mr …?'

'Kane,' James supplied.

'Is your father's name Michael?' Fi continued with a straight face.

'No, it's Kane with a K and no i.'

'Oh, that's a shame. I was just about to propose to you then,' Fi flirted. 'So, Mr Kane – or can I call you Sugar?' Everyone laughed as Fi continued playing to her audience. 'Tell me, if you are not living off your father's international film star money, then what do you do?'

'I'm a trainee solicitor,' James said proudly.

'Are you?' Ruby asked with surprise. 'Where are you based?

'In Staple Inn, near the Chancery Lane tube line. A firm called Trilby, Vine and Pitheringon.'

Ruby sniggered. 'Why is it all solicitors have such funny names? You never see a Brown, Smith and Jones Limited, do you?'

James laughed and added. 'We'd all be Matthews, Kane, Stevens and O'Donahue – hmm, that doesn't sound quite right either.'

'Actually, Rubes, our jobs are very similar. I keep grass off the lawns and he keeps criminals off the streets.'

'Or on them if I get it wrong,' James intercepted.

'Get in there!' George's beloved West Ham had equalised.

He jumped up and nearly knocked all their drinks flying.

Monty appeared sleepily from under the table, then began to bark loudly, until Ruby made a fuss of him enough to resume his siesta.

'Sure you don't want another?' Fi asked during the commotion.

'No thanks,' Ruby said. 'I just want to chill today. It's been a mad few weeks.'

The boys headed to the bar.

'I came on this morning,' Ruby told Fi.

'Thank feck for that. What about the Fairdale Clinic results?

'Clean as a whistle,' Ruby smiled.

'Phew!'

'Ruby got up and threw her scarf around her neck. 'Now, are you sure I can't persuade you back to mine for hot chocolate and some of my yummy football cake?'

Chapter Twenty-seven

April, Job Four: Event Co-Coordinator

'Jaysus, where does she think we're going to get fecking Dendrobium orchids this time of year?' Fi ranted. 'Ruby, get onto The Flower Factory in Chelsea and see what they can do.' She dragged her hair back on top of her head, clipped it into place, and continued, 'And the silly bitch wants pink diamante poodles scattered over the tables now instead of red ones. Make a note of that on the event schedule, will you?'

Ruby took a big glug of water straight from the two- litre plastic bottle on her desk and updated her To-Do list for the hundredth time that week. Her head was spinning. She couldn't believe how much money and effort could go into arranging one birthday party. What had happened to good old Pass the Parcel and butterfly cakes? Mind you, the birthday girl in question was none other than heiress Alexia Ramada, chief socialite and current gossip-column queen.

Despite being the busiest job Ruby had ever had in her life, she did enjoy the buzz and challenge of it all. And, although Fi turned into an even bossier bitch than usual, at least Ruby could swear at her when she felt she was being unreasonable without fear of getting fired.

Ruby felt her biggest achievement to date in this job was finding an ice statue firm willing to create a lifesize version of Alexia herself, wearing nothing but a smile with Versace the miniature poodle surreptitiously covering her lady bits.

She was mid-search on the internet for a hire car company that would stock pink limousines when her mobile rang.

'You'll never guess what!' Sam was virtually shrieking down the phone in excitement.'

'Hey, Sam. It must be good, whatever it is.' Ruby was pleased of the break from the grind.

'There's only talk that Kitwell might play for England.'

'No! That's amazing!'

'I know – we gingers will eventually rule the world,' Sam went on.

'The only downside is, one of the big clubs might realise his true talent and snap him up from Reading,' Ruby added wisely.

'No way, sis, I won't allow it.' She could sense her brother's smile down the phone and it made her feel happy inside.

'How's Mum? she asked. 'Been so busy I haven't spoken to her for a while.'

'She's great. In fact, she's like a new woman. Graham is making a complete fuss of her. I haven't known her this happy since Dad was alive.'

'Bless Mum, that's great news – and how's that lovely doggy of yours?'

'He's amazing, Rubes. Makes my life so much easier. Gets us a lot of attention from the birds too.' Ruby laughed, then looked up and could see Fi gesturing to her from the other side of the office.

'Hey, Sam, I've gotta go. Working on a birthday bash for Alexia Ramada, don't you know.'

He whistled. 'Good on ya, sis. Just quickly before you go – I wanted to see if you're going to come down for the home game on Saturday. We've got Newcastle so it should be a good 'un.'

'Um, I hadn't really thought about the weekend yet.

But why not? Yeah, can you get me a couple of tickets?'

'Will do. See you Saturday. Ben barks hi, by the way.'

'Right back at him. Can't wait to catch up. See ya soon.'

'Ruby.' Fi came over and sat wearily on her desk. 'Can you ring the venue and tell them I've got Alexia's champagne choice? They'll need at least fifty crates of this on standby.' She pushed a list towards Ruby and stabbed her finger on it.

'Pol Roger. Nice.' Ruby said, adding. 'Winston Churchill's favourite tipple, don't you know?'

'Right ... Let's have a look, shall we?' Fi flicked through the printed off email that Ruby handed to her, then digressed. 'I can't wait for you to see Cliveden, Ruby. It's a gorgeous venue.'

'I'm looking forward to it. Going to have a good old snoop around the place. Mum asked if I can take a few shots of the master bedrooms if I could, so I mustn't forget my camera.'

Fi continued, 'OK. Two hundred people ... standing fork buffet. Why don't you just send the two most expensive menu choices over to Alexia's PA, for her to choose? Miss Fancy Pants will think then she's getting the best, and Sparkle will make maximum commission on food and beverage. Everyone's a winner then.'

'OK, will do,' Ruby replied professionally.

'Oh, and Rubes,' Fi added. 'Darling Alexia wants a special menu for the pampered pooch too.'

Ruby screwed her face up. 'You what?'

'I'm not joking. Look on the hotel website,' Fi added.

Ruby quickly keyed in the web address. 'No!' she shrieked, eyes open in amazement. 'It's better than the food I eat at home!' She scrolled down until she found – "The Dog Menu". 'How bloody funny! How about fillet steak and rice, moistened with light gravy?'

'Perfect,' Fi smiled. 'Although you had better check

first that Versace isn't a vegetarian.'

Fi wandered nonchalantly back to her desk, leaving Ruby wondering whether she was serious or not.

Chapter Twenty-eight

At Putney station, James plonked himself down next to Ruby on the South West train service to Reading. The carriage was surprisingly empty for Saturday lunchtime.

'Got any Paracetamol, Rubes?' he asked. 'I've got a stonker of a hangover.'

'Here, this will work much better.' Ruby laughed and handed him a can of cold lager. 'There's a bit of a posse coming along today,' she told him. 'I hope you're ready for the whole Matthews family, guide dog included.'

'Aye, it'll be canny. Thanks for thinking of me for the tickets, Rubes, really appreciate it.'

'My brother is blind, by the way,' Ruby said quietly. 'Didn't want it to be a shock when you saw him. Luckily he won't be able to be shocked at the sight of you,' she teased, taking in James's dishevelled appearance, extra- thick stubble included.

'Got a needle and cotton, pet? I need to sew up my splitting sides.' James grinned and opened the can of lager. He continued softly, 'So has he been blind since birth then?'

'Yeah, Sam contracted a disease when he was just a baby. It still chokes me up, but he has coped amazingly well. The dog in question is his guide dog, Ben, who has literally opened his eyes for him.'

'I can't imagine what it must be like,' James said thoughtfully. 'Good on him though, carrying on a normal life. Must be pretty scary, being amongst a big crowd at a football match, though?'

'He knows no different, I guess,' Ruby added.

James nodded. Then, 'God, this train is slow!'

'I know. Maybe we should have gone via Paddington, but I really couldn't be bothered to Tube it today.' Ruby put her head back on the seat. 'It'll be worth it though, when the Mighty Royals get one past your keeper.'

'In your dreams, lassy,' James smirked.

'Have you always been a Newcastle United supporter then?' Ruby asked.

'Yep. My Da introduced me to the team at the grand old age of five and they've been in my blood ever since. He even named me after their ground, St James' Park – how canny is that?'

'That's wicked!' Ruby laughed. 'Glad my dad didn't name me after Reading's old home. My name would be Elm.'

'Hmm ... Elm Matthews, bit of a mouthful,' James rounded the words slowly. 'So, is your dad going to be one of the Matthews posse there today then?'

'I wish he was. He's dead, I'm afraid.'

'Rubes, I'm so sorry. Hope you don't mind me talking about it, but how old were you and Sam?'

'Well, Sam was only seventeen. I was twenty-seven. Tougher on him, I think sometimes, as at least I knew my dad as an adult.'

James could see the tears welling in her eyes, and, not one for knowing what to do when a girl was in tears, thrust another can of lager at her.

'Hey, get this down you, pet, and lubricate those vocal cords. It'll take a lot of shouting for your boys to get one in the net today, I reckon.'

Ruby opened the can and lifted it in the air. 'Come on, you R's!'

'I could smell you a mile off,' Sam joked as he greeted them at their usual meeting point at the Madejski Stadium. 'Now let me guess ...' He sniffed the air. 'Clarins Par

Amour today, I reckon. Got enough on, you huss?' Ruby had indeed put a little extra on her erogenous bits, just in case of any extra-curricular activities outside of football. James smiled, taking an instant liking to her cheeky younger brother. 'And you must be James,' Sam went on, holding out his hand. 'I've heard all about you.'

'He hasn't, he just likes to embarrass me for no particular reason.' Ruby flushed. 'Anyway, where's Mum? I thought she and Graham were coming too?'

'Well, they were, but then they decided they'd rather go to the cinema instead. They dropped me here about ten minutes ago.'

Ruby noticed his white stick. 'So, where's Ben then?'

'I've given him the afternoon off. I know he's trained, but I don't think it's fair for him to have to sit in all the crowds. You'll have to be my guide bitch for the afternoon like you used to be.' He accentuated the word "bitch" and Ruby hit him playfully on the arm.

'Kitwell for England,' the lively crowd chanted as the ginger striker's first shot at goal hit the crossbar.

'Tosser,' James said under his breath.

Ruby stared at the goalkeeper's bottom. Now he was one American she wouldn't mind getting jiggy with.

'USA! USA!' The crowd was off again as Mark Harman, the goalie in question, made another amazing save. She really must have sex soon, Ruby thought. She was becoming like some frustrated old woman. Every man she was remotely attracted to she had the urge to trip them over and shag them. She shuffled a little closer to James. He, of course, was oblivious to anything other than his boys in black and white.

The whistle for the start of the second half was blown, and within minutes Michael Owen was charging towards the Reading goal. A neat little side kick and in it went, off of one of the Reading players. Despite it being an own goal, the away fans erupted, including James! 'Get in there, you beauty!' he shouted, jumping out of his seat, completely forgetting where he was. Ruby was aware that everyone around them had gone silent.

An 'Oh fuck,' from Sam.

An 'Oh shit,' from Ruby.

An 'I'm in trouble,' from James.

Sam could sense a group of lads running from the hardcore fan area of the stand towards them. Quick as a flash, he whipped off his dark glasses, thrust them on to James's face, and handed him his white stick.

'Don't say a word,' Sam ordered, grabbing his arm for stability as the group, hotly pursued by security guards, approached them. Sam bravely stood in front of James as soon as they were in earshot and said his piece. 'Hey, boys, come on, he's blind. Give him some slack. It was a real mistake.' His voice remained strong and clear. 'He thought The Royals had scored. Of course he doesn't support those Geordie wankers.'

'Shit, mate, we're really sorry.' The leader of the gang backed down when he saw the glasses and white stick. 'Enjoy the rest of the game like.' They all shuffled back to their seats.

James held his head in relief and whispered to Ruby, 'I can't see a fucking thing with these glasses on, pet.' Sam's amazing hearing picked up this and he laughed.

'Welcome to my world. Now shut the fuck up and be grateful I saved your life.'

The match ended in a 2-1 victory to Reading, and Sam and Ruby were jubilant on their walk back into town.

'See, Davey Kitwell does it every time. You better talk to the Gaffer about signing some new players, me thinks,' Sam laughed, as James cuffed him gently around the head.

'*You'd* better talk to your goalie about letting in own goals,' James chided.

'Now, now, children,' Ruby intervened as they reached

Reading station. 'Shall we have a little drink before we go back home?'

'Depends on what time is it,' Sam piped up.

'Five thirty,' James said, looking at his watch.

'I've gotta run then, sorry. I'm meeting someone from college at six. Hope you don't mind.'

'Don't be silly, go on and enjoy yourself,' Ruby replied gently. 'Do you want us to walk you there?'

'Nah, I've got my stick. I'll be fine,' Sam replied, holding out his hand to James, who took it immediately and shook it. 'Good to meet you, James. Shame about your sub-rate team.'

James laughed. 'You wait till you play us at St James', and then you'll be sorry. Have a good night, mate.'

Ruby watched her brother cross the road and felt proud and sad at the same time. James, observing the situation, took her arm gently. 'Come on, pet. Let's get that train home, shall we?'

Chapter Twenty-nine

'Stella, mate?' James shouted through to George, who was watching television in the lounge.

'Yeah, go on then.'

James threw George a beer and leapt onto a sofa. 'Surprised to see you home on a Saturday night.'

'Yeah, well. I got so pissed last night with Arun Gill that I've got to have a quiet one tonight. Not sure if I can even get this one down me.'

George pulled his ring pull as James laughed. 'Arun Gill, eh? Suki will have your guts for garters for corrupting her young boy.'

'He doesn't need much persuading, I'll tell you that.' George took a large swig of lager and burped loudly.

James suddenly noticed what was gracing the plasma screen.

'*Rambo*! Top man.'

'I'm recording it too, in case I do fall asleep,' George stated.

'Excellent.' James rubbed his face and took a sip of his beer.

'See you got beat today. I bet Ruby was ecstatic,' George smiled.

'Beat and nearly beaten up. Forgot which end I was in and started cheering, didn't I? It would have all kicked off if it wasn't for Sam.'

'Sam?'

'Long story, mate, but it involved me wearing the dark glasses and holding the white stick. Genius, actually, but the whole story can wait for another day.'

George laughed out loud. 'Saved from a marauding football crowd by a blind man. That is fucking mad!'

'All right, keep it down, mate. It isn't that funny,' James said, sounding perturbed. 'Sam is a top lad though, isn't he?'

George nodded. 'I can't even imagine being blind, everything just becomes so difficult. Even the little things we don't think about, like knowing where a toilet is on the terraces, or where to head for a beer.'

James nodded this time. 'Yeah, and Ruby is just so good with him. She's a canny lass, George.'

'I know. The more I spend time with her, the more I like her, but she is a tricky one to gauge.' George drained his can.

'I definitely see something between you two.' James added.

'Bloody hell. You sound like old Margaret down the road. She's always trying to fix me up with her too.'

'Ask her out, mate,' James urged. 'Take her on a proper date. Not to O'Neill*s*, dinner or something. You never know, you might like it. Ruby's worth a lot more than just a shag.'

'I know that,' George said thoughtfully and turned back to the TV screen. 'Fuck me, I love this bit.'

Rambo pulled back his bow and arrow.

Chapter Thirty

'Bloody incompetence. I cannot deal with incompetence!' Bentley roared as he and Ruby waited to be seated. Ruby shuffled with slight embarrassment at his outburst and made attempts to smile at anyone within earshot at the Savoy Grill.

She had been so excited when she had realised that they were going to the newly opened Savoy Hotel on the Strand, and it was certainly living up to its grandeur and hype.

'Ah, there you are, man,' the eccentric one addressed the maitre d'. 'Bentley is the name. Table for two.'

Bentley was wearing his long coat and swinging his brass cane. He handed his over-garment to the unflappable maitre d' to reveal a beautifully tailored brown suit with pink shirt and matching cravat. He looked sexy and smart and Ruby noticed many ladies, and even some of the men, admiring him.

Domenic Bentley was so unlike anyone she had been out with before. For one, he was much older. For two, he was incredibly obnoxious, but somehow his curt character made him who he was and it was strangely endearing. She had been taken by him the moment she'd seen him in Piaf's. And when he had whacked her bottom with his cane, she had felt lustful rather than revolted at his perverse antic.

Her charismatic companion took a large slurp of his red wine and sat back in his chair. 'That's better. Needed a bloody drink. Dolly wandered on to the main road completely starkers today. Police had to come and everything.' He coughed loudly and carried on, 'Not bad tits for an octogenarian though.'

Ruby chose to ignore his last comment. 'Poor old Dolly.' She remembered the old lady's dementia and felt genuinely sad.

'Pain in the bloody arse, the lot of them. Dotty old drama queens,' Bentley ranted. 'But they pay the bills and that's what matters. I say that's what matters, Ruby.' He took another big slurp of wine. 'You see, my father died five years ago. He was a game old devil. He was on the bloody job when he went – giving one of the chambermaids one.'

'well, at least he died happy,' Ruby offered.

'Yes – happy and bloody penniless! He spent all the disposable cash he did have on women, wine, and song. And he squandered the rest – ha ha!'

Ruby learnt that Dinsworth House, along with an accumulation of debt, had been left in trust for Bentley to manage. But he was determined to keep the Bentley name going. There was no way that he was going to see the house sold or go to rack and ruin. No wonder he hadn't had the wake for Lucas. Ruby felt guilty for thinking badly of him now.

'And your mother?' she was inquisitive now.

'I know I shouldn't say this about the one who bore me, but she was a complete bloody slut. She and the old man were actually quite well-suited in the promiscuity stakes and that was about all. She ran off with Blears the chauffeur years ago. Never heard from either of them again.'

'Oh, that's sad.' Ruby went to reach for his hand.

'Sadder that they pinched the bloody Roller, I say.' He quickly took another drink, and mellowed slightly. 'You really are a very beautiful lady, Ruby. It came out wrong when I said at Piaf's that you were plain. I was just mimicking that awful wiry yank. You're a perfect English rose, my dear. Yes, that's what you are – a perfect English rose.'

'Thank you,' Ruby replied shyly. It had been such a long time since she'd been complimented.

Bentley continued, 'Your red hair suits your personality. Bright, exhilarating – and I should imagine a bit fiery between those sheets, what?'

His cut-glass accent made Ruby want to laugh out loud. He smirked and she felt a stirring in her sadly neglected nethers. He made her feel incredibly naughty. Sitting in front of her was the man to quench her recent love drought. She glanced down to check she had put some condoms in her handbag. Let the fun commence!

She reached for her companion's cane, gently slid it under the table, rubbed it against his inner thigh, and whispered in his ear, 'Dearest Bentley, the word "bit" doesn't come into it.'

Ruby giggled as they pushed the heavy front door open.

'Sshh.' Bentley put his finger to his lips. 'Don't be waking the old crones now or they'll all want to join in.' Ruby giggled some more. She had drunk a little too much red wine, but just enough to guarantee a fun evening. And after Bentley's somewhat lewd suggestions in the taxi on the way back, she was fully aware of what might lie before her tonight.

Bentley led her to the library, an amazing oak-panelled room that smelt of wood smoke. Ruby stared in awe at the rows and rows of books. She was curious to know if he had any quotation delights amongst the numerous tomes. She particularly loved the fact that there was a ladder on wheels attached to a sort of track that could be trundled along to reach the top shelves.

When her host disappeared to fetch drinks, she couldn't resist having a go on it.

'Wheeeeee!' She launched herself along the back wall

on the ladder just as Bentley appeared in the doorway. She looked down from on high, ready to greet him, and her eyes widened in disbelief. For there was her eccentric companion, naked as the day he was born, carrying a tray of drinks in one hand, and a small white cloth in the other, hiding his huge erection.

Smirking, he walked towards her, drunkenly shouting, 'Think Cluedo, Ruby. Think Cluedo!' Immediately hitting his wavelength, she laughed out loud at his craziness.

'I guess it has to be Miss Scarlett in the library with the lead piping?'

'Bloody spot on, girl, spot on. Now get that smashing little arse of yours down here and let me spank it.'

Chapter Thirty-one

'Jesus is alive and living with Elvis,' Bert hollered from Margaret's front garden.

'Puts "Return to Sender" in a different context for sure, eh, Bert?'

George bounded down his steps, carrying a garden fork and laughing at her comment. 'Sharp as a bleeding tack as always, Ms Matthews.'

'A rusty one at that today. I'm knackered.'

'Been burning the candle at both ends again, have you then?' George questioned.

'Something like that.' Ruby didn't want to allude to last night's antics with Bentley. 'Anyway, must dash. Got my big event today.'

'Let me give you a lift to the station, I'm going that way.'

She hopped up into the van. Montgomery followed and began licking her face wildly. George tooted and waved at Margaret as she opened her front door with a mug of hot tea and handed it to Bert.

'Is everything OK with Muttley here?' Ruby asked, pushing the energetic Jack Russell onto the floor. 'Sorry, life's been so mad; I haven't had time to even think of finding him a new home.'

'Rubes, it's fine. I love having him. There's no way we're taking him to the RSPCA just yet. I couldn't bear to think of him stuck in a cage waiting for a suitable owner. I'll keep my ears open for anyone who might want him.'

'Thanks, George, I really do appreciate it.'

'Where's the event anyway?' he added.

'Cliveden House in Berkshire. It's an amazing venue.'

'Yeah, I'm sure me old dear's mentioned it before. The Profumo geezer and those pros were at it there, weren't they?'

Ruby was impressed that George knew about it. She felt bad that she sometimes didn't give him more credit for his intelligence. He might be a gardener, but he certainly wasn't stupid.

'That's the one. I'm looking forward to seeing all the celebs who may pitch up. It's Alexia Ramada's birthday bash, you know,' she bragged slightly.

'Any spare tickets?' George turned and grinned at her. 'Quite fancy having a go at that Alexia bird myself.'

Ruby playfully whacked him on the arm and jumped out of the van. 'Thanks a lot, George. Have a good day.'

'Oh, and er … Ruby, there was something I wanted to ask you.'

At that moment, Ruby's mobile rang. She put her hand up to stop George continuing. It was Bentley. She started giggling like a school girl as he began to recount their antics in the study the previous evening.

'Catch you later,' Ruby mouthed, going straight back to her conversation.

George screeched down the road, with Montgomery's head sticking out of the window, tongue to the heavens. Feeling a pang of anger, he cranked up his stereo, sped up, and swore out loud. He was relieved that he hadn't asked her out, it would have made him look a complete fool. She was obviously just sweet-talking another man, and he suddenly realised that he didn't like it much. In fact, he didn't like it at all.

'Just a black coffee, thanks, Glen,' Ruby addressed the new waiter in Piaf's. Bless Daphne for taking him on when he so needed a job – she really did have a heart of gold.

Daphne spotted Ruby at the counter and came running

around, showering her with little air kisses. 'Darling Ruby, how wonderful to see you.'

'All OK?' Ruby gestured to Glen.

'He's a lovely man and very hard-working.'

'And you and Norbert?'

'Still at it like rabbits, and dancing like Fred and Ginger, so life is simply fantastico.' The little lady tidied her hair in the mirror. 'What brings you here today, sweet Ruby?'

'Just waiting for Fi. We've got an event at Cliveden today and need to go through the final details.'

'Oh, how simply divine, darling! Right, I must get on. Keep me posted on life, love, and marvellousness.' Daphne swept off up the stairs just as Fi came bounding through the door, hair flailing everywhere.

'Jaysus, get me a fecking coffee, Rubes. I feel like my brain's going to explode.'

They sat in the window, acknowledging Mrs Connolly and Chester when they came in, plus half-watching a busy London morning walk by.

'So, before we start on work stuff, did Bentley bend you over the balustrade?'

'Fi!' Ruby paused. 'Well, OK, yes, he did of sorts.'

'Oh my God – what was it like to shag a wrinkly?' Fi leaned forward ready for the answer.

'He's not that old, and actually, it was bloody amazing,' Ruby replied indignantly. 'Experience over youthfulness any day.'

'Cock size?'

'Huge!'

Fi raised her eyebrows and Ruby suddenly felt selfconscious as the memory of them thrusting away on the huge rug in the library flooded her mind.

'You lucky cow. Anything else you'd care to divulge?'

'Well, the hysterical thing is that when he eventually came – we were both very drunk by this stage – he just kept saying, "You lovely, lovely young thing" over and over again in his posh accent until he fell asleep like a dead weight on top of me.'

Fi was laughing out loud by now. 'So are you going to meet up with him again, dear Rubes?'

'I hope so. He's decent shag and a bloody good laugh, and as there is no one else showing any interest at the moment, then I might as well go with it.'

'And what about George?'

'What about George, indeed. He hasn't given any indication he fancies me. So I'm going to carry on having fun with Bentley for now until the love of my life, whoever that may be, does decide to bang my door down.'

'Ruby!' Fi sounded frustrated with her friend.

'Oh, please don't, Fi. George would just see me as a bit of fun, I know that. And I'm too old for him.'

'You don't know that, Rubes.'

'Well, I'm not making the first move to make myself look a fool.'

Fi knew when to shut up about Ruby's love life. 'OK, troops!' She looked over to Glen. 'On track for the first Heathrow pick up at seven?'

He stuck his thumb up in confirmation. Fi turned to Ruby.

'And, we madam, better go through this party file or Madam Ramada won't be going to the ball.'

'Look at the size of that fountain!' Ruby exclaimed as they were chauffeured up the long drive towards Cliveden House.

'Wait till you see the actual house,' Fi told her as they rounded the corner.

'Oh my God, it's so beautiful,' Ruby breathed excitedly.

'I love the fact that it is so steeped in history too. A plethora of power, pleasure, and politics,'

'Hark at you, Fiona O'Donahue, you'll be writing bodice-ripping fiction soon.'

'No, I just took that straight from their website.' Both girls chuckled.

Ruby was quite overawed when the concierge approached the car and held open the door for her. She wasn't used to such grandeur. Maybe becoming Lady Bentley *was* the way forward.

The massive hallway, with its host of antique furniture and impressive fireplace, was a hive of activity as preparations were in full swing. A beautiful staircase wound its way to her right and a mahogany grand piano, adorned with black and white photos of politicians, royals, and stars who had visited Cliveden before, fronted the bar. The impeccable staff glided around in their morning suit- type uniforms.

'Such a bloody shame we can't stay the night, Rubes,' Fi uttered as she offloaded her heavy bag onto one of the chairs in the grand hall. 'But Alexia has obviously booked the whole place out.'

Ruby oversaw the arrival of the Dendrobium orchids, which she thankfully had been able to get hold of. Pink balloons were strategically placed around the room, and the pink diamante poodles were scattered randomly over the crisp white tablecloths. Goodie bags were put at the back of the Terrace dining room – the main party area. They contained Crème de la Mer beauty products. and a pink Chanel scarf for the ladies, and remote controlled red Ferraris for the men. Torch candles had been positioned outside each of the six sets of French windows to enhance a dramatic vista down to the River Thames. The front drive had been set up with fireworks, which were to go off every time a car came up the long driveway.

And last but not least – the *pièce de résistance* – the ice statue.

Ruby admired the handiwork as the life-size model, a

dead ringer for Alexia Ramada, was brought in. She made sure it was positioned in the centre of the hallway so that every guest could get a good look at it when they arrived. As the delivery guys were putting the final touches to its platform, Ruby let out a gasp. Fi was in earshot. 'What is it?'

Ruby pointed to the poodle that was covering Alexia's groin and they both fell about laughing. The sculptor obviously had a sense of humour as the frozen pooch was sporting a four-inch erection.

'They'll all be too drunk to notice,' Ruby said when they had stopped laughing.

'Alexia won't. She doesn't miss a fecking trick,' Fi said grimly, then, 'Don't worry, my hands are warm. I'll get rid of it.'

The concierge, staff, waiters, and Ruby all stood open-mouthed as Fiona O'Donahue placed her warm right hand over the icy erection and began to rub backwards and forwards until it dripped, subsided – and then disappeared.

'FiFi, darling, I'm here.' Alexia breezed in, with her entourage of hairdresser, make-up artist, and Versace the poodle, wearing a fetching pink velvet jacket, following dutifully behind. 'Oh, just look at my little pooky--wooky made of ice!'

'Yes, just look,' Ruby whispered sarcastically to the head waiter, who happened to be walking past carrying a tray of pink marshmallows. Alexia teetered up closer to the ice statue. 'He's got an indent where his little cock should be, how very PC.'

'Told you,' Fi mouthed to Ruby.

Alexia was wearing tight white jeans and a little pink crop top, tottering on four-inch cerise stilettos. She must have been a size minus two, Ruby thought. Her blonde hair was tied in a high ponytail and she was wearing no make-up. She could quite easily have passed as a paintbrush!

Fi led her into the main party room and Alexia jumped up and down as far as her heels would allow her.

'It's bloody gorgeous, darling. Fit for a princess – just like me. Could you just make the balloon strings five centimetres shorter though? They are just a teensy weensy bit too high.'

Fi smiled a Tony Choi-type smile. 'No problem, take it as done. At Sparkle Events, no request is too big or too small. You know that, Alexia.'

Ruby overheard this and came in, scissors in hand, to assist.

As Alexia, plus entourage, swept upstairs to take occupancy of the best suite in the house, Fi's fixed smile turned into a snarl. 'Fecking bitch. The joy of events, Ruby. Distaste, *not* love, most of the time! Now pass me those scissors.'

Cliveden's walls glowed as the Ramada party came to life. Their last bit of major excitement had been when a premier league footballer got hitched.

Fireworks along the drive went off on cue and the ice statue caused more of a stir than Alexia had ever imagined. Personally, Ruby had never before seen so much silicon, Botox, hair bleach, or Jimmy Choo-wearing in one room before. She was shocked at the goodie bag frenzy and saw at least three mini-skirted bimbettes hiding extra ones under cushions for collection later.

The men, predominantly City boys, millionaires, and models, looked stunning in their black tie attire. They quaffed copious amounts of Pol Roger, as they eyed the scantily dressed stick insects for either eligibility or easiness – ideally both. The elegant waiting staff moved inconspicuously amongst the revellers. Ruby was quite perturbed that the only famous person she had seen was an ex-girl band member. She noticed that Alexia was getting louder and louder the more champagne she consumed.

Viewing this false monied world close at hand made Ruby appreciate her Superdrug moisturiser, Florence & Fred rain mac, and most of all, the people close to her.

It also made her think of the fickle world of Ritsy Rose Interiors. She had not heard from anyone since, her ex-boss's brief phone call on New Year's Day. Yes, she could have called these people herself, but it made her realise that nobody there was actually worth keeping in touch with. She had classed them as friends at the time, but they had obviously been no more than mere acquaintances.

Ruby and Fi, as all good event organisers should, stayed in the background keeping a beady eye on the proceedings. Ruby was just checking with the head waiter that there was enough buffet left for any late arrivals, when they saw Alexia stagger to one of the open French doors and wander out on to the patio. Her excuse for a dress was clinging to everything it could for dear life. She was a very pretty girl but at just twenty-three Ruby thought it sad that Alexia had felt the need for a boob and nose job already. She decided at that moment she was happy to grow old disgracefully.

'Bastard, he said he'd be here by ten,' Ruby overheard Alexia announce to a gorgeous male model who was having a cigarette outside.

'Don't worry, Lexy, his flight's probably delayed, that's all. You know that photographers don't want to miss a trick, especially when the likes of you are throwing a party.'

Then all of a sudden, Alexia let out a loud shriek as she saw said missing person enter the room, camera slung over his shoulder. 'Darling, you made it.' She teetered back inside and rushed over to kiss the handsome arrival.

'To be sure I did. Do you really tink I'd have missed this for the world? I'll have you on the front pages before you can say Pol Rogair.'

Ruby felt her mouth go dry, then thought she was going

to be sick. Because there, kissing the party girl full on the lips, was none other than Mr Ciaran O'Shea.

Before Ruby had a chance to hide behind one of the huge drapes in the room, Ciaran spotted her. He put Alexia down and came straight up to her.

'Heh, babe. Didn't know this was your line of work,'
'I'm nobody's babe, and you didn't bother to ask,' Ruby replied curtly.

'I'm in the UK all week – fancy dinner and sometink sweet to follow one night, maybe?' The Irish one carried on regardless, and Ruby's stomach turned as she remembered the words of her dear father. *There's no such thing as an ugly face, just an ugly person.* And here, standing right in front of her, was certainly one of those.

'I'd rather have dinner with your girlfriend's dog.' The rat of a creature began to yap wildly at Alexia's feet as Ruby sped off to the makeshift staff room.

'Fecking eejit,' Fi said, following Ruby. 'Just ignore him, he's not worth the time of day. In fact, if you want to head home, Glen's in the limo outside - he can run you back into Town and come back for me.'

'Don't be silly, Fi. And don't worry – I won't cause a scene. I know exactly what I'm going to do.'

Chapter Thirty-two

'I'm not sure about this one, Johnny.' Ruby fell back on her sofa, balancing her mobile phone against her ear as she hungrily flicked to the back pages of *Oh Yeah!* magazine.

'Come on, girl. It'll really help out an old friend of mine.'

Another friend? Ruby thought, loving Johnny more than ever.

'For some reason he's having a busier time than usual,' the little man continued.

'And it's just two weeks, you say?' Ruby enquired.

Her eyes widened as she opened the exact page she was looking for.

'Yep. Come on, Rubes. I'll pay your travel on this one too. And you did say you wanted diversity.'

'Hmm, and *d-i-e* versity is definitely what I'm going to get!' Ruby spelt out.

Johnny laughed at his smart little protégée. 'So you'll start Monday? Please say yes.'

'How can I possibly say no to you, Johnny Jessop, when you've helped me so much to change my life for the better?'

Ruby hung up, and turning back to her magazine, hugged her knees in delight. Because there, in full glory on the Celebrity Parties page, was a very ugly photo of Alexia Ramada at her recent birthday party at Cliveden.

Legs akimbo, minuscule pants showing, and looking decidedly worse for wear, Ruby knew that the delectable diva would not be happy with the accredited photographer – one Mr Ciaran O'Shea.

Ruby reached for the digital camera that was sitting on her coffee table and flicked through the photos of Cliveden she had taken for her mother. When she got to the unflattering one of Alexia Ramada, she deleted it promptly and laughed.

Hopefully now the impressionable young girl would see sense and dump him.

Chapter Thirty-three

May, Job Five: Funeral Directors

Lovegrove & Daughter, located on the corner of a street in Bethnal Green, consisted of a pristine front office with two antique green-leather topped desks and a comfortable seating area with a glass coffee table. Brochures outlining all shapes and sizes of coffins and headstones were neatly stacked on a mahogany sideboard. A signpost pointed to a door marked 'Chapel of Rest'.

Mrs Lovegrove was as broad as she was round, with a huge, motherly bust and an even huger backside. She greeted Ruby wearing a black A-line skirt and white V-neck T-shirt, which accentuated her humongous curves. Her hair was pure white and styled in an old-fashioned shampoo and set. She held a crushed tissue in her hand and her eyes were red from crying. When she spoke, Ruby realised she was a true East Ender.

'Oh, Ruby, anuvver one's gone. It's so bleedin' sad. He was only in his fifties.' She let out a strangled sob. Ruby was surprised at her reaction. Surely if you worked in a funeral director's you should expect to deal with death every day? It then suddenly hit her that for the next two weeks this is exactly what she would have to do, and she shivered at the thought.

She had said to Johnny that she wanted diversity – and she was certainly getting that in every assignment she faced. She knew now why Johnny had offered to pay her travel on this one. It had taken her an age to get over to the East End this morning, but she knew she was lucky to have a job at all, and she only had to do the journey for nine more days now.

At least it was a wonderfully warm May day. A job never seemed so bad when the sun was shining, and it was still daylight when you left home and got back.

Mrs Lovegrove showed Ruby to one of the empty desks and explained that her daughter, Lillian, who usually sat there, had taken a last-minute holiday, hence Ruby's employ. She went on to tell Ruby that the spring months had been an unusually busy time for dying. 'Terribly sad, Ruby. Three suicides in a row, two of them young City bankers. This government needs to shake up and get us out of this recession mess, I say.

"More deadies, more readies," Frank says,' Mrs Lovegrove continued. 'I can't be so cold about it meself. Mind you, a bus veered onto the pavement up the road one year – took six lives, it did. We went to the Dominican Republic rather than Colwyn Bay that summer.'

Ruby then realised that this was just like any other business; instead of making money from cups of tea or arranging events, their commodity was death. Somehow when you looked at it in such a matter–of-fact way, it didn't seem such a sombre subject.

'I'm not usually 'ere you see,' Mrs Lovegrove went on. 'Frank – that's Mr Lovegrove, me 'usband – he runs the show with Lillian. I keep 'ouse and do the book-keeping. That's why I get so upset. Not used to it like they are.' She let out another blubbery sob. 'Just dropped down dead of an 'eart attack late last night 'e did. Poor old Alfie. He was a good'un. Worked 'ard all 'is life. Lived just round the corner from us, 'e did.'

Ruby unzipped her handbag and offered a clean tissue to Mrs Lovegrove. Good practice, she thought, cringing at the thought of having to comfort people who'd actually lost loved ones. She would do her very best with this job, but at that moment she wasn't feeling either love or distaste. The best word to describe the emotion was probably 'panic'.

Ruby was brought back to reality by the front door being pushed open by an extremely tall, thin man with bright white hair. He wore a long jacket with tails, a crisp white shirt, and grey trousers. He was slow-paced and lumbering, and reminded her very much of Lurch from *The Addams Family*. He slowly held his hand out to Ruby.

'Lovegrove. Pleased to meet you.'

Ruby was surprised to hear a Welsh accent as his wife was such a broad Cockney. She also thought it quite amusing that this cold-looking character should be married to someone as warm and emotional as Janet Lovegrove.

Mr Lovegrove walked over to Ruby's desk and without wasting any more time on pleasantries, barked his orders. 'We've just got the one in today. His family are coming in at ten tomorrow to discuss the funeral arrangements. Don't think they've got a lot of money so we'll need to be sympathetic but creative.' Ruby nodded terrified at the prospect of her first dealings with the recently bereaved. 'I'm going to tidy him up this afternoon so he's ready for goodbyes tomorrow.'

Tidy him up? Eek, Ruby thought. What did that mean?

Beep. A text arrived loudly to her mobile. She frantically went to put it on to silent. 'I am so sorry, Mr Lovegrove.'

He smiled a wry smile. 'No problem – but make sure it's switched off if you're ever at the graveside.'

Ruby felt slightly sick. She had had no idea that she might actually have to attend any funerals. Sneakily, she glanced down into her bag to read the text.

'Fancy touching a real stiff later you lovely young thing?'

Fortunately, she managed to stop herself from laughing out loud. Pleased that Bentley had contacted her, she replied swiftly, using just one hand under the desk so the

Lovegroves didn't notice.

'It'll have to be a quickie as I really must get some beauty sleep tonight ☺'

'Nonsense, Scarlett. I'll send a car for you at 8.'

Chapter Thirty-four

Ruby was just applying a smudge of red lipstick when there was a loud toot outside her flat. She peered up out of the window to see a beautiful navy blue Bentley, engine running, waiting for her. Sly old devil, Ruby thought. So Bentley owned a Bentley, did he? She remembered back to their conversation in the restaurant when he'd said that his father had left him a lot of debts. Dinsworth House residents must be paying him better than he made out!

'Jesus is alive and living in Scotland,' Bert hollered as she locked the door behind her.

'Are you sure, Bert? I'm certain I saw Him in Gills' earlier,' Ruby called back, grinning at Bert's confused expression.

She was just about to open the passenger door of her impressive carriage when a smartly-suited elderly man eased himself out of the driver's door, tipped his chauffeur's cap, and shuffled around to let her in the back of the car. It was Cyril from Dinsworth House! Bentley was using cheap labour! Ruby hoped that the old boy could keep his arthritic legs – and more importantly, his bowels – under control for the journey!

Ruby pulled her seat belt tightly around her, looked out of the window, and saw George walking slowly down his steps. Unusually, Montgomery was not yapping at his heels. Ruby thought he looked very tired, and he didn't even raise a smile as the car drove past him. The last thing she wanted to do was upset her Gorgeous George. She really must talk to him properly, she thought, just as Cyril put his foot down and careered towards the main road at full speed. Clicking her seatbelt on hurriedly she questioned her chauffeur, 'Are we in a hurry, Cyril?'

'Yes, Miss Ruby. Bentley told me not to spare the horses.'

The journey home was just as frantic. Ruby lay back on the comfortable car seat with thoughts of Bentley wearing nothing but a black shirt and a white dog collar running through her mind. Tonight, he had been Reverend Green in the study with the candlestick!

She couldn't deny that the sex had been fantastic, but she had for the first time in a long time realised that what she wanted was more than just a quick romp between the sheets. She relished Bentley's company, but knew that he wasn't 'the one'. Back in her early twenties, when commitment hadn't been an issue, she was happy to do it anytime, anyplace; but now she couldn't help thinking, why couldn't they just do it in a bed like anyone else? George's handsome face appeared in her mind.

'I must be getting old with these chaste thoughts,' she said out loud.

'No, Miss Ruby,' Cyril piped up. 'When you get to my age you'll know you really *are* old.' And without even flinching he let out a resounding fart.

Due to the lingering stench, Ruby was hanging out of the window when the Bentley pulled up outside her flat. She fumbled for her keys and without looking where she was going, walked down the steps to her front door.

'Bert!' she shouted, almost falling flat on her face as she caught her foot on the body lying there.

'It's not Bert, it's me.' George pulled himself upright, his voice sounding a million miles away. 'Can I come in, Rubes? Something terrible's happened.'

George sat in silence on the sofa as Ruby made him a cup of strong, sweet tea. She joined him and put her arm around him.

'Has something happened to Montgomery?' she asked softly.

'No, it's my old man.' His voice cracked. 'He's only gone and carked it.'

'Oh, you poor, poor love,' she said, feeling tears welling in her own eyes.

'And here I was, thinking you would be my tower of strength.' George managed to raise a small smile. He handed her a tissue and she blew her nose loudly.

'I'm so, so sorry, George. Losing my dad so young too, I just know where you are at the moment and it's not a good place.' She took a deep shuddering breath and carried on softly, 'Do you want to talk about it?'

George nodded and started to tell his sorry tale. 'It hasn't quite sunk in yet, you know, Rubes.' It was her turn to nod. 'It's so bleeding tragic. Yesterday, me old dear went to the hospital as she had been having chemotherapy for breast cancer. It has been a really tough six months for both of them. Well, anyway, she was told she had the all clear.' Ruby bit her lip as George continued, 'They called me on the mobile, laughing and cheering like teenagers. They were so happy.' He paused. 'Me old man is – I mean *was* – ' his voice wobbled, 'he *was* a postie, never had a sick day in his life, but today he thought sod it, he'd take me old dear to their local to celebrate ...' George ran his hand through his hair and his bottom lip wobbled.

'Go on,' Ruby urged gently.

'He was just ordering the drinks when he just dropped down dead. My mum said the barman knew a bit of first aid and tried his best to revive him, but by the time the ambulance arrived, he'd gone. Heart attack. Just like that.' George started to howl like an animal. 'He's gone, Rubes. He's gone.'

Ruby held him to her chest tightly, and could feel the pain of each wracking sob go right through her. There was no word to describe the death of a parent. The feeling of loss was immense and the fact that you could do nothing to change it made you feel desperate. When Ruby's dad had died she felt that there was a hole in her middle that nothing or no-one would be able to fill ever again.

Two years on, the hole was still as big. Grief was an insurmountable emotion. Would George ever get over it? No, he wouldn't. Would time heal him? No, it wouldn't. Yes, the raw emotion would ease – but there would still be major times, like birthdays and at Christmas, where he would still feel his heart burning. And other poignant times too – when Reading got to the premiership, as Ruby knew her dad would have been over the moon. The bottom line was: when someone you love dies, you never get over it; you simply learn how to manage it.

Well, at least now she could be a true friend and help George through this terrible time the best that she could.

When George finally stopped crying, he took a noisy slurp of his now cold tea and stood up.

'I'll have to go, Rubes. I left me old dear sleeping at home in Stepney Green. The doc gave her some sleeping pills, but I don't want her to wake up and me not be there. I'm gonna pick up Monty and stay with her tonight.' He faltered. 'I just had to see you, Rubes.'

She welled up again. He kissed her on the forehead and with a heavy heart, walked out of the flat and to his van.

When she finally got to bed, Ruby lay motionless, feeling very sad indeed. Gorgeous George really was a beautiful person and she couldn't bear that he was hurting so much.

Chapter Thirty-five

Janet Lovegrove was sobbing when Ruby arrived at the funeral directors. Wet tissues were scattered all over her desk.

'Alfie's poor son. Bumped into him last night, he's devastated.' She sniffed – and that was when the penny dropped. East End of London, man in his fifties with a son. It had to be! 'Is Alfie's surname Stevens, by any chance? Did he live in Stepney Green?' Ruby asked in panic.

'Yes, love – why? Did you know him?'

Ruby bit her bottom lip. 'No, but I know his son very well.'

Rita Stevens was a soft and mumsy woman. Ruby could tell immediately where George got his kindness from. Rita was the same height as her son. Her hair was shoulder-length, dark brown, and wavy. Beneath the bloodshot symptoms of crying, her eyes were blue and welcoming, and the laughter lines of years gone by were feathered sweetly around them. She was wearing just a smidge of crimson lipstick and was dressed very plainly in a knee-length black skirt and dark grey, short-sleeved jumper. In case it came as a shock, Ruby had texted George to let him know that she was working at Lovegrove's.

He held his mum's arm protectively as they entered the funeral directors. Mr Lovegrove had rung ahead to say he was going to be late.

'I'm so glad you're here, Rubes,' George said tenderly.

'Pleased to meet ya,' Rita said politely and continued, 'Is my Alfie in there?' She pointed to the door that led through to the Chapel of Rest.

'Yes, he is,' Ruby replied softly. 'Mr Lovegrove will be back soon and he said he will show you through.' George grasped his mum's hand.

Ruby got them both a cup of tea and brought out the biscuits Mr Lovegrove usually saved for his richer clientele. She talked through the funeral options with them and asked whether they would like Lovegrove & Daughter to provide the flowers. She couldn't believe that she was having to do this for one of her friends, but at least she would make sure they would get the best deal, and tight- arsed Mr Lovegrove wouldn't rip them off.

Rita Stevens sat and listened intently to every word that Ruby said. She interrupted Ruby for prices, as she meticulously outlined types of coffin, types of car, whether they wanted the cortege to leave from their house or from the Chapel of Rest, and, of course, whether they wanted a burial or a cremation. It was such an awful time to make all of these decisions that Ruby wondered how on earth anyone actually got an end result. There and then she decided that when her time came, she would be stuffed and put in a glass case. Patrick would already have been stuffed, and if his rigor mortis wasn't too bad, he could be wrapped around her just like Versace, Alexia Ramada's pooch.

Once Ruby had finished going through every alternative, she looked up at both Rita and George questioningly.

Rita lifted her head high and spoke clearly. 'I appreciate you going through all this, Ruby, but do you know what? I wanna to do it in the true East End way. If it's good enough for the Tanners on Market Street then it's good enough for my Alfie.' She raised her voice. 'How much for a couple of horses with black plumes and a glass carriage?'

Ruby hadn't even mentioned this option as Frank

Lovegrove had already hinted that the widow didn't have a lot of money. She relayed the price and Rita swore. 'What are they – bleedin' pedigree racehorses?' She turned to George. He put his hand on her arm. 'It's a lot of money, Ma.'

'Yeah, you're right, son and I'm gonna need all I've got now your dad won't be bringing home the bacon.' Her eyes filled with tears.

Just then, the door opened and Mr Lovegrove pushed his way in front of George and Rita and shook their hands. 'Lovegrove, Frank Lovegrove,' he introduced himself, and added smoothly, 'Now if you're ready, can you just sign here?'

Chapter Thirty-six

Ruby had encouraged Mr Lovegrove to allow her to organise every detail of Alfie Stevens's funeral. She wanted everything to be just right, and for Rita and George to suffer the minimum of stress on the day. Ruby was to be waiting at the Stevens's residence when the cortège arrived.

Rita took deep breaths as they waited outside. George held her arm tightly. A throng of residents from the close-knit community were gathered at their respective front doors to pay their respects. Other Stevens family members filed out of the house. Ten o'clock on the dot, and Ruby breathed a sigh of relief as she heard the approaching clip-clop of hooves on the tarmac. The magnificent black horses, adorned with black plumes, were groomed to perfection, their coats glistening in the May sunshine. The carriage was shiny black and glass. Rita looked at her in disbelief and started to cry.

'You little darlin',' she cried. 'I can't believe you've done this for us.'

'Let's just say it's the perks of the job,' Ruby replied stoically as George grabbed her and kissed her lightly on the lips.

Feeling very sad, but also very chuffed that she'd successfully managed to pull this off, she suddenly stopped short and put her hand to her head. For there, in white carnations, sitting a foot high against the coffin was the word DUD instead of DAD!

Ruby stood with James at the back of the church. They

wanted to show support for George, and even though they hadn't met him, pay their respects to his dad. She had thankfully managed to get the carriage driver to unload the 'DUD' outside so she had time to get the local florist to replace the 'U' with an 'A' before the service started. She was sure George was so grief-stricken that he hadn't noticed. He never need know about this, or indeed the fact that she had paid the additions to his dad's funeral. She knew his pride would be too great to accept this gift.

The ceremony ended and the mourners trailed around to the graveside. Ruby had to head back to work as Mr Lovegrove had texted her to say he was just off to collect 'another one' and his wife had to go to the dentist.

As she wandered back to the undertakers, she thought again about her own mortality. Life was certainly precious – and she was more determined than ever that she would not waste one single moment working at a job she didn't enjoy.

Chapter Thirty-seven

Pinch-faced Pru managed a strangled hello as Ruby passed her in the street.

Margaret banged on her front window to get her attention and then hobbled to open her front door.

'Got a minute, Ruby?'

Ruby walked into the familiar front room, and noticed it seemed emptier, but she couldn't quite put her finger on why.

'How did it go, duck?'

'To plan, thank goodness, but obviously it was awful. Poor George.' Ruby took a deep breath.

'How's the little darling bearing up? I did put a card through his door, explaining I couldn't make the funeral. Thought it would be too much, what with my feet and everything.'

'He'll understand. Don't you worry, Margaret,' Ruby soothed and continued. 'He was really strong for his mum, but I imagine he's in a mess now. He's going to stay the night with her in Stepney Green.'

Margaret went to a sideboard drawer. 'Here.' She handed Ruby an envelope.

Slightly bemused, Ruby opened it. Inside was £150 in used ten pound notes.

'Towards the funeral,' the old lady stated. 'I won't take no for an answer.'

'Margaret! You haven't got the money to do this,' Ruby tutted.

The old lady closed her hand over Ruby's. 'And nor have you.'

Ruby sighed as Margaret smiled. 'I was getting bored of cleaning all that bloody brass anyway.' A Polo shot in and out of her mouth. 'You and young George are like family to me.'

Tears pricked Ruby's eyes. For the first time in years she had actually thought long and hard before using her credit card for the extra funeral costs, and this money would go a long way to clear the balance.

'Now go on, go home and get some rest,' Margaret continued. 'You look shattered, duck.'

Ruby said nothing and kissed Margaret goodbye.

Chapter Thirty-eight

June, Job Six: Ascot Racecourse Private Box Hostess

Ruby yawned as she made her way off the packed train and stepped onto the platform at Ascot station. Where did Johnny say she must go? Down the steps, left into a short tunnel, then straight up the hill. She had always wanted to go to Ascot but had never quite made it. She had seen the fashions on the television before and knew that it was one of the sporting season's great events, along with Wimbledon and Henley. As she walked, she read the notes Johnny had provided her with.

Royal Ascot is one of the world's most famous race meetings, steeped in history dating back to 1711. The Royal Family attend the meeting, arriving each day in a horse drawn carriage. It is a major event in the British social calendar.

Ooh, Royal Family, she thought. Maybe she would bump into Prince Harry. How marvellous!

It was only a five-day assignment as a private box hostess, but Johnny reckoned that if she gave the job her all, she would get more in tips in a day than she would normally earn in a whole week. Ruby set this as her personal mission and had even blow-dried her hair straight before she'd left the house this morning.

She checked into the staff area and was given a uniform of fetching black suit and crisp white shirt with a pale grey cravat. 'Tips, tips, tips,' she said out loud to herself as she checked herself in the mirror. The new grandstand had not been there long and Ruby was in awe of its imposing, modern design. She was ushered towards the lifts by a box supervisor and was then shown the room which would be her home for the next five days.

Ruby was shocked at how basic the box was for the money people paid. This particular one was nearly £40,000 a day! The space itself was no bigger than her living room and kitchen at home. She guessed it could comfortably house around twenty people. A white-clothed table was pushed against the far wall and chairs were placed around the edge. Glass windows made up the far wall that looked out over the racecourse, and a small balcony allowed a complete view of the whole track. A tiny kitchenette was hidden at the back of the box, where two waiting staff were to tend to the racegoers' every whim. Ruby was to ensure that the box operation ran smoothly and to deal with any special requests. She had been informed that the guests were to be treated as if they were royalty.

Today, her box was being rented by Baratronix, a Dudley-based supplier of electronic equipment for the automobile industry. Ruby had been told that there were much bigger boxes, belonging to the likes of Arab owners and trainers. She would probably have to work much harder for her tips here. Her guests were not due to arrive for another half an hour, so Ruby took the opportunity to take in the sights and sounds of the extravaganza that was Royal Ascot.

Peering over the balcony, she could see hats, hats, and more hats. All shapes, colours and sizes, adorned with feathers, twigs, pom poms, veils, and even a huge white rabbit on top of one of them. She could even see top-hatted gentlemen escorting elegant ladies to the Royal Enclosure for their first sip of Dom Perignon. Further along the stand, she noticed groups of men and woman who had obviously hit the lager on the coaches, arriving from other parts of the UK. It was clear that their intention was not to watch the racing but to get as drunk as they could on pints of lager or Pimms.

She had just repositioned herself at the door of her respective box when the guests started to arrive in a flurry. Vince Baratt, the founder of Baratronix, was the first to arrive, with his wife Greta. He was the chalk, a small bald man with tiny round glasses, to Greta's cheese – a tall, gangly woman with straggly blonde hair, brown roots poking through. Their twin daughters, Fenella and Phoebe, were in their early twenties, and wore matching black and white suits and large, black top hats with a white feather sticking out of each. Ruby couldn't imagine how they had managed to walk in their five-inch white stilettos.

Next were four guys from the Baratronix sales team. They had obviously hired their morning suits as two of them had trousers touching the floor and sleeves rolled up nearly up to their elbows. They were already being quite loud and were first to make for the free-flowing champagne. After that was Mr Brown, the accountant, a dull-looking little man with a comb-over, accompanied by a matching dull wife who was dressed in a brown dress, brown shoes, and a brown pillbox hat. Ruby noticed she had a very red nose and wasn't surprised when the woman immediately asked for a very large gin and tonic.

Looking around, she grimaced at the thought of what state most of them would be in by the time the last race came and went. She was also quite perturbed that she couldn't have a single drink until then. Maybe viewing drunken debauchery on such a large scale would make her appreciate sobriety.

'A toast!' Vince Baratt announced in his broad Birmingham accent once they all had hold of a drink. 'A thank you for all of your recent hard work. To Baratronix!'

'To Baratronix.' The group all raised their glasses and started to quaff.

And they're off! Ruby thought.

'Now I wonder where Dom and that wife of his have got to. It's not as if they had as far to travel as the rest of us, is it?' Vince grumbled.

Ruby flitted around, making sure that everyone's glass was topped up and that the food arrived on time. She'd had a chance to study the race card, and after her one lesson from the supervisor, knowledgeably taught the twins how to use it. Josh and Harry, the waiting staff, were actually rather cute. They were working here to earn some money before they went to university in the autumn, so they weren't really taking their job too seriously. Despite their being only eighteen and obviously having serious eyes for the twins, Ruby flirted with them openly – just to make sure that they didn't welch on their duties too much, of course!

She went out on to the balcony to watch the first race and soaked up the real atmosphere of Ascot. Secret Lies won at 10/1. One of the salesmen went so red in the face cheering it home that Ruby thought he was going to internally combust. She congratulated him heartily and headed to the little kitchen to ask for more champagne. While she was in there, Vince's dulcet Dudley drone rang out across the chattering throng.

'Dom, you old bastard, glad you could make it.' She heard him pat the missing guest on the back. 'And Elena, you're looking as beautiful as usual.'

She heard the smack of a kiss. Lucky Elena! It was when Dom opened his mouth that it was *her* turn to internally combust.

'Dear boy, as if I'd miss an afternoon of free champers. I was waiting for Elena at the airport. Now where's that blessed hostess they usually supply?'

Ruby had two options: one – to stay cowering in a small dark space for the rest of the day and not allow anyone to have anything else to eat or drink all afternoon, or two – to face the music and dance. Although the former option was preferable – since Piaf's she could now do a mean rendition of "Non, Je ne regrette rien" – instead she pushed thekitchenette door open with her foot and went forth assertively, carrying a tray full of freshly filled champagne glasses.

'More champagne, anyone?' she announced, boldly going straight over to a now goldfish-mouthed Bentley. 'Sounds as if this is not your first visit to my box, sir.' She stared right into his eyes. 'What a shame you missed the first race. Being a gambling man, I'm guessing Secret Lies would be a favourite of yours.' She turned around and trod hard on his foot on purpose. 'So is this your first visit to Ascot?' she politely asked Bentley's wife.

'Yes, it eez.'

Ruby had expected her to be English and middle-aged. She was neither. Elena Bentley was, in fact, a stunning Russian in her early twenties. She was the same height as Ruby and had naturally blonde hair that flipped up at the ends. She was smartly dressed in a cream trouser suit, wearing a wide-brimmed hat covered in navy roses. Stylish blue patent leather shoes with a sensible heel were her footwear of choice.

The bloody old bastard. His poor wife. No wonder he didn't want to do it in the marital bed!

Ruby Ann Matthews was far too big a person to be anyone's bit on the side! Like father, like son, eh? Just you wait, Domenic Bentley. Just you wait!

Chapter Thirty-nine

'Come on, Frankie!'

The now even redder-faced salesman was on a complete winning streak and was screaming Frankie Dettori and his mount, Clever Dick, home. The horse came in at 20/1 and the salesman ran around the small Ascot box, throwing off first his hat and then stripping off his waistcoat and shirt. Mrs Brown, the accountant's wife, now fully inebriated, lurched forward accidentally on purpose, steadying herself with both hands on his hairy chest.

'A thousand quid!' the salesman shouted. 'Would you believe it!'

Ruby didn't want to be a killjoy, but asked him nicely if he would put his shirt on as it was the rules of the racecourse. Bentley was watching her every move.

'Clever dick. More like lucky dick,' she spat as she walked past him with an empty tray of glasses. She needed a break. Surrounded by all these testosterone-rich, drunk male bodies, she was beginning to feel claustrophobic

'Would anyone like me to put a bet on with a bookmaker rather than on The Tote?' she asked, thinking that this was a great ruse to get some breathing space. The 'live' bookmakers were based on the ground level at the front of the grandstand, so it was quite a journey down from the fourth-floor box to put a bet on there. The advantage for somebody having a bet with one of these 'live' bookmakers was that the odds were sometimes better than on The Tote, a British bookmaker with over 500 betting shops, and outlets on Britain's fifty-six racecourses.

The lucky salesman gave her £50 to put on the next favourite and Mr Brown gave her £5 to put on General Ledger.

'Just going down to the paddock, darling,' Bentley informed his wife, pinching her bottom as he passed her. He dashed to Ruby's side. 'I'll come with you.' They headed to the escalator together.

'I don't really have anything to say to you, Bentley.' Ruby uttered abruptly.

'Oh, come on, Ruby, you and I both knew that it was just a bit of fun.'

'But your beautiful wife – you don't deserve her.'

Bentley knew he was on a losing streak with the feisty redhead and shut up. When they reached ground level, he handed Ruby two fifty-pound notes.

'On the favourite too, please, Scarlett. I'm going to check out the fillies in the paddock.'

Ruby turned around and bumped right into a lady shaking a charity bucket. She made her apologies and then headed towards the numerous rows of bookmakers. She couldn't help but smile at the situation. Domenic Bentley was a philanderer and would never change his spots. But he was a charming philanderer at that – and although she would never admit it to him, she didn't regret a single minute of the time they'd spent together. He did, however, still needed to be taught a lesson.

Ruby put the bets on as requested and the favourite Red Devil came storming home. With a name like that, Ruby kicked herself that she hadn't put some money on it herself. She picked up the winnings for both the red-faced salesman and Bentley. By being party to the real state of Bentley's finances she knew exactly what would hurt him.

As she saw him walking towards her, she smiled and waved his bounty in the air. The lady with the charity bucket was also walking her way. She held out the money towards Bentley and when he was within a metre of her she dropped it swiftly into the Help the Aged container.

'Thank you *so* much, dear. If only there were more young people like you who appreciated our elderly folk,' the charity lady gushed.

Bentley couldn't believe what he had just seen – but even *he* didn't have the gall to retrieve his money.

'That was for scorned wives everywhere,' Ruby triumphed. 'I'm not a knowingly unfaithful person and never will be. If more women had my mentality then it would save an awful lot of heartbreak in this world,' she carried on boldly and flitted back up the escalator.

'Nice one, love,' the red-faced salesman slurred to her as she handed him his winnings. 'Here, take this – you've done us all proud today.' It was Ruby's turn to flush, as there in her hot little hand was £500 in fifty-pound notes.

Chapter Forty

It was a particularly warm July day, and Johnny was sat on his special Piaf's cushion, fanning himself with a menu. It had been two weeks since her Ascot Week job, and Ruby found it hard to believe that she was about to embark on job number seven.

'Johnny, that's outrageous. I can't do it!' Ruby suddenly exclaimed.

'No such word as can't,' Daphne du Mont piped up as she brought coffee and cream horns to their window table.

'It will be hilarious, Ruby. Being honest with you, the company wanted the real thing but because of budget cuts I couldn't find someone for the money they were offering.'

'Johnny!' Ruby shrieked. 'Is this not fraudulent, then?'

'As if I'd do that to you. Really!' He laughed and bit into his cake, covering the tip of his nose with cream. 'The punters won't be paying you directly, so no, it's fine. It's just part of the overall event. Just a bit of fun, really.'

'Hmm. I can't see it being my career of choice out of the dozen.'

'See? You're looking into the future already.' They both laughed out loud.

Chapter Forty-one

July, Job Seven: Fortune-teller

'I see a man. He has an "A" in his name and is wearing a suit. He is going to mean a lot to you in the next five years.' Ruby waved her hands over her crystal ball and tucked a stray hair back under the silk paisley turban she was wearing to match her flowing purple caftan. It was eighty degrees outside and she was boiling hot with all this garb on.

'That must be Danny,' the pretty young girl from Accounts blurted out.

Madame Saskia was wearing dark glasses, as she felt her eyes might give away her inability to lie convincingly. She had taken it on herself to do a bit of research and now felt that she was an expert in 'cold reading'. She had read that cold readers often start by making broad guesses and will refine their statements based on clues supplied by the subject, abandoning any incorrect guesses while reinforcing any chance connections the subject acknowledges. She had searched on Wikipedia and been comforted by the fact that *"the mentalist branch of the magic community approves of reading as long as it is presented strictly as an artistic entertainment and one is not pretending to be psychic".* Ruby had decided that all her predictions would be happy ones, and would be so vague that she could never be outed as a complete charlatan – thus Sparkle Events would retain their crystal clear reputation. The young girl was hanging onto every word that Ruby was saying.

'I can also see you going on holiday. Do you like the sea?'

'Oh, yeah, I love to be by the sea.' The girl offered more.

'Oh yes. Oh yes.' Ruby moaned and waved her hand over the ball again.

'Tell me, tell me.' By now, the lass was verging on hysteria.

'I can see you somewhere hot. I can hear the sea crashing on the rocks.'

'Will I be going with the man with the letter "A", do you think?'

Ruby looked up to the ceiling and started moaning again. 'I cannot be certain, but it is highly likely.'

'Ooh, you should hear this, Angela!' the young girl shouted to her work colleague. 'I'm going to the Maldives with Danny from Marketing soon. I just knew he fancied me!'

Ruby had been in situ for the past hour. She was actually really enjoying her new role as fortune-teller. Johnny had convinced her that this was a good chance to try something completely different. Fi had come to him directly, completely desperate for him to help her out. Madame Rosanna, the bona fide fortune-teller, had blown out last minute due to the death of her pet rat and Fi needed a replacement – for the fortune-teller not the rat, that is – and fast.

Fi hadn't bothered to ask Ruby if she was interested, as one: it was just a week's work, and two: she didn't think for one minute that her straight-talking friend would agree to it. Ruby had told Johnny that he mustn't tell Fi that it was she who had agreed to do it, as Ruby was looking forward to having a bit of fun with her.

The event for Astec Software was taking place in an old hotel/conference centre on the outskirts of Oxford. It was to be a five-day staff conference – half work related, half play to kick off their new financial year, which happened to be in July.

Madame Ruby was available for lunchtime and evening readings and for the next five days was to share a large oak-panelled room with a close-hand magician, a Tarot card reader, a crystal healer, a masseur, and a two life coaches. They were all to be 'the entertainment' for the week.

Ruby knew she would have to catch Fi early as it wasn't likely that she could keep out of her way for the whole week. She was just preparing her thoughts for her next set of lies when the Irish lady in question came rushing past, mad hair flailing everywhere, walkie-talkie in hand.

Ruby made sure that none of her red locks had sneaked out from under the turban and grasped Fi as she bolted by.

'Stop!' she shouted and then continued at a lower decibel, 'Take the weight off your feet for a minute, young lady.' Ruby had assumed the voice of an old woman.

'I'm so fecking busy I don't know if I can,' her friend gabbled. Ruby stood up, put both hands in the air, then slammed them down on the table and shouted, '*Sit!*'

Fi nearly jumped out of her skin, but for once did as she was told. She hadn't had a chance to talk to Johnny about the new fortune-teller and just trusted that she would be fine. However, before she could even introduce herself, Ruby was off.

'That's your trouble, you're like a whirling dervish, my dear. You need to relax more.'

Fi nodded. She actually did love having her fortune told and sod it, she could take five minutes out. She turned the volume down on her walkie-talkie.

'You're a true Irish girl at heart,' Ruby continued. 'You love your family. I can see a brother – Darren or maybe Darryl?'

Fi was wise to cold reading and now kept quiet. She

was actually quite impressed that this slightly mad woman had got so close to Darragh's name.

'Your mother – Patricia – I see her too,' Ruby said dreamily. 'What lovely hair she has. Not the same as yours though, is it? *That* comes from the man she slept with in Papua New Guinea. Your father, I presume.'

Fi began to feel slightly sick. It had always been a longstanding joke about her afro hair in the family, but there was no way that her Da wasn't her Da ... or was there?

Ruby began to moan and wave her hands madly over the crystal ball.

'A woman. I see a woman with beautiful red hair. She says you must buy her a huge birthday present,' Ruby crooned. 'You are close to her. She's saying that she's looking at you. She is saying that she *can't believe you haven't bloody recognised her yet*.'

Fi pulled off Ruby's turban and hit her with it.

'I can't believe it! That was fecking hilarious!' Fi shrieked, then realizing she mustn't blow Ruby's cover, hushed her voice and handed her back the turban. 'Bloody brilliant, Rubes. I'd have asked you meself but I didn't think for one minute you'd do it.'

'Johnny convinced me,' Ruby explained.

'Well, I'm so glad you're here. Load of boring gobshites, if you ask me. Have you checked in yet?' Fi went back into event mode.

'No, not yet. Johnny gave you the name Saskia Tolsky to keep the surprise and I wanted you to change my details with reception first just in case there was an issue.'

'To be sure. Finish off your lunch shift and I'll sort it for ya. Right, I'd better run.'

Fi looked back at her friend. 'Looks like you've got another customer. Yum, don't mind if I do.' She winked. Approaching Ruby was a very good-looking bald man dressed in a smart grey suit.

'Just want to prove to myself what a load of old bullshit this is.' The handsome bald one plonked himself down in front of Ruby. 'My name's Adam, by the way. But I guess you already knew that.' He smirked and Ruby noticed how blue his eyes were. In fact, she noticed everything about him, from his cheeky crooked smile, to his broad shoulders, right down to the engaging bulge in his tailored trousers.

'Ah, yes.' She touched her crystal ball then closed her eyes. 'Adam the …' *Think, Ruby, think.* He was self-assured, confident, and dressed well. 'Salesman, yes. Adam the Salesman, I knew you would find me here.'

He smiled, then frowned, slightly worried that she had got one thing right already. Ruby breathed an inward sigh of relief.

'I see your wife, or is it your girlfriend?'

'See? I knew it was a load of bollocks,' the handsome bald one stated, giving Ruby just the answer she had wanted. Single, as well as sexy? She moaned again and waved her hands over the ball to give her time to think of another lie. Just as she did this, a woman who had been listening behind the bald one, mouthed to Ruby. 'Sister. Her name's Alison.'

Good girl, thought Ruby. She obviously knew what a 'non-believer' her colleague was. 'Ah – no, I'm mistaken. She looks like you … it's your sister, of course it is. Yes. I'm getting the letter "A".' The handsome bald one sat up and listened intently now. 'Yes, yes, yes. I'm getting the name Ali. Is that her?' He nodded slowly. 'She says you are to get off your arse and find yourself a half decent woman.'

He laughed. 'She would say that too. Anyway, that's enough. It's just a coincidence you got that right.' As he went to get up, the woman colleague put her thumb up to Ruby and quickly walked away, laughing to herself.

'Stop!' Ruby shouted, nearly sending the handsome

bald one flying off his chair. 'Now listen to me, Mr Salesman. You will find that half decent woman and she will be a redhead. Maybe sooner than you think, too.'

'A bloody ginger? I don't think so. See, I told you it was bollocks.' He pushed his chair back and gave her a sexy slanted smile. 'Thanks anyway.'

He paused, and looked at the sign above her. 'Madame Saskia.'

Chapter Forty-two

Astec Software's last-night party was well underway in the Oxfordshire hotel/conference centre. Fi was doing her usual flitting around and Ruby had run short of fortunes to tell. Her customers had either gotten wise to the fact that she was a complete charlatan, or anyone who had wanted a reading had already had one.

At ten o'clock Fi told Ruby to call it a day and go to her room to leave Madame Saskia there for good. She'd sneaked a bottle of bubbly into her event office, which would be a good little starter for them.

Ruby had a quick shower and washed her hair. She even managed to dry it perfectly straight. Then, she threw on her one and only little black dress. Plus a cute pair of kitten heels that she had treated herself to with some of her Ascot Week tips.

She'd been on a small spending frenzy of late. eBay had brought her a new coffee and telephone table. Just a set of wine glasses to go and 42a Amerhand Road could be classed as fully furnished again.

The Ascot employ had certainly been the most lucrative job that she'd had to date, and indeed a lot of fun. It was not, however, her favourite. She had to admit that so far she had felt the most love while working at Piaf's and the most distaste at Lovegrove & Daughter.

But it was only July, so she still had five more jobs to go before her mission was complete. She had never known a year to fly by so fast. For the first time in ages she had taken control of her life, which in turn was making her really happy and ooze the confidence she sometimes lacked.

Tripping gaily down the stairs, Ruby entered the bar area, which was alive with music and chatter. Fi beckoned her to the bar and asked what she wanted to drink. 'Glass of sparkling wine if that's OK, thanks.' As Fi was ordering, she heard a familiar voice next to her.

'Ooh, sparkling wine. Sounds like a PR chick's type of tipple to me,' the handsome bald one flirted.

'Nah. PR's not my bag,' Ruby replied confidently, feeling a little flutter of excitement.

'Oh – so what department are you in then? I haven't seen you at Astec before,' he said.

'Surely that was a chuck-up line instead of a chat-up line,' Ruby responded, smirking, and told him, 'Let's just say I'm in futures.' Then she turned her back on him, took the glass of bubbles from Fi, and the two girls swiftly made their way to the event office, where they could both refill their glasses with free booze without anyone noticing. They had a couple of champagnes in quick succession before Fi went on her rounds to check everyone was OK.

Ruby wandered back out to the bar area. She was desperate to bump into Adam again, but also wanted to try and retain her cool. After all, he had said he didn't like gingers anyway. Shallow bastard. She had a quick look around the bar but couldn't see him, so instead she found Fi and helped her clear the entertainment area instead.

It was midnight by the time everything was done. Fi slumped on a chair in the corner of the now almost empty room and flung her shoes off.

'I'm fecking knackered, Rubes. Gonna have to take to my bed in a minute.'

'I'm coming with you. All that lying has made me tired.' Fi laughed as Ruby went on. 'Shame I didn't see the gorgeous bald one again, but it's probably for the best. He seemed a right cocky bastard actually.'

'Yeah. He's probably shagging one of those young girls from Accounts as we speak,' Fi replied wisely.

They said their goodbyes on the landing and Ruby made her way along the winding corridors to her room. She was just putting her key card in the door, when she heard somebody walking behind her. A quiet wolf-whistle flew out into the ether. She swung round and there he was – Adam from Sales. Grey suit still on, white shirt undone, and tie halfway around his neck. He looked deliciously naughty.

'I thought PR girls stayed up all night?' he slurred.
Ruby noticed lipstick on his collar.

'And I thought salesmen were supposed to listen. I told you I was in futures and I know you don't like gingers.' And with that she slammed the bedroom door shut in his face, leaving his ego in tatters and her self-esteem jumping hoops.

The next morning, relieved it was Saturday, Ruby got up leisurely and packed her case. She was due to meet Fi in reception at eleven for the taxi ride back to London – courtesy of Sparkle Events, of course.

Just before leaving, she did her usual scan of the hotel bedroom and noticed a business card that must have been pushed under her door during the night. She picked it up and smiled.

On the front – *Adam Wilde, Sales Director, Astec Software*. On the back – *Guess you know this already, but we're going out for a drink soon. Call me x*

This playing hard to get lark was obviously the way forward!

Chapter Forty-three

Ruby shouted a 'hello' as she turned the key in the door at her mother's house, but there was no answer. That was strange – she was sure she'd said what time she was arriving. The football season was over so Sam should definitely be around at least.

She dumped her bag in the front room and made her way to the kitchen to get a drink. It was then that she heard her mother's infectious laugh filtering down the stairs, followed by what sounded like a herd of elephants chasing her around the bedroom. Oh God, she had caught her mother in some sort of sexual situation and it made her feel weird. She was glad that her mum was happy, of course, but as lovely as he was, Graham would never be able to replace her real dad.

After making herself a cold glass of orange squash, Ruby took it out to the garden. She'd already applied her Factor 50 sun cream and donned one of Sam's football caps to avoid the blazing sunshine. She set herself a limit of thirty minutes before making her arrival known.

It seemed strange to be alone outside her family home. The garden was just a small strip, with a patio one end and grass the other. Weekend barbecues had been a regular feature when her dad was alive. He would put on some sort of comical apron and equally ridiculous sun hat to protect his fair skin, and then admirably take control of the cooking. There was usually some sort of disaster involving burnt ribs or raw corn, but there was always lots of laughter. She realised, sitting out here alone, what it must have been like for her mum in the early days. Yes, Sam had lived at home, but the loss of such a huge character must have made her feel so lonely and desperate. For Sam, too, who already lived in a lonelier world than most, it must have been terrible. Tears pricked Ruby's eyes. Sometimes life just wasn't fair, and that's why she now intended to enjoy every second of it. She would fill it with love, not distaste!

With such fair skin, Ruby couldn't bear to sit out in the sun too long. She'd on numerous occasions either suffered a severe freckle epidemic or turned an unattractive shade of pink. Sometimes both, if she was very unlucky. Neither of these were an option this afternoon, as tonight she was going on a date with the luscious, bald, and handsome Mr Adam Wilde.

Laura and Graham eventually emerged outside, squinting like moles. 'Oh, Ruby, darling. We didn't hear you come in. I'm so sorry,' her mum said.

'It's OK, mother. I know when I'm not your number one priority any more,' Ruby joked, and Laura smacked her playfully on the arm. 'Where's Sam anyway?'

'He's gone to the park with Beth.'

'Beth?' Ruby hadn't heard that name before.

'Yes, a lovely girl he met at the college,' Graham added, sounding much older than his years. 'He's been seeing her for about three weeks now.'

'He kept that quiet, the little devil,' Ruby commented.

'I know, love.' Her mum grinned. 'Don't think he wanted anything or anyone to put a spoke in the works.'

'That's great news. Good on Sam. I guess Ben's with them both?' Ruby enquired.

'Oh yes, Ben still goes everywhere with him. That dog has been a saviour. As has his dog handler.' She looked up at Graham and it made Ruby well up to see her so happy.

'Anyway, what are you up to later? Do you think you'll be staying?' Laura asked.

'That's the plan. It is only a first date, after all.'

'Well, just be careful, love. And if you do decide to stay out just text me and let me know.'

'Yes, Mum,' Ruby dutifully replied, secretly pleased that her mum was showing an interest in her well-being.

Ruby had arranged to meet Adam in his hometown of Caversham. It was just a short taxi ride from her mother's house, so Ruby thought due to this coincidence, the whole chance meeting had to be fate!

Ruby tentatively pushed open the door to the Griffin and began to scour the bar for her date. It was nice to be in a pub that still retained an olde worlde atmosphere, rather than in a soulless trendy bar, which most drinking holes seemed to be turning into these days.

The humid summer afternoon had broken and a storm was brewing. Big drops of rain had forced people in from the garden area and the bar was absolutely heaving. She had decided on a smart casual approach and felt confident and sassy in her indigo straight leg jeans and green smock top, which accentuated both her auburn hair and emerald eyes. She kicked herself that she hadn't worn some sort of mac for later as the rain now began to pour. Just as she was thinking she'd been stood up, the gorgeous bald one was at her side.

'Sorry. Had to nip to the loo. A fruit-based drink for the lady, perhaps?' he jested and Ruby felt a small flip in her heart. He really was a good-looking man.

'So why the aversion to us gingers then?' Ruby openly asked once they had found a seat at the back of the pub.

'You know ... just the general stigma attached. White, clammy skin, freckles everywhere, red, straggly pubes. I could go on.'

'So why are you here then?' She took a sip of her wine.

'Your mate Fi told me that you bang like a barn door on a windy night.'

Ruby tried to pretend she was offended but couldn't keep it up and smiled widely. She actually wouldn't put it past Fi to say something like that though.

Two large wines later, they headed along the road to a Thai restaurant. It had stopped raining and the air smelt fresh and summery.

'I'd have asked if you liked Thai food before booking it normally, but I guessed you'd already know where we were going,' Adam said as they took their seats at a table near the window.

Ruby laughed. 'Please don't remind me. That was one hideous job.'

'And also slightly fraudulent, one could assume?' Adam queried.

'Fraudulent? May I remind you that I knew your sister was called Alison, and I also told you that you were going to meet a wonderful redhead?'

'Hmm. How did you know my sister's name was Alison?'

'Because I *am* Madame Saskia.'

'Give over. You're no more a fortune-teller than I am a premier league footballer.'

'Who do you support then? It has to be the Mighty Royals, living here.' She could tell Adam was impressed by her native terminology.

'Yeah, I do, actually.'

'So, Mr Ginger Hater Wilde, I bet you don't slate the gorgeous Dave Kitwell for his bright red locks, do you?'

'That's different. How come you know so much about Reading's football team anyway?'

'I was brought up here. Actually, my mum and brother live about two miles down the road.'

The banter continued until they were the last to leave restaurant.

'Coffee back at mine?' Adam suggested as they hit the balmy summer evening.

'Not tonight, Josephine I have a headache,' Ruby giggled. There was nothing she would like more than to shag the pants off this charming, good-looking man, but after Dublin she had learnt her lesson. 'Seriously, Adam, if you don't mind I'm going to head back to Mum's tonight, but I'd love to see you soon.'

She leant her head against the taxi seat and smiled. It felt good to be in control.

Chapter Forty-four

'Just going to mow your lawn,' George mouthed to Margaret through her front window. Every couple of weeks, throughout the summer, he had tidied up her garden for her.

'No!' Margaret shouted through the glass, putting her hand up to halt him. George didn't hear her and thinking she was just waving, began to whistle loudly as he wheeled his lawnmower through the side gate and towards the back garden.

The old girl hobbled to her back door as fast as her sore feet would allow, trying to apprehend him there.

George was just unwinding the flex to put through the kitchen window when he heard a very loud snoring noise. The bare-chested gardener looked up, pushed his non-existent fringe back, and let out a huge belly laugh. There, in the middle of the garden, as naked as the day he was born, was Bert lying face up like a star fish, on a sun lounger. His beard looked like it had been trimmed, and he had a can of cider balanced between his legs.

Margaret was breathless by the time she flew out of the back door, and threw a blanket over a still sparko Bert. A Polo was flying in and out of her mouth so fast, that George feared she may cut off her two remaining teeth.

'Oh, duck. It isn't how it looks,' the old girl gasped.

George was still laughing. 'Bang to rights, I say. You're a dark horse, Margaret, I'll give you that.'

Bert stirred, sat up slowly, and slurred, 'Jesus is alive and Maggie May is an angel.' He then promptly fell back, and his snoring immediately continued.

'I let him use the bath and washed his clothes, that's all. I did give him an old apron to put over his bits while he was waiting for them to dry. But I guess he liked the feel of the wind beneath his wings, so to speak.' Margaret suddenly laughed out loud at the scenario. 'What must you think of me.'

'Margaret, I think you're a kind and lovely person and I'm glad you're my neighbour, that's what.' George kissed her on the cheek. 'How about we go inside and get a drink, and when Sleeping Berty decides to wake up and put his "wings" away, then I'll do ya lawn.'

Margaret folded Bert's now dry clothes and put them at the end of the sun lounger.

She came inside, made George an orange squash, and joined him at the kitchen table. She placed her hand on his arm.

'How you doing anyway, darling? Holding up?' George tried not to talk about the death of his dad if he didn't have to, as it upset him too much. However, talking to Margaret was like holding a comforter blanket against his cheek, and he opened up easily.

'Oh, you know. Up and down. Upsets me more when me old dear loses it.'

'I know, duck, must be so hard for you.'

'Some people forget what's happened once the funeral's over and stuff, and of course, it's always at the forefront of my mind.'

'Yes. It will be, darling.' Margaret put her hand over George's. He took a long drink of squash.

'By the way, have you seen Ruby lately?' he asked.

'It's hard to keep up with her. She's been so busy,' Margaret replied, 'Last heard of, being a fortune teller for Job Seven, I think.'

George smiled. 'That girl makes me laugh with her antics.'

'Is that all she makes you do, George?'

'Margaret! Don't start all that again.'

The old lady smiled. 'I don't even know why I said that. She's busy dating anyway.'

'Dating? Anyone we know?'

'Somebody she met at this recent job of hers, I think. He sounds lovely. Lives near her mother.'

'Oh,' was all George could muster as Margaret quietly gauged his reaction.

'She deserves every happiness, that girl,' Margaret said quietly.

'Yes, she does.' George looked thoughtful for a minute then stood up. 'Right, let's see if our intrepid tramp is ready to go back to his wanderings.'

He peered out of the back door. The lounger was empty bar an empty can of cider and a heart made out of pink rose petals.

'The sly old devil. He's not half as stupid as he makes out.' George looked to Margaret, whose eyes were welling with tears.

'That's the most romantic thing anyone's ever done for me since my Stanley.' She suddenly grabbed George's arm. 'Don't lose her, George, will you?'

'Lose her, Margaret! That girl wouldn't know what love was if it smacked her in the face. And, anyway you just told me yourself that she's seeing someone else.'

Without waiting for an answer, he plugged in the lawnmower and started mowing. Since the untimely death of his father, he wasn't prepared to waste an ounce of his life, and he knew now exactly what he was going to do.

Chapter Forty-five

'Happy Birthday, mate.'

Fi ran into the busy bar in Putney and handed Ruby a present, wrapped perfectly in red sparkly paper and a huge red bow. 'I really can't believe you're thirty-nine today,' she said loudly as she studied her friend's face closely. 'Hmm, and I didn't realise crows had feet that big either.'

Ruby swung for her playfully. 'Fiona Donahue, I don't know why I love you so much. You know full well I'm only thirty-one.' Fi gave her a big hug and helped herself to a glass of wine from the cooler on the bar.

Ruby had indeed made an effort on her birthday. She was sporting her little black dress and had treated herself to a pair of killer stilettos.

Ruby undid her present with gusto. She had always ripped open presents ever since she had been a little girl, finding it far more satisfying than delicately opening the folds. Fi made her a personal toast. 'To you and all who sail in you. On that note – is Adam coming tonight?'

'Yes, he is. I'm really looking forward to seeing him, actually.' Ruby put her Crème de la Mer moisturiser in her bag and kissed Fi on the cheek. 'This, my friend, is an extreme luxury, and I love you so much for getting it for me.'

Ruby and Fi had got to the bar early to ensure that they reserved seats for the pending party. James was first to arrive with Sam, Ben, and Beth. Despite Beth being sighted, Ruby had asked the lovely Mr Kane if he minded showing them where to go as they hadn't been here before, and James happily obliged.

Within half an hour, the majority of her birthday posse had arrived. Adam and George were the only two yet to appear. George had already told her that he was going to be late.

Ruby felt really happy to be surrounded by her wonderful friends, Fi, Sam and Beth, Daphne and Norbert, Johnny, Tony from the clinic, and James. Even Justice had popped in for a drink on his way to meet his girlfriend.

She had already had a quick chat with Beth, a pretty, bobbed brunette who Ruby could tell thought the world of her brother. Ruby smelt her appealing scent and smiled to herself. She was certain that would have been the first thing that Sam had noticed about her.

Everyone sat around chatting amiably. Johnny got up and then reappeared with a champagne bucket which was nearly as big as he was. 'Just a couple of bottles of the fun stuff to get us on our way,' he announced, and everyone cheered. The bar was now heaving, making it necessary to shout over the music and hubbub of Saturday revellers. An hour later and Adam came rushing through the door with a bunch of roses. He made straight for Ruby and kissed her cheek. 'So sorry I'm late,' he puffed. 'Got on the wrong bloody train. Happy Birthday, Madame Saskia.'

Ruby did her best to introduce him to everyone and she shoved along so he could share the stool she was perched on.

When everyone was talking amongst themselves, she took his hand.

'Thanks for the roses,' she said. 'Red's my favourite.'

'Thought they would be.' He kissed her on the tip of her nose. 'Got another present for you, actually.' He reached into his rucksack and passed her the gift.

Ruby ripped the blue tissue paper off with gusto. 'Oh my God, that's amazing!' she screeched. 'Sam, Sam, I need to talk you through this!' she shouted at her brother.

'What is it?'

'It's a book about the Mighty Royals, showing and telling how they victoriously reached the premier league.'

'Nice one,' Sam said, already approving of his sister's new beau.

It got to ten o'clock and Ruby suddenly realised that George still hadn't arrived. She turned to James. 'Any idea where George might be?'

'He's just texted. He's on his way down the hill.' Just as James said this, in walked her gorgeous neighbour. Ruby initially beamed, but then the smile was wiped right off her face because there on his arm was a very pretty blonde. She had long, straight hair and shapely legs, which were hanging out of an excuse for a skirt. She looked extremely young, and must have been a towering five foot eleven to George's five foot six.

George immediately went over to Ruby, gave her a kiss on the cheek, and handed her a card. 'Happy Birthday, trouble.'

'Thanks,' was all she could muster. She felt almost tearful and went mute.

Adam stood up and shook George's hand. 'All right, mate. I'm Adam.'

'George.' George shook his hand and continued, 'Me and Rubes are neighbours. This is Candice,' he gestured to the blonde.

Candice! What sort of a bloody name was that, Ruby thought. The blonde looked up from under her eyelashes at Adam and simpered.

'All right?' she piped up. 'Nice place 'ere innit.' She was the epitome of Essex girliness, and Ruby, without even wanting to get to know her, hated her instantly. She looked over at Fi and raised her eyebrows. They hadn't been expecting a cuckoo in the nest.

Candice was actually a very friendly girl. She pulled up a random beanbag and began chatting away incessantly to Johnny. 'Well, who'd have believed it – me mum was having her front bush trimmed and there he was, the lovely George. Just two days ago it was I met him. I said, "Mum, you'll never guess what, but the man trimming your bush is C-U-T-E."' She spelt out each letter individually. Ruby could see James trying not to laugh and caught his eye. He grinned back at her.

'Just look at my little cutey-wutey.' She held her hand out to George, who was juggling his way through the bar with a full tray of drinks.

Ruby ignored her and turned to whisper in Adam's ear, 'I see you have a rucksack, sir. Does that mean you require accommodation for this evening?'

He wriggled a little closer to her and whispered back, 'Only if the birthday girl doesn't find it too presumptuous.'

The Kaiser Chiefs were now blaring out and Tony was running round the table, much to everyone's amusement singing their song at the top of his voice.

'Ruby, Ruby, Ruby, Ruby.' He ran to her side, lifted one of her hands, and kissed it. 'For you.' He handed her a fortune cookie.

'Bless you, Tony,' she said, snapping it in half and pulling out the hidden piece of paper.

'Unlucky to read out to group,' Tony warned her.

'Oh, OK.' Ruby held it up dramatically so nobody could see it but her. *Love, happiness and wealth are coming your way this year.* Well, she couldn't ask for more than that, now could she?

'Is it how you like it, Ruby?' Tony asked.

'It couldn't be better. Thanks again, Tony.'

'Three cheers for the birthday girl.' Adam stood up, holding his glass in the air. Ruby looked up at him. Maybe, just maybe, she had found herself a boyfriend – and a decent one at that. So why couldn't she just be happy for George?

Chapter Forty-six

Ruby awoke to the sun streaming into her bedroom. Turning over, she snuggled into the still sleeping Adam, taking in his wonderful smell and soft skin. She did like a smooth man – couldn't be doing with having to fight through lots of hair. Speaking of which, Patrick made himself known and jumped up onto the bed to begin wailing for food.S he pushed him down. She wasn't ready to leave her love nest just yet.

They'd had an amazing night. Returning from the Rocket Bar, they had cracked open another bottle of champagne and then proceeded to eat every morsel of cheese that Ruby had left in her fridge, accompanied by Rich Tea biscuits as she had no crackers.

After gorging, they lay together on the sofa, which led to some passionate snogging, which led to some real, old-fashioned lovemaking. Ruby loved the feeling of being so wanted.

Adam had seemed such a jack-the-lad on first impression that it was a relief to find such a kind, caring person underneath. He woke up and they made love again. He was completely OK with her safe sex ruling, which gave him even more brownie points. He actually couldn't quite believe how many condoms she had in her top drawer, until she explained that she had worked at the Fairdale Clinic and that Tony had given her loads for free.

'Actually, Rubes, now you mention jobs, I've got something to run by you. I completely forgot about it last night.'

'Go on.' Ruby sat up in bed and rubbed her eyes.

'It involves travel. How do you fancy going to the South of France next week?'

Her eyes lit up. 'Tell me more.'

'Two weeks away, a beautiful villa in the hills above Cannes, with a swimming pool and …'

She screwed up her face and interrupted him. 'What's the catch?'

He chuckled. 'I love the fact I can't kid a kidder! There are two catches, actually; Anya and Penelope. Five and nine, respectively. Your job would be to look after them.'

She looked at him cautiously. 'So are they your children?'

This time, he laughed out loud. 'God, no! They are my Managing Director's kids. He's a really nice guy. His wife can be a bit spiky, but they'll be out of your way most of the time. And …' Adam paused.

'Oh, what else now?' Ruby interrupted jokingly.

'If you like, I could fly out for the middle weekend and see you?'

'Excellent,' Ruby gushed. 'Go on then, I'll do it. 'How bloody exciting!'

They got up at lunchtime and gorged on eggs, bacon, and toast to quench their after-sex hunger. Adam said he had to get a proposal finished before Monday morning so packed his rucksack ready to leave. Ruby gave him a big hug and opened the door, still in her dressing gown. She blew him a kiss as he wandered off to the station. Just as she was about to head indoors, she caught sight of George. She quickly shut the door behind her, ran upstairs, and sneaked a peek out of the window.

Candice, still in her pussy pelmet and stilettos, clutching her big white leather handbag to herself, was trying to get into George's van without showing everyone next week's washing. George appeared with James. They were both laughing as they pushed her into the van.

Comforted by the thought that it would never last, she

turned on the television, fed the now screaming Patrick, made herself a cup of tea, and settled down to watch the *Eastenders* omnibus.

Chapter Forty-seven

August, Job Eight: Nanny

Maison du Soleil was in a perfect setting. Located high above the bustling seaside resort of Cannes, it afforded a picturesque view of the town below. The peace and sea view gave Ruby a wonderful sense of relaxation. The lounge by itself was bigger than the whole of her flat and the patio doors pushed open to reveal a magnificent swimming pool and barbecue area. Ruby's room was bright and airy and had an en-suite containing both a huge round-headed power shower and Jacuzzi.

'Now this is a job I could get used to,' she said as she launched herself onto the bed. It was her first night and Tom and Jayne had said for her to just chill out and acclimatise. She had had a quick bite to eat with them and excused herself as she was weary from travelling. She was to meet the children in the morning as they were both already asleep.

Tom King was exactly as Adam had described him. Mid-forties, five foot ten, black hair with flecks of grey, very laidback, and approachable. Jayne was of similar age with blonde cropped hair. She obviously looked after herself as Ruby noticed her trim figure, manicured nails, and perfect skin. She hadn't done anything yet to show the 'spiky' side that Adam had mentioned, but Ruby had gleaned from the short time they had spent together over dinner, that she was indeed a 'lady who lunched' and had an enviable staff of babysitters, school runners, and various other home help. Ruby was of the opinion that if you had children and you could afford not to work, surely they should be your priority.

She awoke early, got herself showered, and went into the kitchen. The children were both tucking into cereal, brioches, and milkshakes. Tom and Jayne were nowhere to be seen.

'Hello, girls,' Ruby said brightly.

'Who are you?' the smaller of the two girls with blonde bunches enquired.

'I know who you are,' the dark-haired child said cockily. 'Mummy said that we have a lady looking after us and we weren't to say anything rude about your hair.'

'Oh, right,' Ruby said, not sure what to think, as the dark-haired girl continued. 'Yeah. Dad said you were a carrot top and Mummy told him off.'

'What's a carrot top?' the younger girl enquired innocently.

'Well,' Ruby explained, 'sometimes, people like me who have red hair get called it as a nickname, because our hair is the colour of a carrot.'

'What's a nickname?' Little Miss Bunches asked.

OK, she was in the lap of luxury but maybe this wasn't going to be quite as easy as she had thought. Ruby grinned to herself at Tom's comment and imagined the hilarity it would cause Adam when she told him. At that moment, Jayne rushed into the kitchen and saved Ruby from thinking of an answer for her youngest daughter.

'So sorry Ruby, I didn't realise you were up and about. I've just been packing a bag. Tom and I are off to Monaco for the day.' Ruby thought how lovely she looked in her designer white cropped jeans and little vest. 'So you've met our little angels already?' she said fondly.

'Well, I've not been officially introduced,' Ruby replied.

Jayne put her arm on the little one's shoulder. 'This is Anya, who is going to be such a good girl for you today, aren't you, darling?'

The five year old made a funny face. 'Maybe, if you bring me back a present.'

Jayne ignored her and pointed to her nine year old. 'And this is Penelope. Penny will show you where everything is if you get stuck.'

Ruby noticed that Anya was now flicking milk across the table with her spoon.

'Stop it, you cow!' Penelope screeched and threw her fork onto the floor in temper.

'Girls, behave yourselves right now,' Jayne said sternly. 'Now listen, this is Ruby and she is going to be looking after you while we are here.'

'Carrot top, Carrot top,' both of the children started to recite in unison.

Jayne took Ruby to one side, face slightly flushed, completely ignoring their chants. 'We're going to take the car so it's probably best if you don't mind just entertaining them up here. They love the pool, and the fridge is stocked with food. There's also a variety of board games in the cupboard if they get bored of swimming. If you can face it, there's a Nintendo Wii too.'

At this point, Tom appeared and greeted Ruby. 'All set?' he asked his wife. She nodded and they headed to the door.

'See you later, Ruby,' Jayne smiled. 'Any problems, just call me on my mobile. The number's on the table.'

'Don't you worry, we'll be just fine. Go and have a lovely day,' Ruby said confidently, already wondering why on earth she had agreed to this.

The children soon got themselves into the swimming pool and started playing relatively well. It was scorching hot, so Ruby donned her flowery sunhat and plenty of Factor 50, and positioned herself under an umbrella near the pool edge so she had full sight of her charges. She had brought a new book for the occasion. Patrick Gale never failed to impress her and his *Notes From An Exhibition* was no exception. Just as she was getting herself into the story, there was a scream from the pool. How foolish was she, assuming she might have time to read!

'Tell Penny to stop taking the pink lilo,' Anya whined. 'I want the pink lilo. It's mine!'

'You lying little cow, you know it's mine. Mum said you had to have the blue one.'

Anya started to scoop water into a bucket and throw it relentlessly at Penelope. Ignoring Ruby's shouts to stop, the only thing for it was to throw off her sun hat, jump in the pool, and pull the scrapping siblings apart. By this time, Penelope had swallowed a bucketful of water and proceeded to be sick in the crystal clear water.

'Now look what you've done!' Ruby shouted at Anya, who flew out of the pool and stropped off through the apartment, still soaking wet. Ruby soothed Penelope, dried her off, sat her on her sunlounger under an umbrella, and got her a drink of water. She told her to stay where she was and went to Anya.

'Come on, darling. Let's get you dry and I'll get you a nice drink of cold water.'

'I don't want water. I want lemonade.'

'OK,' Ruby said, feeling her teeth grinding together. 'Lemonade it is.' Whoever said "patience is a virtue" was right, she thought.

The children drank their fizzy pop quietly at the kitchen table, while Ruby found a fishing net and began scooping lumps of cereal and orange scum out of the pool. She wasn't sure what was worse; dealing with old people or children – and this was just day one! She realised that her book would most definitely have to wait and asked the children what they would like to do when they'd finished their drinks.

'Wii!' Anya shouted.

'Yeah, Wii!' Penelope agreed.

Hallelujah! Ruby thought.

'I want to play boxing on the Wii,' Penny said bossily.

'But I want to play ten pin bowling,' Anya howled.

'OK, girls, I decide,' Ruby intervened. 'I think bowling would be better as I can play as well.'

'Favoritism!' Penny sneered.

'I heard that,' Ruby said.

'You were meant to. Anya's your favourite, Anya's your favourite,' Penny chanted with venom, pointing her finger at her younger sister as she did so.

'Of course she's not.' Ruby felt the teeth closing in again. 'Now if that's the way you're going to be, Penelope, we won't play at all.'

Anya stamped her foot. Penelope thought for a minute. Reverse psychology saved the day. 'OK then, bowling it is,' Penny said sulkily, 'but I want to make up your playing names.'

The compromise was made and Carrot Top, Poo Bum, and Princess were soon ready for their first bowl. Luckily, Anya had found her made-up name funny and the game commenced. It was actually quite a relief, Ruby thought, to be out of the hot sun and not have to worry if she'd applied enough sun cream to each child – plus, of course, prevent them from drowning each other. Ruby had never played on a Wii before and began to really enjoy it. She ran around the room, lifting her arms in the air and cheering, when she got her first strike. The children joined in, jumping around, laughing, and squealing. Just as Ruby actually thought she was making some progress to entertain them without incident ... *bash*! Anya swung back her arm to set the ball rolling on the screen, sending the controller right into Ruby's face. For such a little girl, she was quite strong. Ruby put her hand to her eye and momentarily saw stars.

'Carrot Top, I'm so sorry.' Anya started to well up.

Ruby sat down; her eye was throbbing badly. 'Hey, come here. It wasn't your fault, just a silly little accident,' she said gently, and put her arm around the little girl. 'Why don't you two carry on carefully and I'll go and get some ice for my face.'

She wondered how many years in prison she would get if she just left them home alone and hopped on the next plane back to England.

Chapter Forty-eight

Over breakfast the next day, likening her to a panda they had once seen at London Zoo, Ruby's black eye caused great hilarity to both Anya and Penelope. Despite Ruby stressing it had been nothing more than a silly accident, Jayne apologised profusely and said that she and Tom would be back after lunch today so she could take some time to relax. The children were adamant that they wanted to go to the beach, so Jayne left Ruby some money for a taxi as she and Tom were taking the car again.

In tune with a military operation, off they set with bags, towels, buckets, and spades. The whole nannying experience was already making Ruby wonder if she would ever have children of her own. It wasn't all sunshine and roses, that was for certain. Maybe Jayne King got it right by having as much home help as possible to ease the pressure.

She ushered her charges along La Croisette until they managed to find a strip of sand that wasn't part of a private beach linked to a hotel, and ably set up camp. Ruby made sure both girls were swamped in lotion and that they were wearing the appropriate sun hats. Due to her black eye, the lotion made her own face sting, so as an alternative in order to avert the strong August rays, she put on her widest Victoria Beckham-style sunglasses and huge floppy hat. A grand sandcastle mission commenced, including some quite complex moat building. After the children got bored of refilling the moat for the twentieth time, they sat down near the water's edge. Ruby could hear them sniggering and whispering together, and then all of a sudden they were running towards her.

'Bundle!' they shouted in unison, pushing Ruby to the ground.

'We are going to take you prisoner and bury you!' Penny shrieked. Anya giggled incessantly as Ruby played along, thinking that anything to keep the little darlings quiet had to be a good thing, and lay down ready for her fate. It would have all been fine, except once she was buried right up to her neck, the girls decided that one of them would wear her hat and the other her glasses. They then began to dance and sing around her, pretending they were singers from The Saturdays. By the time she had managed to force herself out of her sandy prison and capture Frankie and Rochelle, her non-lotioned, non- covered face was now the colour of a lobster on acid. She ran into the sea to wash herself down, squealing loudly when the salty water hit her sunburnt face. Noticing the glamorous women around her, with full facea make-up and designer bikinis, professionally sunning themselves, she felt nothing short of a freak. Both girls, realising that Ruby actually was in pain and feeling as guilty as a nine year old and five year old could possibly feel, for once did exactly as they were told and got dressed in silence.

Thankfully, it had already been agreed that Ruby should have the weekend free, and she was demob happy that Adam was due to arrive tonight. She had agreed to meet him in the Bar des Célébrités at the Carlton Hotel on the seafront. Tom kindly drove her down the hill and left her to it. It was a beautiful evening and the handsome bald one was already sitting at a table with two glasses of champagne when she arrived. He handed her one of them as soon as she sat down. 'Only the best for Madame Ruby on her holidays,' he said.

She lifted her glass. 'Cheers. I cannot tell you how much I need this.' She sighed and took off her sunglasses.

Adam looked closely at her face in amazement. 'Oh my God, Rubes, what on earth happened?' He couldn't help but laugh out loud when she relayed the story.

She noticed how gorgeous Adam looked in his flowery Paul Smith shirt and smart black jeans, and suddenly felt ugly and conspicuous in the plush surroundings, with her shining red face and black eye.

'I'm sorry I look such a freak,' Ruby said once the first soothing glass of champagne had passed her lips.

'It's OK,' Adam smiled. 'I've got a paper bag in my pocket.' Then he chuckled again. 'Look, don't worry about it. It's still the lovely you under there. In fact, I've always quite fancied going out with an Oompa Loompa!'

Ruby hit his arm playfully and grinned. He ordered another glass of champagne and she began to relax. She sat back and lightly shut her eyes for a second.

'Hard work?' Adam enquired.

'The hardest kind. The kids are actually really sweet, but it's bloody constant.'

'Well done you for persevering anyway.' Adam lifted his glass.

'Cheers,' they said, clinking glasses again. Ruby looked around her, taking in the beautiful setting. She noticed the heavily made-up woman at the table next to theirs. She must have been in her late sixties, with a miniature white poodle at her feet. She was wearing a huge diamond ring and earrings.

'This is a bit flash,' Ruby whispered.

'Yeah, I know,' Adam half-whispered back. 'We had a work do here a few years back and I thought I'd like to come here socially one day, so here I am.'

'Yes, here you are.' Ruby reached for his hand. 'Thanks for sorting this, Adam. Sorry for moaning. It has actually been lovely to get out of London.' Relishing her freedom, she livened up. 'What are the bedrooms like here then? I bet they're gorgeous.'

'Well, yes, they are, but I'm afraid we're not staying here.'

'Oh, OK,' Ruby said, trying not to sound too disappointed.

'In fact, we'd better drink up. The waiter has just gestured that our chariot awaits.'

'Ooh Mr Wilde, you do spoil me,' Ruby mocked as they headed to the waiting black Mercedes.

After a half an hour drive, with Adam refusing to tell her where they were going, the car pulled up to what looked like a little shed. A porter appeared and took their bags. As there was no car access, Adam took Ruby's hand and they began the climb up to their hotel. Ruby was intrigued as they walked under stone passageways, passed cave-like shops and restaurants, and clambered up ancient stone steps and walkways. The evening sunshine lit their path and Ruby felt happier than she had in a long time. Adam explained as they walked that they were in Eze, a thousand-year-old medieval village situated more than 427 metres above the Mediterranean Sea. They were slightly out of breath when they reached their destination but it was well worth the climb. They were to stay at Château Eza. Ruby couldn't believe how beautiful it was.

The château clung to the side of the ancient rock walls of the village and the view from the bar was quite simply breathtaking. Because they were so high up, the view of the sea was infinite on one side, with imposing mountains to the other. They were to stay in La Chambre aux Deux Cheminées, aptly named because of its two stone fireplaces.

The bed was queen size and the view from the balcony was of both the sea and the mountains. Ruby thought that she must just be in the middle of a very good dream and in a minute she would wake up. She'd caught sight of the room rates and couldn't believe that Adam was treating her to such luxury.

They dressed for dinner, with Ruby thankful for the extra living room so she could get ready in peace. Despite them running around butt naked the other night, the thought of him actually seeing her pulling her knickers up when he was stone cold sober horrified her. She looked down and checked that she'd shaved her legs. After Adam's comment about straggly red pubes she didn't want to be guilty of this particular crime either. As she looked to check that her bikini line was trim she suddenly thought of George. They would have such a laugh here.

She wondered if it was still going strong with Candice. Even thinking about that name made her feel slightly sick.

She walked back into the bedroom and Adam wolf-whistled. She was wearing an off the shoulder emerald green dress that enhanced her curves, with a simple drop diamante necklace and matching earrings. Her footware was a pair of three inch black sandals, Jimmy Choos, no less – that she had picked up from the upmarket Oxfam on Westbourne Grove for a mere £10. Her hair was sleek and smooth and her Victoria Beckham glasses were firmly in place. She felt confident that at least from the neck down she looked good.

'Not bad for a ginger!' Adam exclaimed, and Ruby hit him playfully on the arm.

'Hmm, yes, I forgot to tell you that Tom told his girls that I was a carrot top! I couldn't believe it.'

'Oh, Rubes, I'm sorry.'

'No, you're not.' She put on a stern face and he wasn't sure if she was upset or not. He rushed to her side.

'Ruby, I really am sorry. I –' Before he could finish she burst out laughing. He grabbed her and kissed her on the lips. 'You! Come on, let's go for dinner.'

Dinner was a ten course tasting menu. The restaurant had one glass side that looked out over the now darkening sea and sky. Just as they were finishing their second dessert, Ruby, still wearing her sunglasses, noticed fireworks going off across the bay.

'How magical!' she exclaimed. She'd always loved fireworks and thought back to her dear father who put on a mini-display every fifth of November, when she and Sam were small. He would describe in infinite detail all the colours and formations in the hope that his blind son would get some sort of enjoyment out of it. God, she missed him.

'Get back to our room and there'll be fireworks all right,' Adam said, and touched her leg with his. She tilted her head coyly. Adam Wilde certainly knew how to make her tick. He then took her hand over the table. 'On a serious note, Ruby, I can't think of anyone I'd rather be here with than you. I've really had a truly wonderful evening.'

'I've had an amazing time,' Ruby replied honestly. 'Thank you so much, Adam.' She felt giddy with champagne. 'Time for a toast, I think.' She held her glass in the air. 'To Madame Saskia, for predicting such a fantastic union.'

'To Madame Saskia,' Adam echoed and they both laughed out loud.

Chapter Forty-nine

It was late on a Saturday evening when Ruby's flight from Cannes landed at Heathrow. She'd had another extremely tiring week with the children and Château Eza seemed like a distant memory. Nannying was definitely not her forte but at least Month Eight, Job Eight could most definitely be ruled out as a future career. She couldn't believe that it was already September. She'd forgotten to call Johnny earlier to see if he had anything for her next week.

She wearily got out of the taxi and dragged her case down the steps to her flat. Patrick was waiting for her outside and he rubbed himself around her legs. George and James had been taking it in turns to feed him.

As she put the key in the door, she heard a woman giggling and somebody running, singing out, 'Georgie Porgie, bet you can't catch me.' Candice's irritating voice filled the street. Pinch-faced Pru's curtains twitched. George, who was chasing Candice down the street, glanced at the taxi and started to cross the road, shouting, 'All right, Rubes?'

'This way.' Candice grabbed his arm and pulled him towards the house. George looked back at Ruby, then disappeared. She turned on the light, dropped her case, and went through to the kitchen to put the kettle on. Patrick leapt up on the couch for some attention and she began to fuss him. She had been born with green eyes, but never before had she felt jealousy – and she didn't like this feeling one bit.

She'd truly had a wonderful time in France with Adam. He was without doubt a lovely man and was treating her like a princess. But if she was really honest with herself, when he said that he couldn't think of anyone he'd rather be with than her, she knew there and then that she would have actually rather been with George.

She drained her cup of tea and devoured two custard creams, then checked the coast was clear and made her way over to Margaret's. She was relieved that her downstairs lights were still on.

The old lady was delighted to see her. 'Come in, duck.'

'Sorry it's so late, Margaret, I needed your ear.'

'Tut, tut. Never too late for you, Ruby, you know that. Come in and join me for a sherry.'

They clinked glasses and Ruby downed her sweet, syrupy drink in one.

'That bad, eh, love? Tell me what's wrong.'

'Oh, Margaret. I had such a lovely time in Cannes with Adam. He did nothing wrong, but I just know he's not The One. And I'm getting too long in the tooth to muck around now.' She put down her glass and ran her hands through her locks.

'So you must finish with this Adam straight away, Ruby. You can't mess around with people's feelings, it's just not fair.'

Ruby wasn't used to home truths so she kept quiet and poured two more large sherries as Margaret continued.

'And as for this stupid age thing, forget about it. It's all written anyway, Ruby. Your life path, that is. You can get the rudder and steer yourself to a degree, but I truly believe what will be will be.'

The old girl drained her glass and Ruby refilled it.

'Put my record on for me, duck, will you?' Margaret started to ramble. 'Did you know, Rubes, that Frankie Vaughan was born Frank Abelson to a Jewish family in Liverpool?'

Ruby shook her head, as the old girl started to slur.

'The name Vaughan came from his grandmother, who used to call Frank "my number one" grandson, in whose Russian accent "one" sounded like "Vaughan". Isn't that lovely, darling?'

Before Ruby could answer, Frankie 'the number vun grandson' Vaughan's voice filled the room.

'I am *so* jealous that George has a girlfriend,' Ruby suddenly blurted out.

'Halle-bloody-lujah!' Margaret shouted. 'It won't last, Ruby. You mark my words. As I always say, it's all written. My Stanley, your dad, George's dad. All up there, they are.' She pointed to the ceiling. 'Watching, waiting, learning. They won't let him leave you, Ruby,' Margaret slurred, the alcohol suddenly taking effect. 'Follow your heart, you dizzy lizzy.'

With that, her head lolled forward, a Polo fell out of her mouth on to her shelf-like breasts, and she started to snore loudly.

Ruby stood up slightly shakily, as both tiredness and the sherry started to hit her. She pulled the blanket that was resting on Margaret's legs up over her, turned off the gramophone, checked the back door was locked, switched out the lights, and quietly crept out of the front door.

Margaret might wake up with a stiff neck, but Ruby thought it safer having her sleep downstairs than trying to move her with a belly full of sherry and two dodgy feet.

When Ruby eventually got to bed, she couldn't sleep. Margaret was right, she had to follow her heart and stop mucking about with some stupid material wish list, which ultimately would never bring the happiness she both wanted and deserved.

Chapter Fifty

September, Job Nine: Shop assistant – Oxfam

'Ruby, it's Mum.'

'Mum? Is everything OK? Sam all right?' There was panic in Ruby's voice. This was the first time her mother had called her at home for at least a year.

'Darling, of course it is. I was actually ringing to see how you are.'

'I'm fine, ta. Don't faint, but I'm hand washing my cushion covers. Dry cleaning is *so* overrated these days.'

They both laughed.

'I was just watching the evening news, it's a nasty business all these job cuts,' Laura Matthews continued.

'Tell me about it, Johnny hasn't got anything for me yet this month either. I'm thinking of maybe even going to the Job Centre tomorrow.'

'Well. That's really the reason for my call, love. Hopefully, I can help *you* out for once.'

Joanna Glancy, the vicar's wife, ignored Ruby as she walked ino Oxfam in the Berkshire market town of Denbury. The woman's mauve twin set and pearls didn't sit right on her big, manly figure. She had a deep and booming posh voice which she was projecting down the end of the shop to another lady, whose beige Chanel suit clung to her skeletal frame, making her resemble a whippet.

As Ruby walked up to the counter and opened her mouth to speak, Joanna Glancy lifted her palm. 'One moment, dear,' she said dismissively.

If it wasn't for Ruby catching sight of a pair of Prada shoes on the rack beside her, she would have walked out there and then at the sheer rudeness of the woman.

'Well, of course, Marjorie,' the booming continued. 'You can imagine my shock when he was accused of creaming off thousands from the church collection. I've never heard of anything so ridiculous in all my life. My dear Henry, pillar of society – a thief?! We're suing, of course.'

Marjorie the whippet just nodded wildly.

'I'm sorry to interrupt.' There, she'd got the manly one's attention. 'I'm Ruby. I spoke to you yesterday. Two weeks holiday cover for Mrs Pemberton-Smythe, remember?'

'Oh, I'm so sorry, dear. I thought you were just a customer.'

Ruby smirked inside. The charity might be taking its first steps towards a more fashion-conscious image but the staff here certainly could do with some people skills training.

Laura Matthews had been walking in Denbury when she had noticed the advert in the Oxfam shop window. She'd been really excited to tell her daughter about it, and with nothing else in the offing, Ruby had readily agreed to call and try and get herself an interview. Just one mention of the word Cliveden and snobby Joanna Clancy gave her the job on the spot.

After her recent visit to the Westbourne Grove branch of Oxfam, Ruby was excited about what treats she might be able to pick up here. However, the Denbury store hadn't quite had the same overhaul yet.

She had spotted a few designer one-offs and an area where clothes had been updated by young designers from the local fashion college. But there were still quite a few oversized floral skirts and slightly battered shoes,

Looking around her, Ruby could already see where she could improve the layout of the store and was hungry to get going.

The vicar's wife continued, 'Well, Ruby, it is lovely to meet you and I simply cannot wait to hear all about your lovely little event at Cliveden. But one must fly, Ladies who Elevenses meet in Henley in ten and I can't be late. Marjorie here will show you the ropes. Toodlepip.'

Ruby was just thinking that she had never heard anybody say 'toodlepip' before when she was startled by the sound of Joanna Glancy's brand new and gleaming Rolls Royce roaring in to life outside.

'Either God has given them a substantial pay rise or they are going to need a very good lawyer,' Ruby said politely to Marjorie, who threw her a warm smile.

It was wonderful to have her mother to herself for a while. Sam had gone on holiday with Beth, and Graham was on a Guide Dog training course. It was even nicer to come home to a home-cooked dinner.

'So, how was it?' Laura was waiting eagerly at the front door.

'It was interesting,' Ruby smirked. 'Do you know any of the women who work there?' she carried on, praying that she didn't.

'No, far too do-gooding for my liking,' Laura replied.

They moved through to the lounge and Ruby filled her mum in.

'It was actually bloody hysterical. Joanna Clancy, the vicar's wife no less, is more corrupt than one of the Great Train Robbers, and her sidekick Marjorie has so much money she doesn't know what to do with it – but is so bored with life that her three-hour daily stint in the shop is the highlight of her life.'

'Denbury is a bit like that. Graham says that it's only the haves and have lots who live there.'

'Which is why its Oxfam will hold such rich pickings for a skint little magpie like me. I get paid a pittance per hour but I am allowed to pick two outfits before I leave as a perk of the job.'

'I'm so glad I could help you for once, darling. If you do need to borrow any money you will ask now, won't you? You know your dad left me comfortable.'

'Yes, thanks, Mum, but I am managing OK at the moment.'

Laura went to the kitchen and came back with two mugs of steaming tea. She sat down next to Ruby on the sofa. Ruby could tell she was uncomfortable with what she was about to say. Mrs Matthews cleared her throat.

'Look, love, I feel that sometimes since your dad died I haven't been that much of a support to you. It's only since meeting Graham that I feel so much happier. It was as if I was in a deep gloom for a long time.' Laura blinked back the tears. 'I just couldn't see my way out. I'm so sorry if I let you down.'

Ruby burst into tears and Laura leant over to comfort her.

'It has been hard. I felt sometimes you didn't care,' Ruby blubbed. 'But, then I would realise that you were probably going through a much worse time than me.'

'Oh, Ruby, you silly girl. I wish you'd have confronted me earlier.' Laura now had tears rolling down her face. 'Good old Ruby. Strong old Ruby, that's what Sam and I always see in you. You've been so independent since you moved to London. I just didn't realise how you felt.'

Taking in this special moment, Ruby smiled through her tears.

'I love you, Mum.'

'You'd better,' Laura jested. 'And I promise from now on I will be here for you whatever the weather.'

It was the start of Ruby's second and final week at Oxfam.

Joanna Clancy, realising how much of an asset Ruby was, had taken herself off to a spa retreat in Dorset for a few days.

Marjorie the whippet, already feeling able to confide in the affable Ruby Matthews, was happy to tell her that the Area Manager was coming in the following Monday and she just knew that the vicar's wife would take all the credit for her hard work.

'Do you know what?' Ruby said. 'Let her take it. I think she reckons that just because she's the vicar's wife, she gets an instant pass to upstairs.' Ruby pointed to the ceiling. 'But I believe in karma so she might be knocking for a very long time at those Pearly Gates.'

The store was now looking very different indeed. From Day One, Ruby had immediately got busy, and had picked some of the best designer pieces and dressed them in the window professionally. She had created separate areas for women and men, and by observing the buying habits of some of the elderly members of the community, she kept the old-fashioned floral numbers and battered shoes together.

Ruby had also met a couple of the students from the college who had taken away particular pieces on her suggestion to revamp them.

Marjorie had been a great help and as Ruby noticed her start to come out of her shell and be less timid, the more she gave her to do.

What Ruby loved best was when people came in and asked for her advice on putting outfits together. She had a natural flair for colour and styles, and found it easy to find outfits to suit different body shapes. Word of the 'personal dresser' got around the close knit ladies who lunch community, and from Day Three Oxfam's takings had doubled.

Ruby was taking great delight in trying on a few outfits on her last day when she heard Marjorie whisper through the changing curtain.

'Ruby, quick. Sally King, the Area Manager, is here. She's a day early.'

'Joanna around?' Sally asked briskly as Ruby appeared from the changing cubicle.

'No, she's taken a few days off. I've been holding the fort.'

Sally smiled. 'Ah, makes sense now why the figures are so good. I cannot believe the changes here. Was this down to you?' She looked at Ruby, who nodded.

'Well done. Ruby, isn't it? Joanna did mention you were going to be covering for her and you've done a splendid job. Thank you very much. This is just what this place needed.'

Ruby swelled with pride.

'Now I take it you realise the hourly rate is not high?'

Ruby nodded. 'Yes. Joanna's left me an envelope with my wages in the till.'

'I can't give you any more money, but how about you take three outfits away with you from that colourful section there?' She pointed to the tidy women's designer section. 'And Marjorie, the same applies to you. Well done. Oh, and when you do see Joanna on Monday, tell her to ring me immediately.'

Oh, such love and not distaste for this particular employ, Ruby thought as she waited for the train to take her back to London.

Chapter Fifty-one

October, Job Ten: Divorce Lawyer Administrator

'Jesus is alive and living in Gretna Green!' Bert hollered from the end of the road, adorned in the new brown Armani suit that Ruby had gotten him from Oxfam.

'Don't tell Ruby that or she'll be taking you there to get married,' George joked as he ran down his steps, carrying a hoe.

'All right, missus?' he asked as Ruby drew level with him. 'Haven't seen you for ages.'

'I've actually been staying in Reading with Mum.' Ruby felt her heart beating faster.

'All OK with Adam?' he asked genuinely.

'Fine, fine,' Ruby lied. 'Candice?'

'Still lovely as ever,' George replied.

Bitch.

'Right, I'd better get going bird, I've got to be in Richmond in twenty.'

'Nice arse, by the way!' the gorgeous one shouted out of the window as he sped off up the road in his van, music blaring.

Ruby didn't know whether to laugh or cry.

Trilby, Vine & Pitheringon were based in smart offices in Staple Inn, a beautiful little enclave off Holborn. James, who worked there as a Trainee Solicitor, had overheard somebody saying they needed a temp for three weeks as holiday cover for an administrative assistant in Divorce Law. He had immediately thought of Ruby. As a trainee solicitor, James was moving around departments; he was currently working for the Wills and Probate department on the third floor.

Annabel Vine met Ruby in the stark reception area. An upright woman, with a thin face and severe brown bob, she reminded Ruby of Mia Wallace from *Pulp Fiction*. She was wearing a smart pin-striped trouser suit and was immaculately made-up. Speaking in a proper English accent, she held her hand out to Ruby.

'Hi there, you must be Ruby. Welcome to the madhouse.' She turned for Ruby to follow her to the stairway. 'Don't dither, girl. We have a bucketful of work to get through.' She ushered Ruby to a leather-topped desk that housed a PC and a wilting spider plant. It was positioned at the door of a huge office.

'Now this is where you'll sit, and I'm just in here. If the door is shut, please do knock first.' The feisty lawyer walked into her own huge office, addressing Ruby once more. 'I feel lost already without Jennifer, but I'm sure you'll do. You come highly recommended by the agency, so that's good.'

Ruby hadn't realised that she was going to be working for one of the partners of the firm. With Annabel Vine's attitude, she predicted a difficult assignment. But she would stick with Khalil on this one. No distaste, just love. After all, she was only here for three weeks. With this being Job Ten, her end goal was in sight, and she was going to embrace everything thrown at her in good humour and a positive spirit.

Ruby actually couldn't quite believe that she had already reached month ten of her twelve-month mission. She had decided that over Christmas she would have a good think about all the positions and areas she had worked in and analyse them with a scoring system. She would rate the twelve positions firstly by writing LOVE or DISTASTE next to each. She would then eliminate the

DISTASTES, take the ones with LOVE, and allocate points against them for happiness and willingness to get up in the morning.

'Stop daydreaming, dear, will you, and get me some coffee?' the loud voice boomed from Annabel's office.

'If you say please, then maybe I might,' Ruby replied just as abruptly as she had been spoken to. For some reason, instead of Rubygetting another biting comment from her rude new boss, Annabel Vine firstly flinched, and then smiled wryly. Sometimes these feisty characters needed showing that you were their equal, Ruby thought.

With a newfound respect for her temporary assistant, the divorce lawyer said more politely, 'Black,two sugars, *please,* Ruby. Out of the office, turn right and down the corridor to the kitchen. To the left for the lavatories.'

Ruby returned with two coffees to find all hell breaking loose in front of her desk.

'Over my dead body will I allow him to take Bertie to Barbados, especially with *her*,' a smart middle-aged woman, wearing a black trench coat, matching trilby, and sporting thick-rimmed, dark glasses, screeched at Annabel. A bedraggled-looking Bassett Hound on a lead next to her began to howl loudly. 'Well, that's it. You can tell that swine he'll have to find him first. I'm going to hide him somewhere.'

Annabel remained silent as the woman continued her rant. 'This is getting bloody ridiculous. I don't think I'm being unfair. Did you know that he's even requested his ten-year-old nose trimmer back? Tell him he can bloody have it back! I've been trimming my pubes with it for years anyway.'

Annabel screwed her face up in distaste while Ruby tried not to laugh and Bertie Basset continued to howl.

At this point, the lawyer took control. 'Look, I'm really sorry, Mrs Darling-Smythe, but you know I cannot comment on anything as I am representing your husband. I would really appreciate it if you left.' The woman went to say something else and Annabel intercepted harshly, '*Right now.*'

The woman huffed and strutted purposefully to the door. Annabel, unaware that the irate woman was not yet out of earshot, looked to Ruby and said, 'The husband's bit of stuff is allergic to the bloody dog anyway, so I can't see her even allowing it to go to the Bahamas with them.'

Mrs Darling-Smythe stopped in her tracks, smiled, and turned around. She walked back to Ruby's desk, placed the dog's lead in her hand, and addressed Annabel. 'If he wants to be a bloody-minded sod then so can I. Let the sensitive young tart sneeze her way to the sunshine. Good day, Mrs Vine.'

And with that she tilted her hat and stormed off the premises, leaving an open-mouthed divorce lawyer, a laughing assistant, and a loudly barking basset hound.

Chapter Fifty-two

Fi met Ruby outside the solicitor's office after work. Ruby immediately handed her Bertie's lead.

'What the feck?' Fi asked.

'One of our clients called Mr Darling-Smythe – love that name – is shagging some young tart, and the soon to be ex-wife–'

'Mrs Darling-Smythe?' Fi queried.

'You got it. Well, they were arguing over custody of the dog, and she left young Bertie with us as she learned about the girlfriend's dog allergy and wants her to suffer.'

'Cool! But why on earth have you got him now?'

'Because my stroppy boss insisted that as we couldn't locate Mr D.S. that I should take him home tonight. She didn't want him doing anything untoward on her shag pile.'

'Cheeky cow. How does she know you haven't got good carpet to ruin?'

'You know me, Fi. I'm too soft sometimes.'

Fi bent down to stroke Bertie's big soft ears. 'He's lovely, isn't he?' With this, Bertie opened his mouth and began to howl.

'Come on, Rubes, let's find ourselves a bar that will take pooches. Have you got a muzzle?'

'No, I haven't. Come on, good boy. Come on, Bertie,' Ruby urged.

But Bertie had plonked himself down on his back haunches and would not budge. Both girls coaxed and pulled, but to no avail. The miserable hound would not move for love or money.

Luckily, just as they were about to give up and leave the stubborn dog on the pavement, James appeared. Word had got around the office about what had happened, and he laughed at their predicament. As he did so, Bertie decided it was time to get up and pee against a lamppost.

'Thank Jaysus for that!' Fi exclaimed. 'I need a fecking drink. You joining us, James?'

'No, got football practice tonight. Gotta dash. All OK with the job, Rubes?'

'Fine, thanks.'

'By the way, I was handed Lucas Steadburton's will earlier. Shouldn't really tell you because of client confidentiality, but George told me how close you were to him.'

'I'd love to see who he left everything to,' Ruby stated. 'Monty was my early gift. He probably left the rest to Battersea Dogs' Home.'

'Well, come and find me tomorrow and I'll see what I can do. The young hound at least has a right to know if his master left everything to a dog's home and not him.'

Ruby laughed. 'Exactly! Thanks, mate. See you tomorrow.'

Ruby and Fi found an old pub in a side street that didn't mind dogs. Luckily, they managed to keep Bertie quiet by placing him under the table with three packets of pork scratchings.

'It's so lovely to see you, Rubes.' Fi said, well content to be spending some time with her best buddy. 'Feels like its ages since we saw each other. So, tell me – how is the gorgeous Adam Wilde?'

Ruby relived her tale of France. Fi couldn't believe that she'd been taken to Château Eza.

'You know it?' Ruby enquired.

'Course I do, Rubes! You're talking to Miss Sparkle Events here. Footballers and the like quite often stay there.

It's somewhere I've always wanted to go, you lucky dog!'

'Well, I didn't see anyone famous. But it is a breathtaking place.'

'So's he obviously found your hole then?'

Ruby tutted and laughed. 'Do you have to be so coarse, Fiona O? As it happens, we did it the night of my birthday.'

'Ooh, look at you, second date girl.'

'Getting good, aren't I?' Ruby joked

'That's such a loada old bollocks anyway,' Fi asserted. 'I say if you fancy 'em, you fancy 'em. No man in his right mind will not carry on seeing you if you put out on the first date. If he likes you then he likes you.'

'Yeah,' Ruby agreed. 'But when I do meet The One, I think I actually would like to wait and get to know him better first. Makes it a bit more special when you do get round to doing the do, I reckon.'

'So Adam's not The One then?' Fi took a sip of wine and looked quizzically at her friend.

'Oh, Fi, he's so lovely. I can't quite put my finger on it what it is, but …' Ruby suddenly felt uncontrollable tears welling in her eyes, as she continued. 'I haven't seen him since we got back from France. He's been trying to set up a date to meet but I keep avoiding him.' She wiped her eyes.

'Don't get upset, Rubes. You can't help the way you feel – or don't, in this instance.' Fi put her hand over her friend's.

'I just feel so guilty, especially after the way he treated me in Eze. Adam *is* really lovely, but the *but* is a big one – and I really do think that I should nip the relationship in the bud before anyone gets hurt.'

'For once, Rubes, you are learning. It is all right to let go of love, you know. Just be truthful with him, let him know exactly where he stands.'

Ruby smiled through her now clearing tears. 'I will do.

In fact, I'll call him later. It will then open me up to my next dilemma.'

'Dilemma?' Fi questioned.

'It's George.'

'George? What's the matter with him?'

'Nothing the matter's with him, Fi. The fact is, I am insanely jealous that he's seeing that blonde thing.' She took a big slurp of wine. 'And I feel really confused as to whether it's because he's my friend and not there for me as much, or that maybe … I …'

Before Ruby had a chance to finish her sentence, Fi put her hand over her mouth and started gagging. Ruby soon followed suit. At that moment, Bertie appeared from under the table. If a dog could smile, then Bertie was definitely smiling.

It appeared that copious amounts of pork scratchings accelerated the workings of a Basset Hound's stomach lining. Both girls looked down at the steaming turd under the table, and as if embroiled in an awfully bad dream, remained motionless.

'What should we do?' Ruby whispered.

'Fecking run,' was all Fi could muster.

Bertie's ears were flailing in the wind as they dragged him behind them. By the time they reached the end of the road they were laughing their heads off.

'Jaysus!' Fi exclaimed.

'I feel terrible,' Ruby said. 'That poor barman will have to clear it up.'

'Well, it could have been worse,' Fi shrugged.

Ruby screwed her face up questioningly.

'He could have done it on Annabel Vine's shag pile.'

Once they had stopped laughing, Fi announced that she was heading home. She patted Bertie on the head and put both arms loosely around Ruby's neck. 'It's been lovely to have the craic with you tonight.'

'You too, you old tart.' Ruby smiled.

'And about George, Rubes.' She looked into Ruby's eyes. 'Just follow your heart, mate. It usually speaks more sense than a head that thinks too much about everything. And then, when the time is right for you, you just have to tell him how you're feeling.'

'OK,' was all Ruby could muster, then, 'But?'

'No buts, Ruby. Men are not mind readers. They need to be told.'

Fi pulled away from her. 'Right, let's get you a cab. You've got a busy couple of days ahead, Ms Matthews, and I want a full update on progress. Good luck!'

Ruby hailed a cab and kissed her wild-haired friend goodbye, thinking that maybe Fi was Margaret's secret love-grandchild, as they sure seemed to spout the same scary advice.

Chapter Fifty-three

'Watch that smacked-arse of a face don't rot your shoulders, ginger!' Bert shouted out, lumbering down the street and supping on a can of cider.

George ran down the steps of his flat, shovel in his hand. There was a gust of wind, and a swirl of red and yellow autumn leaves whirled around them.

'Hey Rubes.' George noticed her red-rimmed eyes. 'What's up, darling?' He threw the shovel in the back of the van and came to her side.

'I'm fine.'

'Hmm, even I know that in girl speak that means you're not all right at all. Want to talk about it?'

'Not really.'

He raised his eyebrows. 'You sure? I've got ten minutes.'

Ruby reluctantly jumped into the cab of his van. This wasn't how this was meant to be. She had wanted to set a time and a place to tell the gorgeous one how she felt about him, but she guessed now was as good a time as ever.

She placed the pint of milk she'd just bought on the dashboard. 'I'm OK. It's just I finished with Adam last night.' She couldn't believe she was telling George this. But that was one of his qualities she loved. She could actually talk to him about anything.

But it was them she should be talking about, not her now ex-boyfriend, she thought, struggling to find the words.

'How did he take it?'

'Pretty badly, actually. I felt terrible, especially after he spent all that money on me in France.'

'Did you go and see him then?'

'Of course I did. I'm not that shallow to not tell them in person,' Ruby snapped. She put her hand on George's knee. 'Hark at me, the moody old cow.' She managed a smile. 'Look, George, I did actually want to talk to you about something else.'

'Knock, knock, knock, is this a private party or can anyone join?' Candice's face appeared at the driver's door window.

As George wound the window down, Ruby felt her whole body retract in horror. Talk about timing!

'Course not, angel, just telling Ruby that us men are not worth it. She finished with Adam last night.'

'Oh shame,' Candice said with the sincerity of a dead rabbit. 'Anyway, here's your flask, lover. You left it in the kitchen.'

Ruby grabbed her milk and hopped down from the van as the gorgeous one and the blonde said their sloppy goodbyes.

As George drove off, Patrick appeared in the street. Candice bent down to stroke him and Ruby noticed how long and toned her legs were in her skinny jeans. Bitch!

'Int he lovely?' the blonde one whined. 'Such good-natured things, cats.' At that moment Patrick took a swipe at Candice's hand and drew blood with his claws.

'Oh, Candice, I'm so sorry,' Ruby said, thinking at this moment just how much she loved her feline friend.

'It's OK, Ruby, honest. I've gotta 'nother one, ain't I? At least it was my right hand. Wouldn't want it to be the other one, would I?'

With that, she held out the unscathed digits of her left hand. A sparkling diamond ring sat proudly on her wedding finger. Ruby gulped and did her best to hide her shock.

'We're getting married, Rubes. I'm surprised that George didn't tell ya?'

Ruby's scarf fell down from her face and she felt herself welling up. She coughed to try and regain her composure.

'Oh, I've been really busy, Candice,' she blagged. 'I don't really see that much of George any more, you know.' She turned her nose up. 'I guess he didn't deem it important enough to make a special effort to tell me.'

Relishing Ruby's pain, Candice smirked and offered more information. 'Well, you're on the guest list. The invitations are being printed as we speak.'

'How very organised,' Ruby felt like she was being strangled. 'So … umm.' She paused, not really wanting to know the answer to the next question. 'So, you've set a date then?'

'Oh yeah,' Candice giggled. 'A romantic Christmas wedding, with fur and bells and glittery things everywhere. In less than three months, I will be Mrs Candice Stevens.'

'Wow. You haven't wasted any time.' Ruby thought she was going to be sick.

'Why wait, eh?' Candice went on. 'When that ol' devil called love shows 'is face, grab 'im by the bollocks, I say.'

She flicked back her locks. 'Right, I must go. Shoes to buy, flowers to choose. Laters.'

The blonde one teetered off towards the station as Ruby, eyes now streaming with tears, abandoned her milk mission and walked slowly across the street to find solace with her dear friend, Margaret.

Unable to quite yet grasp a complete sense of normality, Bert was in the old girl's front garden, sitting up in a quilted sleeping bag and doing *The Times* crossword.

'She's not here, ginger,' he said politely for once.

If Ruby hadn't felt so distraught, she would have fallen over in shock at Bert's smart appearance. The suit she had got him from Oxfam fitted him perfectly and he was wearing a crisp white shirt.

'Not here?' Ruby questioned almost hysterically. Margaret was always here!

'At the dentist, I think,' Bert replied and turned back to his paper. 'Five down, six letters. Trouble and, dot, dot, dot, dot, dot, dot. What could that be, Ruby?'

Ruby let out a racking sob and ran back across the road.

'Strife!' Bert shouted at the top of his voice. 'Means wife, see?'

Ruby saw completely and God, it hurt.

Chapter Fifty-four

'Morning. Ruby.'

Annabel Vine rushed past her desk with a cup of coffee and an armful of files. She was dressed very smartly, in an olive green pencil skirt and a green and white striped shirt. 'Come in. Come in,' she shouted once she was sat at her large mahogany desk.

Dutifully picking up a pad and pen, Ruby joined her boss, who began speaking very quickly. 'Mr Darling-Smythe is coming in at ten so we've got some preparation to do. Ring the kennels, can you? He's made provisions for that blessed Basset Hound to come out this afternoon.' Ruby began scribbling. She felt like she was back in the pressurised environment of Ritsy Rose Interiors, and didn't like it at all.

'You will need to type up the notes from this morning's meeting, and here,' Annabel handed Ruby an audio tape. 'I did these last night. If you can counter-sign for me and get them in today's post, that would be great.' Ruby got up to go back to her desk. 'Oh, and for your info I've got a client lunch at midday today. Back threeish, I expect.'

Ruby was so raw from the wedding incident that she was tempted to say, 'Stick a broom up my arse and I'll sweep the bloody floor too, shall I?' But she instead replied with an assertive, 'No problem at all.'

Mr Darling-Smythe came and went in a flurry of swear words and expensive smelling aftershave. He was pleased that he could collect Bertie from the kennels that afternoon, albeit he had to go via the pharmacy for allergy tablets and a surgical mask for the girlfriend.

Annabel handed Ruby a list of actions as she whisked off to lunch with another client. Ruby rang down to reception to get James's extension number. She recognised his Geordie accent on answering.

'I'm all alone,' she told him. 'Fancy coming to my office so you can show me your last willy and testacles?'

James laughed. 'What are you like, pet! I'll take you out for a drink. I've got something to tell you that you are not going to believe.'

'If it's about George and Candice then I already know.'

'No, it's not that, but great news, heh, Rubes? Glad he told you. He's been meaning to since Saturday.'

Ruby knew her breath would be wasted talking to George's best friend so she let the whole thing go. She had to get her head around the fact that she had lost him. It had been her own stupid fault for not seeing something good right under her feet.

They found a seat in the York Minster. James had insisted they have an alcoholic drink, as by the end of what he had to tell her, she would need one.

'James, if you don't tell me what's going on, I shall scream.' Ruby took a large slurp of her Pinot Grigio.

'Look at this.' He shoved the Last Will and Testament of Mr Lucas Geronimo Steadburton into her hand. In fact, he handed her two.

'I can't be arsed to read through everything,' she objected. 'Can't you just tell me what you've found?'

'No, you've got to read this yourself.' He pointed to a paragraph on the first will.

I bequeath my precious Jack Russell, Montgomery Rasputin Daffodil Clift, to Miss Ruby Ann Matthews of 42a Amerhand Road, Putney. Ruby nodded.

'He sent me a letter saying this,' she said, and then exclaimed, 'Bless Monty having middle names too!'

'Now read down.'

Ruby did as she was told.

I bequeath my Wordsworth poetry book, containing the poem "Daffodils", also to Miss Ruby Ann Matthews of 42a Amerhand Road, Putney. The residue of my estate I leave to The Lake District Mountain Rescue Search Dogs.

'The book is such a lovely gesture. But I'm not quite sure why you have got yourself so excited about the whole thing,' Ruby said.

'James handed her will number two.

'Now read this one,' he ordered.

I bequeath my precious Jack Russell, Montgomery Rasputin Daffodil Clift, to Miss Ruby Ann Matthews of 42a Amerhand Road, Putney.

'And?' Ruby stopped reading.

James got a little annoyed with her flippancy. 'Ruby, will you just read on!'

I bequeath my Wordsworth poetry book, containing the poem "Daffodils", to Mr Domenic Theobold Bentley of Dinsworth House, Twickenham. The residue of my estate I leave to Mr Domenic Theobold Bentley of Dinsworth House, Twickenham.

'Well, everyone has a right to change their minds, I guess,' Ruby said innocently.

'Ruby, you are so sweet but I am going to fight your corner on this one. This Domenic Bentley, whoever he is …'

Ruby went a deep shade of pink.

'Ruby?' James looked at her questioningly.

'He's the owner of Dinsworth House.' Her face was now scarlet.

'You kept that one quiet, you dark horse,' James said intuitively and smiled at her. 'Anyway, the will was changed within days of the first one being sent to us. Was this man ill before he died?'

'Yes, he was. I sat with him the day he passed away.'

'And what date was that?' James was intent now.

'I feel like I'm in court.' Ruby squished her face up and

thought. 'It must have been January 28th. Yes, it was, Your Honour, as it was the last day of my assignment at Dinsworth House.'

'Hmm.' James rubbed his chin. 'This will was changed the day before he died.' He looked for the witness signatures. 'Did you come across a Dolly Herriot at Dinsworth House?'

'Yes, dear old Dolly. She's got Alzheimer's. A lovely lady but completely barking. She was always wandering off.'

'And I'm guessing Elena Bentley is Domenic's wife or daughter?'

'His wife. So, Inspector Clouseau, what do you deduce from your enquiries?' Ruby assumed a French accent.

'I deduce that your lover …'

'Ex-lover,' Ruby was quick to correct him.

'… I reckon that he changed the will to his benefit while the poor old boy was on his death bed. I mean, look at Lucas's shaky signature.'

Ruby was on the case too now. 'Hmm, and it makes sense that he sent me a separate letter concerning Montgomery, so he could try and stop me seeing the will.'

'Exactly.' James bashed his hand down, sending his pint glass shooting down the table.

'So, how come it's October and you're only just looking at the will now?' Ruby questioned.

'As the only executor, maybe Bentley thought he'd let the dust settle before he came to us. Or maybe that the initial will would be disgarded. Who knows? But what I do know is that if it wasn't for me knowing you, then he'd have got away with it.'

'I think it's really awful. I mean, I'm not bothered on my own behalf but as for duping poor old Lucas … I know how much the Lake District meant to him too.'

'It's OK though, pet. We will get your book and Mr Bentley won't get a penny.' Again, Ruby looked quizzical.

'The witness signatures won't stand up in court. Dolly Herriot is not of sane mind. Domenic's wife is also not a viable signatory as she could be classed as a benefactor. Plus, of course, Lucas was a very ill man at the time and probably wasn't even aware what Bentley was making him sign.' James took a swig from his pint of lager. 'Something else doesn't add up either. He states "the residue" of his estate. Where has the rest of it gone to?'

'Ooh, I feel like Daphne from *Scooby Doo*!' Ruby suddenly exclaimed.

'She was the red-headed one, wasn't she?' James laughed.

'You can be Shaggy, Fi isVelma, George isFred, and Montgomery isScooby.'

James shook his head in disbelief as Ruby went off to buy them a couple of cheese rolls.

Chapter Fifty-five

It had been a busy week and Saturday came around quickly. Just as Ruby was finishing some toast and peanut butter there was a knock at the door.

'Alreet, pet?' James walked in. 'You ready?'

'Almost. Just need to nip to the loo and grab my coat. You driving?'

'Yep. It should take us less than twenty minutes to get to Twickenham with no rugby on.'

Bentley's face was a picture when they arrived. Luckily, he was out on his drive tending to his car so had no place to hide.

'Guess you know why we're here?' Ruby asked without even saying hello.

'I do hope it's a social call. I've missed you, darling girl.' He went to pick up her hand to kiss it and she pulled away.

'This is James. He works for Trilby, Vine and Pitherington.' She could see the colour drain from Bentley's face. At that moment, Elena came to the front door.

'Welcome to Dinsworth House,' she greeted them warmly.

Bentley pushed past his wife.

'We're going to the library,' he told her curtly. 'Have some coffee brought in, will you?' Ruby was so glad that her relationship with him had been nipped in the bud early.

The intrepid duo sat opposite Bentley, who was holding court at a big walnut desk. He shoved a pile of books out of the way and they fell to the floor. Ruby looked around her and cringed at the sight of the big rug. She found it hard to believe that they had made love on it all those months ago, and realised now that this hadn't been one of her better encounters.

'We're here about Lucas Steadburton's will,' James said boldly.

'Yes, I realise that. I take it everything is in order?' Bentley shifted in his seat.

'Well, no, it's not.' James jogged Ruby's knee with his, and she quickly pushed the record button on her phone as James had instructed. If things didn't go the way they planned, at least they would have some evidence of this conversation.

'Dolly Herriot has Alzheimer's Disease. Her witness signature does not count.'

'But she can read and knew exactly what she was doing when I asked her,' Bentley defended.

'Did Lucas know what *he* was doing when you asked him?' Ruby added, suddenly feeling really cross.

'Of course he did, Ruby. Ooh, I do love it when you get feisty on me,' he flirted. She wished his cane was in sight so she could beat him with it.

'Additionally, Mr Bentley, your wife could be seen as a benefactor so not even her signature counts,' James announced.

Bentley stood up and banged the table with his fist. 'Trust you to meddle in this.' He glared at Ruby, all pretence of flirting and flattery gone. James alsostood up and positioned himself in front of Ruby.

'You would never have got away with it.' Ruby raised her voice slightly. 'I would have had to have seen the will at some stage, as I was mentioned with regards to Montgomery.'

'So what now?' Bentley said defiantly. 'Are you going to call the police?'

'Actually, no,' Ruby said bluntly. She took the second will and testament of Mr Lucas Geronimo Steadburton and ripped it up, then threw the fraudulent remnants onto the smouldering open fire. 'Call me a fool but I feel sorry for you,' Ruby uttered. 'You've got enough problems with running this place – I know that.' She could hear Bentley sigh with relief as she continued, 'A word of advice would be to trade in your flash car for something smaller, and make the residents' wing bigger. Love your wife and stop treating people with disrespect.'

'When you've quite finished, Marjorie bloody Proops – ' Bentley boomed, realising that she was quite right, and not liking that at all.

James stepped in. 'All we need from you is the poetry book that Lucas mentioned in the will. As the executor, you know where it is, I take it?'

Bentley mumbled something about going to his study and came back with a brown envelope containing the poetry book. 'You'd better take the silly old bugger with you as well,' Bentley said gruffly, and handed her a wooden box containing Lucas's ashes.

'Good work, Shaggy,' Ruby congratulated James as they drove down the impressive drive from Dinsworth House.

'Yes. And well done for staying so strong.' He paused and looked over at his friend, who was hanging on tightly to the box. 'He was a bit old for you, wasn't he?'

'Big dick though,' Ruby said matter-of-factly.

James just nodded knowingly and concentrated on the road.

Chapter Fifty-six

'All right, Raj?' Ruby greeted the shop owner with a smile. It was only the beginning of November, but advent calendars and lengths of tinsel were already adorning the shelves.

'Ruby! How lovely to see you. *Oh Yeah!'s* magazine' shares must have gone down it's been so long,' he joked.

'I know, I've just been so busy.'

'How's the job mission going then? Suki and I feel bereft of our update.'

His pretty wife came through to the counter and greeted her. 'Yes, dear. Come on. What's the chosen career to be then?'

'Well, to be honest I'm not sure yet. But what I do know is that I definitely *don't* want to work with dead people or children.'

The couple laughed out loud.

'So, what can we tempt you with today then, madam?' Raj said jovially.

'I need some cat food and most definitely a bottle of your finest Sauvignon Blanc.'

As Ruby paid for her bounty and headed for the door. Raj shouted after her, 'Two months to go and you will have completed your mission! We're really proud of you, Ruby.'

She turned around. 'Bless you both, that means a lot to me.'

And it really did. She couldn't quite believe it herself. Ten jobs down out of the twelve she intended to complete. Soon it would all come to an end, and then hopefully she would know where her true vocation and happiness lay.

To date, it had certainly been a rollercoaster of a ride, and she definitely wasn't thinking of getting off before the twelve month, twelve job mission had been accomplished.

Back at home, Ruby kicked off her shoes, poured herself a glass of wine, and lay down on her sofa with the plastic wallet containing the Wordsworth book. Patrick jumped up next to her and started licking his balls.

'Do you *have* to do that so close to me?' she tutted at her furry friend before turning her attention to the wallet. She had such special memories of Lucas. Bless him for leaving her the poetry book. Even though she had known him for such a short time, she had become very fond of him. He had such a depth and kindness to his personality.

Ruby took out the Wordsworth anthology and opened it reverently. Feeling a lump in her throat, she immediately found the page for the "Daffodils" poem, and suddenly her eyes widened. Attached to the page with a staple, was a blue Basildon Bond envelope with "GINGER" written on it in a shaky hand. Ripping it open, she found a short letter and two keys. She began to read hungrily.

Dearest Ginger,

You promised me you would go to the Lake District and now you shall.

Millbeck is very small, and Daffodils has a yellow gate. You won't miss it.

Now, the smaller key is our little secret. There are three bedrooms: go to the one with the dressing table and look behind the oval mirror.

You gave me great joy in my last days, Ginger, and I will never forget that.

Just a few more things before you start calling me a rambling old fool.

Throughout your life you must only regret the things

you don't do. Make the ornaments of a house the friends who frequent it, and most importantly, without fail, always *follow your heart.*

I can't say I'm in a better place now, but if I do happen to bump into your dad I will tell him what a beautiful young lady you've become.

Big kisses for Montgomery.
Toodle pip,
Lucas xx
PS. Make sure I'm scattered somewhere gorgeous, darling.

Tears rolled slowly down Ruby's cheek. 'Looks like I'm off to dance with the daffodils, Patrick. I'd better get my ornaments together.'

Chapter Fifty-seven

November, Job Eleven: Ruby Matthews Inc.

Johnny had been struggling to find anything for Ruby's eleventh-month mission.

So she checked her bank balance and took it upon herself to sell nearly all of her designer bags on eBay.

Possessions that not so long ago she never would have contemplated letting go had brought in a tidy sum – and the decision was made to dedicate month eleven, job eleven to working on Ruby Matthews Inc's future.

The will and George episode had made her tired, and with this in mind, Ruby thought it an ideal time to take a few days away from it all and visit Lucas's cottage in the Lake District.

Fi and James were all set to come, and when James had told her that Candice was going to be on her hen weekend, she thought it an ideal time to invite George along and get back on track with the friendship they'd had before the blonde one had come into their lives.

They all agreed that a few days in a cottage in the Lakes was just what they needed. With Ruby's renowned dreadful sense of direction, they had all insisted it was on the proviso that James did the driving and George, the map reading. Margaret had agreed to feed Patrick.

Full of excitement at what she might find behind the oval mirror, Ruby was up with the larks the morning they were due to leave. She hurried across to Margaret to give her a spare key and cat food, plus to drop off some shopping she had gotten for her the night before.

Margaret was ironing when she knocked on the window.

'Hello love,' Margaret greeted her warmly. 'Let me go and turn this iron off.'

Ruby followed her through to the lounge and was shocked to see a snoring Bert in 'her' armchair with the worn arms. A welcoming fire was burning in the grate and Bert, with his trimmed beard and clean clothes, had a look of serenity on his sleeping, weathered face. Margaret put her fingers to her lips to shush Ruby, who, with wide eyes, followed the old girl to the kitchen, put her supplies on to the worktop, and sat down at the pine table.

'Now, young Ruby, no lecture required. I've cleaned him up body-wise, clothes-wise and sometimes drink-wise. He's got a PhD, you know. In fact, he's a really interesting man and he's been keeping me company.'

Before Ruby could interject, Margaret continued. 'There's no funny business going on, and all I can add is what a joy it is not to feel so lonely. He's even started doing a bit of DIY for me.'

Ruby beamed at her. 'Margaret, you have never once judged me, from the day I met you, so why on earth would I judge you now? Your intuition is miles apart from mine, and if it feels right then do it.'

Margaret lifted Ruby's hand and kissed it. 'Bless you, duck.' Then she chuckled. 'Now I know our Bert isn't quite the Burt Reynolds look-a-like I *was* after, but at least he's sort of his namesake.'

Ruby laughed out loud. 'Right, I am going to have leave you to it. James will be along with the hire car in a minute.'

'OK, duck. I'm pleased you're getting away for a bit, especially with George. I still can't get over the fact he's marrying *her* and not you!' Bert let out a loud snore as his companion continued. 'Forget that blonde thing anyway. I told you, Ruby, they're all up there watching and waiting.'

The old girl pointed to the ceiling. 'As much as I don't want the young lad to get hurt, he won't stay with her. You mark my words. Now, away with you. Have a marvellous time and I want to hear *all* about it when you get home.'

James had hired a people carrier so they could suffer the long journey in some sort of comfort. The boys took turns to drive and they kept themselves amused by singing Cockney songs and playing word association games. It was getting dark by the time they reached Keswick, and George had them all looking out for the signs to Millbeck. They eventually turned off a main road and into the tiny village. They parked up so that Montgomery could relieve himself and they all got out and stretched their legs. They could hear the sound of a rushing stream.

'The address is simply Daffodils, Millbeck, so we just need to look out for the house name and its yellow gate.'

As Ruby announced that to the group, a Land Rover pulled up in the gloaming. An old boy with a shock of white hair poking out from under a yellow Sowester wound down his window.

'You OK, the lotta yers?' He breathed a plume of white into the freezing air.

'Yes, thanks,' George replied politely, adding, 'Do you know where Daffodils is, by any chance?'

'Gerald's old place, you mean? It's just up the hill on the left. Won't be in very good order, I expect. The garden's a mile high. Lucas hasn't visited as much lately. I live at the farm down the road here.' He pointed down the road. 'Any problems, come and see us.' With that, he wound his window up and drove off.

'Bloody hell, Rubes. I was expecting four-star, at least,' Fi said to Ruby, raising her eyes in jest as they pulled up outside the cottage. The yellow gate was faded and weathered and the garden was indeed unkempt. Ruby turned the key in the stiff lock and pushed her way in. She flicked the light switch – nothing. Damn. She hadn't for one minute thought there would be no electricity. James produced a torch from his bag.

'Look at you! Quite the Boy Scout,' Fi teased as James pushed past her and found an old-fashioned pay metre in the corner of the kitchen.

'Got fifty pence, any of you? We need to get this fed. It's bloody freezing in here.'

As everyone emptied their pockets and purses, Montgomery ran about barking, stopping to sniff anything that might remind him of his old master. The lights came on with a whirr and everyone cheered.

The cottage inside was absolutely beautiful, with a huge inglenook fireplace, big kitchen table, and a completely refurbished bathroom containing a free- standing roll top bath. Ruby didn't think somehow that Lucas would have anything short of perfect. It wasn't his fault the garden was overgrown. He probably hadn't even thought to get somebody to tend it when he fell ill. Each bedroom was adorned with Versace-style curtains and cushions, and Ruby noticed that each bed was made up beautifully with crisp white Egyptian cotton sheets.

'Bless Lucas,' Ruby said aloud, thinking that he had probably left it like this last time he came here, as considering the state of the grounds it obviously wasn't used as a holiday let. Adorning all the available stone wall space were a plethora of photos of the old lates and greats of Hollywood, including Montgomery Clift and a beautiful photo of the young Elvis in his army uniform. No wonder he felt so at home at Dinsworth House, Ruby thought.

The central heating was going to take a while to heat the whole house, so George took it on himself to light the fire while the others ran to choose their respective bedrooms. The back room with the dressing table was a twin. Ruby eyed the oval mirror on the wall and staked her claim on thar one. Fi was happy to share with her. James opted for the single bedroom as he was sure in daylight he'd get the best view of the valley, and George was left with the master suite housing a magnificent four-poster queen-size bed.

The fire was roaring by the time Ruby and Fi had unpacked, and Montgomery was chewing a rubber bone on the white fluffy rug in front of it. The boys were already chilling out on one of the sumptuous burgundy velvet sofas, drinking beer.

Fi, ever the event organiser, had guessed they would arrive late and had brought a box of food and drinks with her. They were all starving and agreed on hearty sausage and mash for their dinner. While Fi was busily peeling potatoes and the boys were involved in a heavy conversation about football, Ruby snuck off up to her bedroom. She reached into her jeans pocket for the smaller of the keys that Lucas had left her and tentatively removed the oval mirror. It was heavy and she struggled to place it glass down on the nearest bed. Behind the mirror was a safe set into the wall. She stood on the bed so that she could reach the lock. Not knowing what on earth she would to find, she turned the key with a shaky hand

'You all right, Rubes?' George called up the stairs, nearly sending her flying off the bed in shock.

'Yeah, fine thanks,' she called back. 'Just getting changed.'

She slowly opened the safe door, coughing at the dust that flew out at her.

As she peered inside, her heart began to beat faster in anticipation.

Firstly, she pulled out a whip with a diamond-encrusted handle. Smiling to herself, she threw it onto the bed. Then, a plastic wallet containing a yellowing script of Shakespeare's *Henry V*. She quickly flicked through a battered old photo album, and tears pricked her eyes as she could see how happy Lucas had been with his precious Gerald here in the Lakes. Finally, right at the back, there was a large brown envelope.

She replaced the photos and script and managed, using all of her strength, to reposition the mirror. Just as she stepped back on to the floor, she heard footsteps approaching along the landing. Shoving the whip under the bed and envelope under her pillow, she greeted George at the door. She had to remain true to Lucas – until she knew what was going on, anyway.

'Just checking to see if you were slipping into something a little more comfortable, Ms Matthews. Oh, and I needed the bog too,' George told her with a wink.

'You really are foul, George Stevens,' Ruby smirked, relishing that they still hadn't lost their familiar rapport.

'Part of my charm, and you love it.' He went off to the bathroom. She changed into leggings and a sweatshirt so as not to arouse suspicion.

Once downstairs again, she poured herself a glass of wine and went to help Fi chop onions. The boys had restarted their conversation about Newcastle United needing a new manager.

Never failing to cement her best friend status, Fi asked George the question that had been on Ruby's lips all day. 'So, what does the lovely Candice think about you coming here with two beautiful ladies?'

'She's fine about it. She'll be partying hard in Ibiza anyway,' George informed them all.

Ruby took a deep breath, then kicked herself into positivity. She would make the best of being in close proximity to Gorgeous George for now. Maybe living with him for a whole week might make her realise that she didn't really want him after all.

Chapter Fifty-eight

Despite playing cards until the early hours, Ruby woke early. While everyone was still sleeping, she took the chance to take the envelope downstairs and read the contents in peace. The heating had not come on yet and she shivered. Pulling her dressing gown around her, she threw a couple of logs on the fire and lit them with some old newspaper that was in the coal scuttle. Then she made herself a cup of coffee using the jar of Nescafé she had brought from home, and settled herself down on the comfy sofa.

She felt almost fearful of what she might find, and instead of ripping open the envelope like she normally would have done, she opened it slowly and deliberately. Inside the brown envelope were two smaller white envelopes. She gasped on finding a massive wedge of £50 notes in one of them and then quickly opened the other to find a letter in Lucas's now familiar scrawl.

Dear Friend

Whoever is reading this is now the proud owner of Daffodils. As you will already know, I have no living family and I wanted to make sure that whoever I left this property to would be worthy of its history and surrounding area.

Forgive me for not addressing you personally, but as I sit here writing this overlooking the natural beauty of fell-flanked Derwentwater, I do not know who you are yet.

I do, however, know that you will be rich in spirit and kind in heart. You will be unassuming and have no doubt made my life pleasurable during the little time I have left in this wonderful world.

Somehow, the thought of dying doesn't seem so frightening sitting here. Almost as if being up this high puts me on the bottom rung of where I am going next.

I shall try my best to get the key to my magical cottage to you without anyone knowing. Maybe then I can save you from the bloody stupid inheritance tax. However, I'm guessing the sort of person I've chosen to be reading this is probably a damn sight more honourable than me. Whoever you are, you must do what you see fit and share your gift with your friends and loved ones.

The other envelope contains the residue of my inheritance. I would like this to go to The Lake District Mountain Rescue Search Dogs. There is a leaflet in one of the kitchen drawers which will give you all the details on how to do this.

Enjoy every single minute of your time at Daffodils as I did.

I wish I was here with you to see your face, as I know you will be most humbled by this gift. You deserve this and don't ever think that you don't.

And on a final note, in the glorious words of Mark Twain – Dance like nobody's watching; love like you've never been hurt. Sing like nobody's listening; live like it's heaven on earth.

Love and all that jazz,
Lucas Geronimo Steadburton (good middle name!)

Tears streamed down Ruby's face. Montgomery ran to her, jumped up on the sofa, and began to lick the salty stream from her cheeks. She fussed him and then stood up and started to laugh tearfully. 'We are going to enjoy every second we spend in this joyous place, Montgomery Rasputin Daffodil Clift.' Monty began to bark incessantly as she jumped up and down, clapping her hands in joy.

'What's all the noise?' George appeared, rubbing his eyes.

Fi followed shortly. 'We're supposed to be on holiday, Rubes, it's only nine o'clock.'

Then James. 'Bloody hell, pet. Can't we muzzle him or something?'

Ruby continued grinning inanely.

'What is it with you, bird?' George asked, looking in the fridge for the milk.

'You look like the cat that got the fecking cream,' Fi said grumpily, attempting to throw another log on the fire. She missed and it went rolling across the carpet instead.

'Steady on the carpet, not sure if I can afford the upkeep.' Ruby went to pick up the log.

'What you on about?' James added. 'Have you been smoking wacky baccy or something? You're making no sense, and if you smiled any wider you'd split your jaw.'

Ruby couldn't keep it in any longer. She began to run around the lounge, talking at one hundred miles an hour. 'You're never going to believe what happened. You know that Lucas left me the Wordsworth book in his will?' They all nodded. Monty carried on barking and nipping at Ruby's heels. 'Well, he also only left me the key to this place too,' she squealed. Daffodils is mine. Dear Lucas has left it to me. I cannot bloody believe it.'

'Oh my God, Rubes.' Fi jumped up to hug her friend. 'That's amazing. Good on you.'

'And the will makes sense now,' James said sensibly. Ruby handed him the letter.

He took his time to read it. 'Inheritance tax. I can help you with regards to all of this.'

'Bloody hell.' George had caught sight of the wedge of notes. 'Is this yours too?'

'No, this is to go to The Mountain Rescue Search Dogs,' Ruby replied.

'Would anyone know if it didn't?' Fi said cheekily,

holding down Monty's ears so he wouldn't hear her.

'I would,' said James, 'And I am the lawyer.'

'I am going to honour exactly what Lucas wanted,' Ruby said stoically. 'I'm still in total shock that this beautiful place is now mine.' She hugged herself with both arms.

'Have you taken a look outside yet?' James asked.

They all went to the front window. It was a frosty November morning and the sun was trying to break through the clouds. They were faced with an amazing view across fields, with a wooded area to their right. There was a stream running right through the garden.

'It's beautiful,' Ruby said dreamily.

'Let's get out there,' James suggested.

'Yes. Today we are all going to climb Skiddaw and look over Derwentwater,' Ruby announced. 'It's just where Lucas would have wanted to end his days.'

Fi made a face. 'How fecking high is this Skiddaw hill then?' Ruby laughed and threw her one of the walk guides on a shelf in the kitchen. Fi read out loud, grimacing as she did so, 'Skiddaw is a mountain in the Lake District. Its summit is 3,054 feet above sea level, making it the fourth highest mountain in England. Rubes, are you sure about this?'

'Carry on reading,' Ruby urged, sounding a lot more knowledgeable than she was; she'd only gleaned what she knew from the same source.

Fi did as she was told. 'It is the simplest of the Lake District mountains of this height to ascend (as there is a well-trodden tourist track from a car park to the north-east of Keswick) and, as such, it is fine for the occasional walker wishing to climb a mountain.'

'See,' James piped up. 'It'll be fine. Come on, let's wrap up warm and get up there. We'll be back down for a pint by mid-afternoon.'

It was so nice to be out of the madness and smog of London, and everyone was in a buoyant mood as they began to climb. They had all wrapped up warm and James had insisted they took water and a supply of bananas from Fi's food parcel. They decided that they wouldn't take Montgomery for fear of losing him in the fells. James had been to the Lakes quite often on childhood holidays, but to the other three this was a new adventure. Ruby couldn't believe the beauty that surrounded them as they continued up the imposing Skiddaw. The colours, sights, and sounds of the winter landscape touched every sense and the air felt fresh and clear. When they reached a point where they had the most amazing view of Derwentwater, Ruby made everyone stop, while she took off her rucksack and removed a plastic sandwich box. She dislodged the blue lid to reveal that it was full to the brim with grey ash.

George laughed. 'I don't know what your beloved Lucas would have thought about being put in there.'

Ruby smiled. 'Look, he'd have realised that a bloody wooden box was too heavy to lug up here. Now, quiet, everyone, a little respect please.' She cleared her throat and quoted Wordsworth with passion, ending with,

'And then my heart with pleasure fills, And dances with the daffodils.'

As she finished, she lifted her arm up high and the remains of Mr Lucas Geronimo Steadburton were scattered amongst the magnificent fells that had given him such pleasure. He had told her of the many walks he and Gerald had been on around here, and she knew he would be happy with her choice of resting place for him.

Once every single piece of ash had caught on the wind Ruby said softly, 'Dance away, Lucas, nobody is watching.'

They continued to scale the hill. By lunchtime, Fi sat down abruptly on her bottom like a spoilt child. 'That's it,' she announced dramatically. 'I don't want to go on any more.' She puffed and panted. 'I'm fecking knackered.'

'Oh, come on, Fi. Imagine the view when we get higher,' James urged.

Fi looked around her. 'The view is great from here, ta. I can see all I need to. If I go any fecking higher, it'll just be the same but further away.' Ruby knew they were on a no win situation here, as once Miss O'Donahue had made her mind up, that was it. She was as stubborn as a mule. Her idea of a holiday was to be relaxed and comfortable, and Ruby knew she had just fallen out of her comfort zone.

'Look, why don't you two go ahead?' James voiced to George and Ruby. 'I've been up here before and you have to keep going – it's amazing when you do get up really high.'

'Oh, James, are you sure?' Ruby asked. 'It's just I really would love to get to the top if we can.'

'Of course. I wouldn't think of our precious cargo going back alone.' He poked Fi in the ribs, she giggled, and he continued, 'We'll go back in the car. Have you got your mobile?' Ruby nodded. 'Good, just give us a call when you're nearly done and I'll come back to fetch you from the car park at the bottom. Remember, it gets dark around four, so give yourselves time to get back down.'

'Yes, Dad,' Ruby grinned.

James and Fi made their way back down the slope. 'Looks like it's just you and me, bird.' George linked arms with Ruby. 'Come on, let's do this.'

They walked and talked and as the slope starting getting steeper they huffed and puffed. They laughed and even cried a bit when they both talked about their dads.

Ruby felt so easy in George's company. It was as if she had known him for years. The going got tougher and at one point, they were scrabbling on their hands and knees. Once they had reached the top of a difficult part they sat down to have a rest and sip some water.

'Good job your Candice isn't here.' Ruby put on her

voice. '"Ooh, Georgie, my nails are getting dirty, my white stilettos are too high for this hill."'

George, loyal to the core, saw red at Ruby's comment and suddenly turned from his usual affable self to a very angry man.

'Do you know what, Rubes? You need to take a look at yourself before throwing stones at other people.'

Ruby was taken aback and said nothing as George continued his rant. 'At least Candice is honest, and I know where I stand with her. I couldn't think of anything more harrowing than going out with someone like you, who has no idea what they want.'

George became more and more expressive with his hands. 'Don't get me wrong, I like you as a person, Ruby – in fact, I *love* you as a person. You are kind and funny and generous, but where affairs of the heart are concerned, you're a complete fuck up.'

Ruby felt like she was in some sort of terrible dream. She tried to stick up for herself, but George was unstoppable.

'I'm so glad I met Candice – because, you, Ruby, *you* were tying me in knots. One minute we were in bed together, the next minute you were in bed with – now let me see, a married man old enough to be your father. Yes, James told me about it. Then you go to Dublin and God knows what happened there, but I know it wasn't good because I know you so bloody well, Ruby. And then when you do eventually find a good man in Adam, you throw it away. Why? I can't see any good reason. He was a decent guy and you obviously really liked him. Commitmentphobia is a really sad thing, and that's all I can put your actions down to. And if it's not that, then what the hell is it?'

'I love you,' Ruby whispered.

'What?' George squinted, the light was getting poor.

'I LOVE YOU, GEORGE STEVENS!' she shouted at

the top of her voice.

'Don't waste my time, Ruby. Too little too bloody late. You wouldn't know what love was if it smacked you in the face. You had your chance with me and you blew it. I don't think you realised just how much you hurt me.' With that, he picked up his bottle of water and stormed off down the hill.

With tears pouring down her cheeks, Ruby watched him go. He was right, she didn't realise how much she'd hurt him. He should have told her. But then, she should have told him how she felt, too. She remembered Fi's wise words – *men are not mind readers. Men need to be told.*

Well, she had told him now, but he was right, it was too late. He was marrying somebody else in a matter of weeks.

When she had said those three little words she usually found so hard to utter, they had poured out from the bottom of her heart without thought. The honesty felt good, but the loss she felt now was more than terrible.

She wished she'd just kept her mouth shut, as she was sure she would lose his friendship too now, and a life without George Stevens in any capacity was one she didn't like the prospect of.

She pulled herself up. A mist seemed to have descended from nowhere. The visibility was so poor that she couldn't even see the direction George had gone.

Even the light her mobile created just glared back at her, the smog was so intense. She tried to call James immediately, but there was no signal. The text she sent would not go through either. She hoped that it would only be a matter of time before he and Fi realised that she was in trouble, and prayed that they hadn't got carried away tucking into the alcohol back at the cottage. If not, she knew that George would surely come back and find her.

She took a deep breath. 'Don't cry, be strong. Don't cry, be strong.' Various thoughts rushed through her mind. She thought of her darling mother and her brave brother.

She thought of her wonderful father and how sad it was that his life was taken so early, and then she thought of Lucas. Despite her woollen gloves, her hands felt like blocks of ice and she wrapped her arms around herself to try and keep the rest of her body warm. Her teeth chattered loudly as she began to recite from "Daffodils", as if in doing so, Lucas, with his knowledge of these hills, would somehow look down on her and protect them.

I wandered lonely as a cloud
That floats on high o'er vales and hills,
When all at once I saw a crowd,
A host, of golden daffodils;
Beside the lake, beneath the trees,
Fluttering and dancing in the breeze.

After what seemed like hours, Ruby heard the sound of a dog barking and torch lights flashing through the gloam. She didn't think she'd ever felt so relieved in her whole life. She suddenly thought how ironic it was that the very same mountain search dogs that Lucas was leaving his money to were now helping her.

Maybe Lucas had been right in his note. She *was* standing on the bottom rung of where she was going to next. It just wasn't her turn to go there yet.

Everything the gorgeous one had said made sense. Adam was lovely and yes, she had been too blind to see how much she had hurt both him and George. It was the wake-up call she needed.

'Ruby? Ruby Matthews?' A kindly voice came through the fog.

'Yes, that's me,' Ruby uttered now weak with cold and tiredness.

'Everything's going to be just fine,' the voice carried on.

'Yes – yes, I think it is,' Ruby replied, gripping on to the warm, gloved hand that now clasped hers.

Chapter Fifty-nine

Three weeks later, the Christmas shopping frenzy had already started in Central London, and Ruby loved people-watching from her warm window seat in Piaf's.

The cuckoo clock on the wall came to life at ten a.m. Norbert waved at them as he rushed out of the door to a rehearsal, and Mrs Connolly waltzed past them with Chester, kissing Ruby on the cheek as she did so.

When Fi began shuffling in her seat, looking very cagey, Ruby knew her too well not to know something was up.

'Fiona O'Donahue, tell me this minute.' Fi smirked and Ruby continued, 'Go on. I'd know that smutty look from a million miles away.' She tilted her head in anticipation.

'I slept with James at Daffodils,' Fi blurted out.

'No!' Ruby exclaimed. 'You kept that bloody quiet.'

'Well, we guessed we should, considering you were suffering from hypothermia up a fecking mountain at the time.'

'That is hilarious. You wait till I see that Mr Kane. I'll give him a piece of my mind.'

Ruby paused. 'So, was it a one-off?'

'I hope not.'

Ruby had not seen her friend this gooey for quite a while.

'He knows what makes me tick, Rubes.'

'I can see you two together, actually,' Ruby agreed. 'He certainly won't take any nonsense from you, I know that.'

'I guess that's why I like him. It's about time I had

someone to keep me in order.'

Ruby nodded. 'Hats off to him if he takes you on, and that's all I'm going to say on the matter.'

Thinking back to that awful day, Ruby finished off her coffee and sighed deeply. It was George who had said to call the rescue team. When she had eventually got back to the cottage, he had already left for the train station.

'Heh,' Fi said gently, knowing by the sad look on her friend's face that she must have been thinking about George. She reached for Ruby's hand. 'It'll be OK, you know that. At least you can scrap that feckin male wish list of yours and we can hang out at the Chelsea Flower Show rather than Harvey Nic's wine bar now.'

Ruby laughed.

Fi changed the subject. 'So – looks like you may not have a job for the December mission either. Heard anything from Johnny yet?'

'No, not yet. But I'm not worried. I'm still managing with my eBay bounty.'

'And we mustn't forget you are now also a property owner. Daffodils must be worth a mint.'

'Well, yes. James is just tying up all the legalities for me at the moment but I am indeed a very lucky girl.'

'Will you sell it, do you think?'

'No. Well, not in the foreseeable future, anyway. As you know, it really is a joyous place and I know that Lucas would want me to keep it.'

'Well, I christened it for yez anyway,' Fi trilled.

'Yeah, you bitch. My turn next.' Ruby flicked a crumb across the table at her and called Glen over to order more coffees.

'How are you feeling about George and the wedding now?' Fi broached, realising that her friend had been avoiding the subject.

Ruby took a deep breath, and just as she prepared herself to give her outlandish friend the latest wedding update from Margaret, she suddenly put her head down and began rooting in her handbag. Fi looked around and saw Candice walking in with another blonde short-skirted girl. Without noticing either Ruby or Fi, Candice sat at the next table with her back almost touching Ruby's.

Ruby raised her eyebrows at Fi and mouthed, 'I've got nothing to say to that girl.'

'OK,' Fi mouthed back. 'Shall we move?'

'No, not yet.' Rub took a sip of her fresh coffee.

'You're marrying him?' Candice's companion squawked. 'In two weeks' time? I can't believe it!'

'Let's listen,' Ruby mouthed urgently.

Luckily Daphne had disappeared upstairs so as not to blow their cover. The companion continued, 'But you've only known him five minutes.'

'Yeah, I know,' Candice said. 'But I've spun him a right line. He's smitten and I've got 'im just where I want 'im.'

Both Ruby and Fi's eyes widened in shock. Fi grimaced at Ruby as she accidentally knocked her mobile phone on to the floor.

'What do you mean?' Candice's companion asked innocently.

'Well, 'e's always going on about how he wants a love like his old dear and old man used to have. I've just said everything he wants to 'ear. He's vulnerable at the moment, you see. Since his old man popped his clogs.'

'I don't get it,' the companion said. 'The way you're talking it's as if you don't even like him.'

'Oh, 'e's nice enough but I'm not after 'im,' Candice blurted out. 'No, I'm after his money. I figure keep 'im sweet for a year then fuck off.'

'Money?' Fi mouthed to Ruby, who shrugged her shoulders.

'I thought he was just a landscape gardener?' the dumb one pursued. Fi put her thumb up to Ruby, ready for the impending answer.

'He is, but evidently even though his old man was just a postie, he kept a savings plan running since George was a baby. And with 'im being an only child, it's worth thousands. My dear, darling husband-to-be will receive the money in January. So, as long as I make sure not to blow it all before I divorce 'im then I'll be laughing.'

'You are *so* clever, Candice.'

'Yeah, I know,' the blonde one smirked. 'Now get that weird old bag's attention and order us some hot chocolates.'

'You finished up then, Ruby?' Daphne reappeared and asked chirpily. Damn, Ruby hadn't seen her. Well, if you couldn't beat them …

'Yes, thanks, Daphne. We're just off.' She placed a ten-pound note on the table and pushed her chair back noisily, knocking into the perpetrator.

'Oh, hi, Candice. I didn't notice you there,' Ruby said in faux surprise. Fi acknowledged her with a smile. If Candice had had pale skin before, she was now whiter than the driven snow that had started to gently fall outside. Ruby put on her best Tony Choi Cheshire cat smile. 'I bet you're excited. Not long to go now.'

And with that, Ruby and Fi got their coats, kissed Daphne, Mrs Connolly and Chester, and made their way into the throng of Christmas shoppers in the huge Covent Garden market.

Chapter Sixty

Ruby arrived home, tired and wanting a drink. She pushed open her front door, throwing her shopping bags on the floor as she did so. After feeding a purring Patrick, she poured herself a generous glass of wine and put her feet up on the sofa. She was just about to watch a recorded *Gavin & Stacey* when there was a knock at the door. It was James.

'Hey, pet.'

She kissed him on the cheek. 'Hey. Not working today?'

'Day off for Christmas shopping. I'm done now, wondered if you fancied a beer?'

'Got some Stella here to save us battling through the Christmas drinkers if you like,' Ruby offered.

'Canny, pet.'

Ruby handed him a can and took a slurp as he stretched out at one end of the sofa.

'Did Fi tell you about what happened at Daffodils yet?' Ruby hesitated. 'It's OK, I knew she would,' he went on immediately.

'Good job you didn't both fall asleep. I'd have been an icicle,' Ruby smiled.

'Shit - I know, Rubes.' He put his head back on the sofa. 'George told me about the row. Are you OK?' he asked softly, knowing it was a touchy subject.

Ruby looked up to the ceiling to suppress her tears, and told him, 'I knew deep down that he was the one for me, James, but George is right – when it comes to relationships, I don't know my arse from my elbow.'

'Oh, Rubes,' James said sympathetically. He had grown very fond of his red-haired neighbour.

Ruby said tearfully, 'I do think that it has something do with losing Dad, you know. I'm frightened of the feeling of loss, so I won't take chances with long-term lovers. The only chance I did take was with Dean, but that was because I knew that he loved me far more than I would ever love him.'

'That's so sad, Rubes. You have so much to offer, you should be far more confident in yourself and not presume that everyone is going to leave you.'

Ruby took a sip of wine.

'I know, I know. I just wish George had told me how he felt when he was feeling it. But I met Adam, and when I did actually realise that Gorgeous George here was meant for me", he was besotted with the bloody bitch of a blonde bimbo, and now it's too late.' She ran her hands through her hair. 'So stupid of me. I should have just been straight with him in the first place, and now things are going to get even more complicated.' Ruby fought back the tears,

'More complicated? Why?' James asked with interest.

'Well, I've just overheard none other than darling Candice telling her mate that she's only after George for his money. Evidently, he is getting some from his dad's will.'

'No!' James said, shocked. 'But between you and me, he asked me to look over the will last night.'

'Why so late with the will?' Ruby quizzed. 'His dad died months ago now.'

'His mum only just found it; in the garden shed of all places,' James confirmed.

'Oh, right,' Ruby replied. 'That makes sense now.'

James frowned. 'I can't believe that of Candice, she seems such a sweet, unassuming girl.' He then became a little stern. 'Ruby, you're not just saying this to split them up, are you?'

'No! Of course I'm bloody not,' she said defiantly. 'Fi heard it too. Go on – ask her.'

'It's all very well saying that, but who is George going to believe? As you say, he's besotted with the girl. I reckon even if you use Fi as a back-up, he might not believe you. The little cow has obviously put on a good bloody act.'

Ruby downed her glass and sat back on the sofa despondently. 'My name is Baldrick, and I have a cunning plan,' she quoted from *Blackadder* and managed a smile.

'Oh God. What now?'

'James, *you* must tell him that *you* overheard her.'

'And when exactly did I overhear her?'

'In Piaf's, of course.'

'But I was so obviously not there. In fact, I never go there, Rubes, you know that. George knows that too.'

'Well, can't you tell him that I told you and that you believe me?'

'As if he'd believe that after all the water that has gone under the bridge with you two!'

'You have to, James. It's the right thing to do by your friend. You cannot let him marry that money-grabbing little bitch!'

Chapter Sixty-one

It took an age for Ruby to get to Daffodils. She had hired a car especially.

George was getting married the very next day. Candice had taken no chances by arranging everything within a few months, convincing George that winter weddings were all the rage now. Ruby knew that she had to be as far away from them as she could, as it would be too much for her to bear.

James was right: despite her and Fi telling him exactly what they had heard, George, now completely besotted and taken in by the young girl's charms, would have none of it. There was no way that he was going to confront his fiancée as he didn't believe for one instant that she would be so callous. James, eventually believing the two girls, also urged him to reconsider, but George stuck his East End feet into the ground and would not be moved.

When Ruby had asked Johnny if any work had come in for December, he had told her that it was still very quiet and she should do as she saw fit. She knew that she had to get as far away from the wedding chatter as she could, so she told Fi where she was going and promised her mum and Sam that she would definitely be back for Christmas Day.

The last time they had been at the cottage, Ruby had arranged for one of her new neighbours to look after the place in her absence. She had rung ahead to say she was coming and breathed a sigh of relief when she saw the outside light was on, and was even more relieved that the heating was cranked up high.

They had even left her bread, milk, and tea bags. Even a little Christmas tree with lights perched on the fireplace. The garden was now at a manageable height. Bless them, Ruby thought. There was a community spirit here and it made her warm inside. She lit the open fire and snuggled on the sofa with her recent copy of *Oh Yeah!* This made her think of the kindness of the Gills, and how lucky she was to be surrounded by people who cared about her. She somehow felt that by being this far away from George and that calculating bitch, that she couldn't take the blame when it all went tits up. She was also very angry at George for believing that little trollop over his friends.

With James being best man, Fi had taken it on herself to support him. At least Ruby would get a full account of the proceedings.

Ruby awoke to the sound of the stream flowing through the garden and the incessant chatter of birds. She luxuriated in the comfy queen-size bed and snuggled down again to relish the tranquillity. She actually loved the fact that there were no televisions here, and she decided to keep it this way. She had heard Vivienne Westwood once say that there was too much distraction around in the world today. Ruby agreed. She loved having time to think and be at peace with herself, and realised that this trip would be good for her in more ways than one. It had been quite a year for her.

She lay flat on her back, looking at the ceiling and thinking over the past year's events in her head. She smiled as she thought of the wonderful, eccentric Daphne and her doting lover Norbert. She grimaced as she thought of Ciaran O'Shea and Pouting Pamela. She grinned when she thought of her stint as a fortune teller and felt tearful when she recalled how grateful Rita Stevens had been for the true East End send-off for her beloved Alfie. She actually felt sorry for Domenic Bentley. He was one of life's lovable rogues. Not malicious in any way, just struggling to keep what belonged to him. She would never forget the image of him wearing nothing but a tea towel, nor would she forget the lovely Adam and their clifftop dalliance in France.

Tony Choi also made her smile. Never again would she listen to the Kaiser Chiefs song, without thinking of him running around the Rocket Bar singing 'Ruby, Ruby, Ruby, Ruby' on her birthday. His fortune cookie had predicted love, happiness, and fortune. She had definitely been fortunate, with her dear friend Lucas leaving her this wonderful cottage, but the happiness and love elements still needed a bit of work. This brought her thoughts back to Gorgeous George.

She imagined him at the flat with James right now, getting ready for his big day. She bet he would look gorgeous too, all dressed up in his wedding day finery. It made her feel sick just to think of it. She couldn't be cross with him – she was just really worried for him. How dare that young girl fleece him then break his heart. Ruby suddenly felt guilty that maybe she should be there to try and make the blushing bride confess, but she had honestly tried everything she could via James to get it through to George that Candice was no good – so why should he suddenly believe her, today of all days? Candice must have thought that Ruby hadn't overhead her conversation in Piaf's, and even if she had, the devious one would have realised there was no physical proof. The bottom line was, Candice was clever enough to wrap George around her little finger, whatever the argument, and she knew that.

Once his anger had subsided, she hoped she could still be his friend and help him through the trauma when shit hit the fan. She did, however, realise that now she was losing him, albeit temporarily, just how much she did love him. She had fought her feelings for all that time, and wished she'd listened to her lovely friends a bit more and just followed her heart so much earlier.

When she looked back, she realised that George had always been there for her. The morning she had woken up with him after their drunken night out had felt so right. Why had she been such a stupid cow and not just grabbed the moment then?

She felt comfortable with him and as she had got older, she realised that this was what a relationship was all about. Yes, you could still have the passion, but the fact that you could sit in bed and have a cup of tea together the next morning, discussing anything that came into your head, now that was reality. Whoever said that love is friendship set on fire was right, Ruby thought.

What on earth she was waiting for? Some sort of knight in shining bloody armour? Adam on paper had actually ticked most of those boxes, but it was George who had won the battle. He was kind, thoughtful, caring, and honourable, but still maintained that joyous cheeky boyishness and raw naughty streak that made him stand out above the rest. Life without George Stevens would not be right. He was the love of her life, and she wanted to spend the rest of hers with him.

A branch bashed against the bedroom window, startling her out of her thoughts. She looked across the room at the black and white photo of Montgomery Clift looking all handsome and proud. She could see why Lucas fancied him. Bless Lucas. She had only known him a short time but he had touched her life greatly. There was something about him, so much depth to his personality – a joy to be around. Just being in the room with him made her feel exhilarated and strong enough to take on anything. The fact that he had left her this place – had set her up for life – made her think that everything did happen for a reason. Lucas Steadburton was without doubt her guardian angel, and Daffodils was her heaven on earth.

She looked at her watch. She really ought to get up. She was meeting Mr and Mrs Cole, her new neighbours, at eleven. She wanted to discuss terms with them, as they had readily agreed to continue looking after Daffodils in her absence. By the sound of it, they too had been very fond of Lucas, and had also spoken very highly of his partner Gerald.

After discussing things with Jamesthey had agreed that it would be a shrewd move to rent the cottage out as a holiday home. She would still allocate certain weekends and weeks out of the calendar for herself, so that she, along with her friends and family, could still reap the benefit of such a beautiful abode. A regular income would pay the bills and allow her to follow her career of choice without having to worry too much about money. In fact, it was a perfect situation, one that just a year ago Ruby would never have dreamt of being in. So much could happen in twelve months and this was certainly a year to remember for Ruby Ann Matthews.

She got dressed and put on her thick coat, scarf, and gloves. It was a perfect winter's morning. The tree branches glistened with frost as the high winter sunshine shone through the white sky. Selfishly, she hoped it was raining on Candice's parade down south. Fi had promised her she would ring later with a full rundown, but Ruby had actually told her not to bother. No, she would remain in her sanctuary for at least a week. She would return when the excitement had subsided and Mr and Mrs Stevens were well into their Caribbean cruise honeymoon.

Blocking the scenario from her mind, she walked down the hill towards the Coles' house. Once she was at the bottom of the hill, she heard a squawking noise. Looking to her right, in a field with various coops and cages she saw an array of ornamental ducks, a wallaby, and a kangaroo. How bloody bizarre, Ruby thought.

Mr Cole appeared wearing a worn yellow Sowester. He had a ruddy face and a huge tummy under his green weatherproof jacket. His shock of white hair stuck out under his hat just as it had done the very first night they had arrived in Millbeck. 'Oh, hello, young Ruby. How be you today?'

'Great, thanks, Mr Cole.' She pointed to the wallaby and made a questioning face.

'Oh, that's Walter,' Mr Cole laughed. 'I've got a penchant for me different animals. The kids love 'em in the summer and me birds produce all sorts of tasty eggs.'

'That's really lovely,' Ruby said honestly.

'Gotta have an interest, pet. Keeps you sane when you get as old as me. Only so many walks and crossword puzzles you can do.' Ruby smiled broadly as he carried on, 'Come on, follow me, dear. Maud's got kettle on t' stove.'

It was two o'clock by the time she left the Coles' farm, feeling at least a stone heavier. Mrs Coles' hospitality had almost hospitalised her! It was no wonder that Mr Cole had such a big tummy. They had started with tea and homemade scones and cream. Lunch was big chunks of crusty bread with blocks of cheese and a huge boiled duck egg, followed by a wonderful fruit cake, and washed down with fresh goat's milk.

During the feast, they had discussed the running of Daffodils and Ruby knew that she could trust this wholesome couple with her life. They had exclaimed that she was offering them too much money to help, but Ruby insisted that without them it would be impossible for her business to take off as she lived so far away.

She started to walk back up the hill to the cottage, thinking that a lie down in front of the fire was very much required. She noticed Christmas trees in people's windows and suddenly felt a bit sad that she wasn't sharing this wonderful time of year with anybody else.

George would be married by now, and the happy couple would be on their way to the reception. Just the thought made her feel sick.

She lit the fire and lay down on the sofa. Within minutes she was asleep, only waking when a log spat loudly on the fire. She dozed, taking in the silence around her, and realised that maybe being alone wasn't all it was cracked up to be after all.

She tried to call her mum and Fi but there was no signal. She reached for her magazine instead, but seeing the marriage of a celebrity chef to an ex-model did nothing to heighten her mood.

There was only one thing for it. She went to the fridge and opened a bottle of freezing cold Sauvignon Blanc, then grabbed a family bag of Walkers Sensations from the cupboard. Suddenly, life didn't seem quite so bad!

Chapter Sixty-two

Bang! Bang! Bang! Ruby sat up in bed with a start. Sluggish from her heavy slumber, she couldn't fathom where the noise was coming from. She quickly switched the bedside light on and looked at her watch. Three a.m. The banging continued. It was too loud and persistent to be a stray branch against a window. She felt groggy. She had drunk the entire bottle of wine then sloped up to bed. She tried to wake herself up.

Bang! Bang! Bang! Her mouth was drier than the Sahara, her palms sweaty, and she could actually see her heart pounding through her nightshirt. Oh God, this was it. She was going to be killed in her bed in the middle of nowhere. The Millbeck Murderer was going to strike again. Who would find her? She had visions of her mother putting her photo in the *Reading Post* with the headline 'MISSING.'

Even worse, Patrick would become obese after gorging on the five packets of custard creams stashed in her cupboard and wouldn't be able to get out of the cat flap to seek more food.

She took a big glug of water from the glass by her bed. How did she always manage to remember this lifesaver, however drunk she was? Bang! Bang! Bang!

Too frightened to peer through the window, she quietly got out of bed and searched around her for a suitable weapon. Suddenly remembering Lucas's whip, she retrieved it from its hiding place and held it tightly in her hand. She had never heard of anyone getting thrashed to death with a diamond-encrusted horse whip before, and hoped it would act as a deterrent if nothing else. She was just about to dial 999 on her mobile when amongst the banging, she heard a familiar voice.

'Ruby, for fuck's sake will you open this door!'

Chapter Sixty-three

'George? What the hell are *you* doing here?'

'Come down and let me in and I'll tell ya. I'm freezing me bollocks off out 'ere, bird.'

Ruby ran downstairs wearing just her nightshirt. She noticed how cold the cottage was, and shivered. She opened the door to find a quivering George, snowflakes glistening in his dark hair. He threw his arms around her.

'Ruby, I am so sorry.' He was in tears. 'I've been trying to call you all the way here. Fi was going spare that she couldn't reach you. I had to come, bird.' He kissed her forehead. 'I can't believe I've been so foolish. You were all trying to tell me, and I didn't listen.'

Ruby ushered him onto the sofa and went down on her knees to light the fire. He was still wearing his wedding suit.

'So what made you realise we were telling the truth?' she asked, her teeth chattering.

'It was Fi. She came running round to ours this morning, thrust her mobile into my hand, and told me to listen.'

Ruby screwed her face up. 'Listen to what?'

'Well, evidently you two had been in Piaf's and Fi dropped her phone, which somehow turned the message record function on.'

Ruby raised her eyebrows in relief.

'I heard every word, Rubes. The bleeding cow. Thank God I found out before it was too late. Bless Margaret too, she kept on that I was making a huge mistake, and I just thought she was playing the matchmaker as usual. I can't believe I was so deluded.'

George joined her on the rug in front of the fire. He pulled her towards him and kissed her, the most passionate and loving kiss Ruby had ever experienced in her whole life. She pulled away, almost giddy with emotion. How life could change in the blink of an eye. This morning she thought the love of her life was lost and marrying someone else, and now here he was, kissing her. She suddenly became serious.

'You can't just stop loving someone like that, George Stevens.'

He kept his hold on her, looking right into her eyes and whispered, 'No. You can't.' He cleared his throat. 'Ruby Ann Matthews, I realise now that I loved you from the minute you drunkenly fell into my bed.'

'So why carry on with Candice then?' Ruby questioned, still not quite believing what was happening.

'I think I made that quite clear when we were up the mountain.'

Ruby raised her eyes to the ceiling.

'Men! I should have just hit you over the head with a frying pan. Me Jane, You Tarzan and all that. OK, I know now that I should have just told you outright, but I was scared of my own feelings, and then Candice came along.' Ruby's voice tailed off.

'She showed me love when I needed it – or I thought she did anyway. But I realise now, none of that was real,' George confessed.

He let Ruby go and put both his hands in hers. 'What's real is someone arranging your dad's funeral for you, with her own money – yes, James told me.

'And Margaret contributed,' Ruby added.

'Really? Bless her heart!' George exclaimed.

'She sold her brass,' Ruby added.

Tears pricked George's eyes. 'That's just the kindest thing.'

Ruby kissed him on the nose.

'What else is real is someone holding me whilst I sob, and understanding exactly what grief feels like, close up. And what's really real is hearing the raw emotion of someone saying that they love you, even when they know that there is little chance that it will be heard.' He hesitated. 'Do you really love me, Ruby Ann Matthews?'

'Of course I love you, George Stevens – and don't you ever forget that.'

While they lay holding each other, the fire suddenly spat fiercely.

'Ouch!' Ruby cried out. 'Shit, that hurt!' She jumped up and rubbed her calf. 'Something just flew out of the fire and burnt my leg.'

George started to laugh.

'I really don't think it's a laughing matter, George Stevens,' she said crossly.

'It's never going to be like the movies with us, is it, Rubes?'

She pretended to swipe his head with her right hand.

'Small, dark, handsome Cockney meets stunning, unemployable redhead. I really don't know what you mean.'

She shivered. 'Sod getting this fire going. It's five in the morning, I'm freezing cold and in need of some sleep.' She yawned. 'And in the morning, maybe we can reenact a scene from *Top Gun*, eh, Tom Cruise?'

Chapter Sixty-four

'Johnny, you are really testing me now.' Ruby was quite serious.

'Oh, come on, Rubes. It will be a laugh.'

'Maybe for you and half of Richmond, but certainly not me,' Ruby said sullenly.

'Pretty please. One of my boys is off sick and there is no way I can find a replacement for him at such *short* notice.' She could sense Johnny grinning down the phone as he carried on, 'It's for charity too, so come on – say yes. I'll get you a big Christmas present.'

'So you're saying you want me to do this for free too!' Ruby exclaimed.

Johnny was laughing at his feisty friend. 'Ruby Ann Matthews, if you do this for me, you will definitely be nothing *short* of magnificent.'

Chapter Sixty-five

It was the Saturday the twenty-first of December, and Ruby was relishing every moment of putting shiny red baubles on her three foot Christmas tree. She had turned a corner with regards to missing her dad, and had recently been feeling happy as she remembered all the good memories instead than the sad ones. She was comforted when she thought of him living on through her, and for once, felt quite peaceful about the whole situation.

Her old passion for Christmas had returned. She adored anything to do with Christmas and sang along loudly to "Do They Know It's Christmas?" as it blared out of the radio. Patrick, who had been charging around the lounge with a piece of tinsel, stopped, and looked perturbed at the unnecessary disturbance of firstly his mistress's singing and then the shrill of her "Jingle Bells" mobile ring tone.

'Gorgeous George,' Ruby answered.

'Get your glad rags on, bird you're going up West. A taxi will be with you in thirty.'

Before she had time to ask where to and why, George had hung up.

Ruby had never been to The Ritz before and had to stop herself from yelping in delight at the sight of the magnificent festive decorations in reception. The cab driver had told her that once inside that she should head to Palm Court. The smart concierge directed her to where the institutional afternoon tea was being served.

The excited redhead grinned a Tony Choi grin when she saw her welcoming committee, nearly falling over when Margaret smiled to reveal a full and perfect set of false gnashers.

The old girl was wearing a navy blue, long velvet dress, and her white hair was neatly tied back in a fashionable chignon. She looked beautiful. George stood up and pulled out a chair for his girl.

'I told you she was at the dentist,' a clean shaven, suited Bert chipped in, as Ruby sat down and opened and closed her eyes in amazement.

'Margaret, I can't believe it, you sly old fox! You look bloody great.'

Margaret couldn't stop smiling. 'And, that's not all, dear.' She nodded to Bert, who stood up, and helped her out of her seat. With both of them humming Frankie Vaughan's "The Garden of Eden", they waltzed perfectly around their table, with Margaret not missing a step.

'Your feet!' Ruby pointed downwards, shocked.

'Your George,' Margaret replied, out of breath.

Ruby looked to her handsome beau.

George shrugged. 'Margaret always believed in us, bird, but neither of us listened. The least I could do was get her bunions sorted, and try to stop that annoying Polo habit of hers.'

They all laughed.

'You're a little darling, George Stevens.' Margaret showed off her pearly whites again. 'But do you know what? The biggest present for me is seeing you two together. It makes my heart smile.' She squeezed George's cheek. 'I told you they were all watching you, Ruby.'

'What?' Bert and George said in unison.

'Clotted cream, anyone?' Margaret replied, winking at Ruby as she did so.

Chapter Sixty-six

December, Job Twelve: Actress

They were all there for the momentous occasion. Daphne, wearing her best black dress and fur stole, clung onto Norbert with baited breath. Sam and Beth canoodled, feeding Ben popcorn under the seat. Ruby's mum and Graham chatted incessantly and Tony hummed 'Ruby, Ruby, Ruby' to himself. Justice and his girlfriend (who had long since forgiven him) were in the front row, along with George, James, and Fi, who was on the verge of wetting herself with laughter already. George's mum, Montgomery's proud new owner, stroked his ears while he slept soundly on her lap. Raj and Suki Gill sat awkwardly behind them. The Lovegroves were sat in the cheap seats to the side and for some reason Margaret and Bert had insisted they looked on from the wings. None of them would have missed it for the world.

The curtain went up to rapturous applause. Ruby felt her heart beating faster than a frightened bird. She straightened her beard and pointy hat as Johnny pushed her forward onto the stage.

'Hey ho, hey ho,' she began to sing. And there was Ruby Ann Matthews, her twelve month, twelve job mission to happiness almost over, standing – or rather, kneeling – on the stage of a Richmond theatre, dressed as Grumpy, one of Snow White's seven dwarfs.

'Jesus is alive and laying in a manger,' Bert hollered.

New Year's Day

'Happy New Year, Grumpy!'

Bert, sat up in his quilted sleeping bag, tilted his bottle of cider, hiccuped, then promptly slumped back against Margaret's door. Margaret opened it and he fell backwards into her hall. She clipped him round the ear and dragged him inside, waving at Ruby and showing off her film star smile.

Despite her hangover, Ruby managed a rousing, 'Happy New Year, lovely Margaret!'

She ran up the steps to George's flat. He opened the door and kissed her on the lips as she placed a carton of milk in his hand. 'Well done, bird,' he said. 'Mouth's like the bottom of a parrot's cage.'

Fi appeared from upstairs, hair flying everywhere, steadying herself on James's shoulder.

They all tucked into the huge fry-up George had made.

'So, my darling fiancée. You must know what the million dollar question is?' George asked.

Ruby slurped her tea, her hangover state not allowing her to compute what he was on about.

'Twelve jobs, twelve months – what's it going to be?'

Ruby sat back in her chair, smiling as she deliberated. 'Oh, I get you. Now let me see.' She drummed her long, red-painted fingernails on the table. Everyone leaned in.

'Fluffer for Brad Pitt perhaps?'

'No, come on – seriously, Rubes?' James, ever the sensible one, asked.

'Well, of course I'm going to manage Daffodils as a holiday home. That will bring in a tidy income, and, actually if you'll have me and Patrick, we'd love to move in here so that I can rent my place out and ...' She suddenly leapt up and became animated, 'say yes to the course I've been offered at the London School of Fashion!'

'London School of Fashion?' Fi screeched. 'Bejaysus, Rubes, you kept that one quiet.'

'I wanted to wait and tell you when I'd been accepted,' Ruby beamed. 'Working in Oxfam made me realise that I have a flair for fashion and it's something that I really do enjoy. I'm so excited.'

'Going back to school and living with a young gardener in rented accommodation! Oh, what a difference a year makes,' George joked.

Ruby leaned over and kissed him on the cheek, happiness exuding from every pore of her being.

'And then ... Gorgeous George ... when I've graduated, who knows what I'll do?' She paused and added, 'I guess, if all else fails, I could always cover for Dopey next year.'

Everybody roared.

Other titles

For more information about **Nicola May**

www.nicolamay.com

Printed by Amazon Italia Logistica S.r.l.
Torrazza Piemonte (TO), Italy

13110266R00189